BENEATH

BY CHERYL GORDON

Book Design By: Cheryl Gordon

Printed By CreateSpace

For bulk purchasing information please contact

Gordon Publishing

Po Box 846, Valleyview, Alberta T0H 3N0

thetridentseries@gmail.com

Summary-Morgan finds herself thrown into a world she never knew existed and is forced into roles she does not welcome. She must choose between her duties as an Atlantean princess, her longing to return to the only home she has ever known, and a forbidden love that could destroy what remains of the Atlantean people

ISBN 978-0-9879150-1-6

BENEATH : The Trident Series - Book One

[1.Supernatural -- Fiction 2. Young Adult-- Fiction 3. Fantasy-- Fiction 4. Mythology--Fiction 5.Teen--Fiction]

Chapter 1

"It's morning," Morgan murmured as she nudged her back into Lucas's chest. He did not jump from the bed and head for the door, which had become the routine. Instead, he wrapped his muscled arm around her torso, pulling her against his chest.

"I know," he said, his warm breath lingering against her earlobe. "I love you," he whispered, nuzzling his face against her neck.

"I love you, too," she replied. With a quick and unexpected swoop, Lucas flipped her body, pressing her against the wall so she faced him.

Morgan rubbed her face, trying to clear the daze of sleep from her mind. She noticed Lucas's normally bright blue eyes were creased and bloodshot. He looked like he hadn't slept a wink.

"No, Morgan, I mean I'm in love with you," Lucas confessed as his tired gaze turned to one of hope and desperation. He gently raised her chin and pushed his eager lips against hers.

Morgan's hand shot out and rammed into Lucas's chest. His body fell from the bed and landed with a loud *thwomp!* on the floor.

"What the hell?" he said.

"What do you mean 'What the hell'? I should be the one who gets to say 'what the hell'! You tried to kiss me! Why'd you do that, Lucas? You're like my brother!" Morgan demanded. Morgan's mind was reeling as she studied her best friend, his chest heaved the way it always did when he was upset. Morgan felt utterly betrayed by his sudden confession. She and Lucas had been friends since they could walk. Morgan had no siblings or any type of father figure in her life, Lucas had been the one she always leaned on. He taught her to ride a bike when they were seven and bandaged her knee when she fell onto the pavement, he taught her to drive a car when they were sixteen and helped her fix her mom's mailbox when she ran it over. But, they had both decided after an awkward escort to their grade seven dance, five years ago, that dating each other was definitely not an option. Now with Lucas's one crazy impulse, their entire relationship was careening off the rails.

"I...am not...your brother," he growled.

Rising from the floor, Lucas gazed at Morgan with longing.. She could actually feel the friendship they had built over the years shatter around them.

They stared at one another silently, each of them scared to say the wrong words.

"You're my best friend, Lucas, but that's all you'll ever be. Please don't ruin what we have," she said. "And quit staring at me like that," she added, pulling the covers up tightly beneath her chin.

"I can't just turn off how I feel about you Morgan. I've tried....believe me. I'm done pretending there's nothing more than friendship here. No more games Morgan. Make a choice. You're the only girl I want to be with. Give us a chance... please?" Morgan remained silent. She just couldn't give him the answer he needed.

He nodded his head in defeat, signaling that she need not kill his heart with the words he already read across her face. He pulled at her large wooden framed patio door and stood on the threshold.

"I'm sorry, Lucas. Please don't leave like this. Come back in and we can talk some more," Morgan pleaded.

Without looking back he spoke, "You know I have to go before your Mom wakes up and finds me in your room. I will talk to you after Easter Break. I'm going with my family to Hawaii for a while. I need some time to think Morgan…I'm not sure where we go from here."

Morgan watched the defeated boy as he slipped past the garden and squeezed through the back gate. His mass of blonde curls atop his head shone gold against the sunrise. She waited for him to look at her. She desperately wanted to fix the tornado that had just ripped between them, but he marched off without as much as a glance in her direction.

Chapter 2

"Single! We have a single! Are there any other singles?"

"I'll just pay for two tickets!" Morgan yelled at the yellow-toothed Ferris wheel conductor.

"Sorry, Miss. No single riders," The man sneered as he pointed his grease-covered finger at the faded metal sign she'd wished she noticed beforehand.

She pulled at the long metal bar that secured her into her seat and was about to free herself from the humiliation when a boy stepped out of the crowd and onto the loading platform. Morgan took a quick study of him as he swiftly slid into the seat beside her, ending any chance she had of escape. She wondered how he could possibly be a single rider. His short preppy-boy blonde hair, framed his prominent cheek bones and square jaw, perfectly. His eyes shone the most vibrant blue she had ever seen. He smiled sweetly at her as he scooted his body in closer to her on the hard metal bench. . She quickly turned away, pressing her body into the farthest edge of the seat, embarrassed by her single rider status. She refused to give her co-rider the time of day. He was undeniably gorgeous, but she had too much male drama in her life already to even consider talking to another guy. The seat jerked and swayed as the ride started pulling them skywards in a backwards motion.

"Wow, isn't it beautiful up here?" came the smooth, husky voice beside her. Morgan felt a shiver ripple along her spine as he spoke. She looked out across the Santa Monica pier and nodded her head; it was pretty, she'd allow him that.

The two large, boys with long dark shaggy hair in the seat ahead of them rocked their seat back and forth as they mocked the ride. They kept turning around and smiling at Morgan which made her very uncomfortable. She could feel the boy beside her tense up as they carried on.

"Hey Ethan! Who you got beside ya?!" came the voice of the larger boy in front of them.

"You know them idiots?" Morgan blurted before she could stop herself.

"No" he answered. She could feel anger radiating from him as his face turned rigid and he glared at the boys who began to hoot, whistle and make kissing noises in their direction.

"You should know better than to take your girl on a big dangerous ride like this. Anything could happen." The other boy threatened, his cold green eyes narrowed to slits.

Morgan felt a chill shoot down her spine. Her instincts told her to get the hell out of this situation, but where was she to go? She was sitting at the top of a Ferris wheel!

"Ethan is it? Can you tell your friends or whatever they are, to stop?" she demanded as she turned to face him. She grabbed the security bar to help shift in her seat.

"Wait! Don't move!" Ethan shouted.

A bright flash came out of nowhere, stinging Morgan's eyes. She turned to Ethan and heard a small click as the bar she leaned on to shift in her seat, suddenly released from its lock and swung open.

Morgan gripped the bar for dear life as she fell forward through the air. She screamed as her body swung away from her seat and she dangled over the screaming crowd below. Ethan held to the back of his seat so he did not fall out too.

"Hold on! I'm going to try and swing the bar back in. Just hold on." He shouted. Morgan's hands burned as she clung to the steel rail, desperately trying to keep her body from plummeting to a grotesque, carnival death. There was no time for her life to flash before her eyes or any of the other near death experiences she had heard about. All her concentration was there and now. She had to swing back to the seat. She could see the people gathering beneath them through the tears that streaked down her trembling cheeks.

"Help me, please!" she begged the stranger who now held her life in his hands. Ethan grabbed the security rail close to the hinge with one arm as he held himself against the back of the seat with the other. He gave the rail a speedy yank, sending Morgan swinging toward him.

"Don't let go, do you hear me? Hold onto that bar. I'm going to try and grab you."

"I'm slipping, don't move me, don't move me! Please, don't move me!" she screamed. Her hands moved down the bar.

This is it. This is how I'm going to die. Morgan's hands were sweating against the metal, making it hard to hold the bar as her body swung in towards Ethan. She felt his hand clasp her wrist. She wanted to feel relief but she didn't know how he was going to help her with only one free hand.

"Okay, I've got you. Let go of the bar," he said.

"You're going to drop me!" she screamed

"Look at me..." he urged "open your eyes and look at me." Morgan hadn't even realized her eyes were squeezed shut until Ethan had said that. She forced her eyes open and looked into the stranger's gentle, yet confident face. He smiled.

"I know you don't know me but I can do this. We can do this. You're going to be fine, I promise. You have to let go of the bar, when you do, you will fall downwards but don't be scared. I've got you and I'm going to quickly pull you up and into the seat. When I do, you grab the bar, swing it in and lock it. Okay?" he said, tightening his grip on Morgan's tiny wrist. Morgan nodded. "On three then?" he suggested. Morgan was so scared she thought she might pass out as the numbers echoed in her head.

"One...Two...THREE!" he yanked her hand from the bar, her body swung down with force as the words - *don't drop me, don't drop me, please god don't drop me* screamed in her head. In a quick, smooth motion he yanked her upwards and into the seat as he had promised. She scrambled for the bar pulling it in and locking it. The sound of lock clicking into place was the best sound she had ever heard in her life.

"WE DID IT!" she yelled and she heard cheers echoing from the crowd below. She grabbed the boy beside her and yanked him into an embrace. "Thank you Ethan, thank you so much." She cried.

"Get us off this thing!" Ethan yelled down to the ride operator.

The Ferris wheel hummed into motion as the riders quickly got off, chair by chair.

"Well this is no fun is it Trenton? I was hoping for a little more guts and gore." The larger boy in front of them said to his co-chair.

Morgan had almost forgotten about the two morons in front of them.

"Well brother, we all know Ethan is sooo handsome AND strong, but wow, lifting a girl up with one arm like that. Impressive. Have you been working out Ethan?" Trenton added with a wicked grin.

"You guys have a one seat head start. Use it wisely." Ethan warned the nasty boys in front of them. The air was thick with hate.

"Did they unlock our bar somehow? Are they responsible? I know it was locked when we got on, I don't understand what happened, did you see the flash of light right before it unlocked? Were we hit by lightning?" Morgan's mind raced as she tried to figure out exactly what happened. It felt like the jerks in front of them had something to do with the accident but she didn't know how. Ethan never offered any explanation.

The boys chair reached the platform and they shot for the exit. "See ya around Ethan!"

Ethan shook the bar holding them in, Morgan knew he was impatiently waiting to throttle those jerks before they got away, but as their chair finally reached the platform she couldn't see the evil brothers anywhere.

When the ride attendant unlocked the bar to release them at last, Ethan turned to Morgan, "Are you alright?" he asked. He looked her up and down. She nodded,

"I'll be back in a few minutes. Will you wait for me at the entrance?" he asked.

Morgan was still trembling and knew she must be in shock. She nodded to Ethan again. She wanted to get as far away from the pier as physically possible, but Ethan had just saved her life.

 He placed his hand on hers. "Thank you, I won't be long, I promise." Ethan shot from the platform and before the Crew of medics reached the rides entrance, Ethan was gone.

Morgan obliged the Medics, allowing them to check her over thoroughly before her friend Nala arrived. Morgan spotted a mob containing park management officials, the police and reporters stampeding towards her. She didn't want to explain what happened, she honestly didn't know. Her best guess would be the flash of light she seen before the bar opened was a random strike of lightning. But the sky was perfectly clear, so she decided it would be best to keep her hypothesis to herself.

"You have to get me out of here." She whispered to her dear friend Nala.

Nala, the red-headed spitfire, seen the oncoming crowd and needed no further explanation, she grabbed Morgan's hand and led her through the crowd, successfully dodging the camera toting men, storming down the pier. Morgan stopped when they reached the entrance. Nala came to a halt when she realized Morgan no longer followed.

"Come on Morgan, Let's get you home." Nala prompted.

"I can't leave yet Nala, the boy who saved me told me to meet him here. He'll be here any minute, he promised." Morgan explained. She found a bench and pulled the hood on her sweatshirt up to cover her from the news crews. Nala sat beside her.

"Okay we'll wait a few minutes but you're still shaking and I'm sure you're still in shock, so if he doesn't show soon, I need to get you home."

Morgan nodded in agreement, but refused to budge even an hour later.

Morgan scanned the park for Ethan but she couldn't see him. The officials shut down the park for inspection and people were clearing the area quickly. Even the press gave up on the story and drove off after an hour or so. Still no Ethan. Morgan shook her head.

Of course he isn't going to show, he probably just said he would meet me so he could get the hell away from me as soon as possible. He had to risk his life to save me and I was hysterically screaming and bawling like a baby- of course he blew me off and doesn't want to see me again.

Despite coming to terms with the idea that Ethan officially blew her off. She still felt bad leaving. She hadn't even told her rescuer her name (not that he even asked). The park was completely empty and it was getting dark. He was not going to show.

"I'm sorry Morgan but I have to get home. My mom just texted me, she seen the Ferris wheel accident on TV and she is freaking out. I'm guessing when your mom sees the News she will go into panic mode too. We really have to go now. I'm sorry but if that boy hasn't shown by now, he's not coming" Nala stood up and extended a helping hand to Morgan. Morgan took one more hopeful look around then accepted Nala's ride home.

***

It was the first day back to school after Spring Break, Morgan hadn't talked to Lucas since he dropped the "I love you" bomb a week ago. She didn't care what happened between her and Lucas anymore, all she cared about was fixing it. Funny how hanging for your life, over a carnival ride, really puts what actually matters into perspective. She had sent him so many texts in the last week she knew she'd officially qualify as a stalker. But Lucas had not returned a single message! She knew he checked his texts and email compulsively, no matter where he was, so being on vacation did not make for a very good excuse. He was definitely ignoring her and that was really starting to tick her off.

How could her best friend be such a jerk? She had almost died and she couldn't tell her best friend about it, she was beginning to wonder if he'd even care. When he got back, she was going to let him have it.

Enduring the past seven nights of hellish nightmares without him lying next to her had been horrible but the thought of losing his friendship was far worse. She couldn't believe how much his absence affected her, but she was determined to just suck it up and find a way to cope with her dreams in some other way, a way that no longer involved Lucas. She just prayed their friendship remained salvageable.

Her first nightmares started a few days after her sixteenth birthday. They were so horrifically realistic she became scared to close her eyes, no matter how briefly. Lucas showed up on her doorstep that Friday with an arm full of Tom Cruise movies (so not her choice). He laid beside her the entire night, watching movies in the living room as she slept...nightmare free! For the last year and a half, he has done everything in his power to sneak into her room at night without their parents noticing and sleep platonically by her side. Until now.

She dug out well-worn Levis and a soft white GAP t-shirt from her overcrowded closet. Fashion had never been her thing. She stuck to jeans, t-shirts and the occasional hoodie. She brushed her golden blonde hair up into a ponytail then swiped on a little mascara to accentuate her large sky blue eyes. She piled her textbooks into her backpack and headed downstairs.

"Good morning, missy! Did you sleep at all? You look exhausted." Morgan's mom Lynn, questioned her with concern as she added another sausage to an already monstrous pile of breakfast food.

"I slept...a bit." Morgan grabbed a slice of toast from the stack of food in front of her. "Is someone here I don't know about?" she asked eyeing the overloaded breakfast buffet. Plates of crispy bacon, scrambled eggs and toast filled the counter.

"No, why?" her mom answered in confusion.

"Mom, you made enough food to feed the entire block and I don't even like breakfast. Neither do you!" Morgan said.

"Breakfast is the most important meal of the day. Oprah says children should eat a complete breakfast every morning. She did studies showing that kids who ate breakfast did better in school."

Morgan shut her mouth. She knew better than to argue over the sacred words of an Oprah rerun. She was just thankful to hear the hum of Nala's car pulling into the driveway.

"Oh darn! Nala's here Mom," she said and attempted her best look of fake disappointment as she pushed the giant plate of breakfast sausage aside. "I better run... Love you!" Morgan said. She grabbed her backpack and headed for the door.

"Wait! Take some food for the road. Maybe your friends are hungry," Mom suggested as she fussed and filled a plastic lunch bag with toast and strips of low-salt bacon. Morgan took the breakfast-to-go reluctantly and kissed her mother's cheek before she ran out the door.

Morgan greeted the entire gang as she crawled into Nala's powder blue Volkswagen Beetle. Nala had been the first one in their little group to get a car, she told Morgan it was one of the perks to having divorced parents. They had made a competition out of trying to buy her love. Nala had become the appointed chauffer but she never seemed to mind; she was always the friend that kept the gang together. She was the event planner, counselor, and fashion designer for the entire group.

In the back seat, Ava and Jen, the dark-haired, large-breasted, divas, peeked up from their chronic texting and gave a smile. "How was your week off? What did you do without Lucas attached to your hip?" Ava asked curiously. Morgan was happy Nala hadn't told them about the Ferris wheel incident. She just wanted to forget it. The news crews never tracked her down so she was officially the 'unidentified girl' on the Ferris wheel and she wanted to keep it that way so she swore Nala to secrecy. Morgan hadn't even told her mom, which made her feel guilty, but she didn't see how stressing out her already overprotective mom would help matters.

"Not much," Morgan mumbled, not wanting to reveal her fight with Lucas since she knew that conversation would definitely end with an "I told you so" from Nala.

"It's weird seeing you without Lucas. Good thing it's only for a few more days, it feels like half of you is missing." Nala added. Her curly red hair bounced against her small pale shoulders as she drove.

"Good grief Nala, I hardly think I'm half a person when Lucas isn't around, that's insulting!" Morgan snapped.

"I wasn't trying to insult you. I'm just saying, I think this is the first time I have seen you two do something separately. You're always together."

Morgan shrugged and turned her attention to the scenery. Ava quickly changed the subject back to the topic she loved to discuss most- herself. She prattled on as they drove. .

When they turned into the school parking lot Ava stopped her gossiping long enough to let out an ear-piercing squeal. "O.M.G! Look what the Easter Bunny brought us!"

A tall, muscular, blonde-haired boy climbed out of a surfboard-filled, crimson Jeep.

Jen eyed the empty parking spot beside him. "Park there! Park there!" she screamed. Morgan sunk down in her seat, sure that half the school could hear Ava's shrieking from the backseat. The overstuffed Volkswagen swerved quickly into the empty stall and screeched to a halt.

Nala, Jen, and Ava all barreled out of the car through the driver's door at jet speed. They were fussing with their hair and smoothing their outfits in preparation for meeting the hot new stranger on the other side of the car. Sadly, the girls' plans were foiled when their three football player boyfriends spotted them from across the parking lot. The three girls appeared absolutely sober with disappointment when their boyfriends whisked them away before they had even gotten the new boy's attention. Morgan peered out her window and snorted.

"God, Nala, if you'd parked any closer to him, we'd have to call an ambulance," she grumbled to the empty car.

Morgan let out a little curse when she realized that there was no way to open her door without bumping the new guy who was busy looking in his vehicle for something. Sure, she enjoyed looking at hot guys as much as the next girl, but she didn't enjoy the awkward and usually idiotic tendencies she had when it came to talking to them. She couldn't talk to them. Her mouth would dry up and full sentences would disappear from her dialogue. She was so incredibly shy and uncomfortable around male strangers, that she usually felt the urge to crawl under something and disappear when a cute boy approached her. She guessed it was because her mother had never dated much over the years, so no adult male figures had ever played a role in her life. Lucas was the only boy she'd had more than a two sentence conversation with. She sure wished he was here. He would tell the new guy to get the hell out of the way so she could get out of the car. She pulled at the door handle and gently tried to open it without disturbing the boy.

Crap! I bumped his side. Why is he still standing there? "Excuse me please," Morgan mumbled, desperately trying to keep her head down and avoid all eye contact.

"Sorry, I didn't realize I was in the way," he apologized as he turned to face her and pulled open her door.

"Oh my god, Ethan!" She panicked and wanted to literally kick herself for waiting around like an idiot for him at the pier when he was trying to blow her off. She never thought she would see the guy again, let alone have to speak to him. She felt her stomach spin with queasy shyness as he stood there smiling.

"Let me help you," he offered acting as if he had never even met Morgan before. He swung around the outside of the door and stood in front of her. Not waiting for a response, he grabbed her overstuffed bag from the floor of the car and threw it over his shoulder. Morgan stepped out of the car and shut the door, still not looking up at him.

"That's fine," she mumbled and held her hand out. "Can I have my bag back, please?" She could feel the eyes of the entire student-filled parking lot, glued on her and Ethan's every move.

"That's okay, I already have it. Besides, today's my first day and I was thinking it would be great to have someone show me around. What do you say, can you help me out?" He flashed a bright smile of perfect teeth acting as if it was the first time they had ever met. Could he possibly not recognize her? She had trusted him enough to put her life in his hands.

She met his eyes and wished she hadn't. She felt goose-bumps spread across her flesh as she became locked in his gaze. She wanted to run off to her own comfortable world, but she didn't have the heart to dismiss Ethan. His extraordinarily blue eyes revealed a hypnotic swirling ocean of sapphires and ice. He took a step closer, and she sensed a strange kind of electricity between them—a cerulean light radiated in a soft silhouette around his chiseled body. The silhouette grew as she watched what she could only describe as a visible glow of energy pulsing between them. A multi-colored wave passed out of her body and into his and her knees grew weak. More colored waves escaped her body as she gripped Nala's car to steady herself. The energy pulse increased its intensity, changing shape to mimic small lightning bolts. As each bolt shot from her body it weakened her further and further. Her knees began to buckle beneath her and she crumbled to the ground. Ethan reached out to help her, but his touch seemed to draw another wave from inside her, incapacitating her even further. Morgan wanted to push Ethan away but her body turned completely numb and unresponsive, then everything went dark.

***

The scent of sandalwood and linen filled Morgan's nostrils as she slowly gained consciousness. She felt distant and confused as she opened her eyes. She tried to lift her head, but the dizzying rush she had experienced earlier quickly returned.

"Easy, Morgan, you took quite a spill." The deep, soothing voice echoed in her mind.

She surrendered to it, helplessly lowering her head till she met with a chest hard against her cheek. A surge of panic set in as her mind cleared and she realized she was in his arms!

"P..p..put me down!" she stuttered with embarrassment.

"I don't think that's a good idea," he answered.

"Set me down right now you big moose!" she yelled.

She sensed the eyes of the entire school and she was mortified. She wondered if it was possible to actually die of severe humiliation?

"I'll put you down when we get to the nurse's office. You'll soon learn that there's no point in arguing with me, Morgan. Now, where *is* the nurse's office?"

"How do you know my name? I never told you my name. I would have told you, but you stood me up" she snapped, trying to struggle free.

He did not reply.

She dropped her head back against his hard, muscular chest in a futile attempt to hide her face from the onlookers.

She had always tried to stay under the radar. She never craved the spotlight like most girls her age. Now this stranger had thrust her into her own Broadway production in her first five minutes back to school after Easter break.

She gave in to Ethan's demands, just wanting to end her torture. "The nurse is the second room on the left," she answered dryly as she closed her eyes and waited for the torture of the football teams hooting to cease.

He lowered her to the bed in the nurses' room and pulled away a little slower than she thought necessary. She felt the warmth of his breath on her cheek as he hovered over her.

"What the hell are you trying to do?" she burst at him, having had enough of his mysterious, hot guy, bull crap.

He looked at her and the swirling in his eyes stopped. He shook his head as if he was bringing himself out of a dream.

"I... I'm sorry, I didn't mean to. I...my..." he stammered, like he was the vulnerable one who had passed out into the arms of a complete stranger.

"My name's Ethan Scott. I transferred from Vancouver last week. I apologize for making you uncomfortable, Morgan. I can sense that you don't like to draw attention. Although, you're so beautiful, I'm not sure how going unnoticed is even an option."

Morgan noticed he hadn't apologized for standing her up at the pier and grunted at his false flattery. She never thought of herself as ugly but she had also never been called beautiful by a boy before. He studied her in a puzzled way. "You don't believe me?" he asked with surprise. "You will, my sweet. You will."

He stepped close enough to sweep the hair from her forehead with his fingertips then headed for the door. "I'll come back and check on you after first class." He grinned then disappeared through the doorway.

What the hell just happened? She played the bizarre scene in the parking lot over and over in her head. *My Sweet? Who the heck is this crazy guy? This crazy, smoking hot, chiseled-like-a-god, guy? And why is he talking to ME? After ditching me after the Ferris wheel, I'm surprised he didn't leave me lying unconscious in the parking lot. My Sweet? Really? Who says that?*

Morgan closed her eyes as the school's elderly nurse entered the room. She explained what had happened (for the most part anyway), and allowed the kindly lady to check her over.

The nurse came to a conclusion quickly. She told Morgan that she needed to start eating more for breakfast. Morgan laughed at the irony of the situation.

She thought guiltily of the breakfast her mom had prepared that morning and knew if she ever told her mom about fainting she would get an "I told you so" and an even bigger breakfast-filled lunch bag tomorrow. She swore to never tell her mom about her fainting spell, but she would listen and start eating more breakfast. Heck, she was determined to eat like a linebacker from now on if it meant not having to face the humiliation of fainting in the arms of a complete stranger ever again!

One idiotic damsel in distress moment per lifetime was enough for her.

She reached into her worn nylon backpack, pulled out the breakfast in a bag, snatched out a piece of bacon, and gnawed at it diligently.

Morgan peered at the clock and realized she had two minutes till the end of first period. She darted from the office leaving the doting school nurse dumbfounded as to her sudden energy burst.

Morgan wanted to get out of the infirmary before Ethan returned to check on her.

He was totally confusing, and she had more on her plate than she could handle—except maybe food. Until Lucas got back and everything was cleared up with him, dating was definitely not an option. She wished Lucas was here now and not gone on holiday's for another stupid week. They had always been one another's safety net. This morning's drama would never have happened if he had been in the car with her. Lucas played on the football team like Nala, Jen, and Ava's boyfriends, who were the reason Morgan's friends incessantly tried to push her and Lucas into coupledom. Morgan understood that it would make the group outings a lot easier. Sometimes she wondered if she should just give in and date him—it was what everyone wanted. Everyone but her. Something just felt wrong between them; there was no chemistry. She'd always felt a strong bond with him and she loved him, but not in any way that meant she should be his girlfriend. She hoped her feelings about their bond being an unbreakable one were right or she feared she may have lost Lucas for good.

She felt warmth behind her as she fumbled through her locker and somehow she knew exactly who it was.

"So, this is Morgan in a nutshell, always doing what's best for the group? Who is this Lucas?" he whispered into her ear as he stood behind her.

Slamming her locker, she spun around to face the new guy. She was done with his antics. "What? What's going on here? Who are you? Who's been telling you things about me?" she demanded, feeling the dizziness of this morning rushing back to her head.

"Whoa, easy," Ethan said, as he reached out to support her arm.

She pulled her arm back roughly, accidentally slamming it into the locker behind her. "Stay away from me! I don't know you and I don't want to! All I do know is when you're around crazy things keep happening to me."

Her mind began to fog over again. She shoved Ethan an arm's length away from her, thankful to spot Nala and the rest of the crew approaching.

"Wow, Morgan, if that's how you treat your rescuers I would hate to see how you treat your enemies!" Nala mused as she eyeballed Ethan.

Morgan looked downward, embarrassed and confused by her own behavior. She tried to figure out why this guy stirred up so much anxiety in her. She hated feeling so out of her comfort zone. She was being an idiot and completely rude, but for some reason his simple presence seemed to mess with every emotion in her body.

"Hi, I'm Nala, Morgan's friend," Nala offered as she extended her hand to Ethan. Morgan felt unexplainable anger swelling inside of her as Nala and Ethan's hands touched. Without thinking, she suddenly jumped between them and pushed Nala back into the lockers.

"Wow, Morgan, possessive much?" Nala grumbled rubbing her arm in the spot Morgan had pushed her.

Morgan couldn't believe what she had just done. How could she get so irritated over her best friend touching some crazy guy she didn't even know?

Nala continued a little more cautiously. "This is Ava and Jen," she announced as she pointed at the two girls while they did sleazy curtsies in his direction.

"Hey," Ethan said in an uninterested mumble, his gaze never leaving Morgan.

Ava and Jen wandered off amazed and disappointed. They were always the prettiest and most desired girls in the school. Every boy noticed them. Every boy but Ethan.

"Hmm," Nala mumbled.

Morgan noticed that even Nala was surprised by Ethan's lack of interest in their friends. She couldn't help but smile. She had never considered herself as being in the same league as those two girls with their tall, voluptuous, spray-tanned bodies and perfectly manicured hair and nails, they exuded a sexiness Morgan never dreamed of possessing. Heads always turned when Ava and Jen walked in a room, so receiving all the attention in spite of them standing before him in mini-skirts and designer heels, felt pretty darn good.

Nala turned to Ethan but was careful to keep her distance when she spoke to him this time. "We are going to the diner by the Santa Monica Pier after school. You should come with us. Morgan can buy you a milkshake to thank you for rescuing her this morning," she suggested as she nudged Morgan repeatedly and awaited his response.

Ethan stared at Morgan and smiled. She studied his face, knowing that he knew that she could not refuse the invitation when Nala phrased it like that.

Ending the awkward silence growing between them all, he finally responded, "Well, that's up to Morgan, of course. I wouldn't want to make her..." He paused and took a step back, breaking his intense stare, "unhappy," he finished, looking hurt by the words uttered from his own lips.

"No...I mean yes..." Morgan fumbled. "No. I don't mind. Yes, I do owe you a milkshake for your trouble. Repayment by milkshake is a custom we have around here. You should come with us after school," she answered, inviting him before she changed her mind. "Please forgive me for being so snippy this morning. I'm just not myself today. I guess I'm not used to getting hauled around by complete strangers."

"Well, we aren't strangers anymore, I'm your rescuer remember?" he said. "See you after school." He winked then spun on his heel and walked down the hall.

Morgan collapsed against the locker desperately needing to catch her breath. She gave herself a little mental reminder to kill Nala after school for the whole "come to the diner" bit.

What the hell is she trying to do? I have enough going on with Lucas! Nala is the one who keeps nagging me to go out with him, and now she's throwing Ethan in my face!

Uuuggh Ethan! How did he know what I was thinking earlier, and what the hell even happened this morning? The thoughts whizzed around Morgan's head till she felt a headache coming on.

Morgan decided to put it all out of her mind until after school. Which was no easy task since despite her best efforts, Ethan seemed to be all she could think about since the Ferris wheel. She scooped up her AP books and headed to class.

Chapter 3

When the final bell rang, Morgan sat at her desk a few extra minutes, hoping to prolong the inevitable. Nala poked her head in the doorway.

"Come on, Morgan. Mr. Muscles is waiting for you!" Nala chuckled at Morgan's torment.

God, why am I friends with her? Morgan thought as she pried herself from her seat and headed for the door.

Jen and Ava were already in the parking lot casually leaning against Nala's car with wide smiles across their devious faces. Morgan rolled her eyes at the troublesome duo as she nudged past them and opened the car door. She just wanted to get this over with. Jen swooped in as the door opened and plunked her butt in the front seat.

"Shotgun!" she yelled out.

"Oh, I just remembered the boys wanted me to ride with them. I will meet you guys there," Ava schemed.

"Cows," Morgan grumbled as she turned toward the backseat, knowing exactly what she would find.

Ethan was scrunched up, sitting patiently in the tiny hatchback. Morgan couldn't help but let out a giggle at the sight of this massive guy packed into the back of a Volkswagen Beetle.

He grinned. "I amuse you?" he asked with a deep, warm, smile that spread upwards to his ocean blue eyes.

"Yes, you do. You amuse me, and confuse me, and frustrate me!" she confided. "Wouldn't you prefer taking your own car?" she asked hoping he would take the hint.

His smile disappeared and he answered her with a single word. "No."

When they arrived at the Oceanside Diner they were greeted by the familiar smell of fries mixed with the salty air. The girls piled out of the front of the vehicle and ran off to meet their boyfriends.

Morgan wished Lucas wasn't on his stupid family vacation. Using him as a fake boyfriend at her convenience wasn't fair, but it sure came in handy when she was faced with situations like today.

After clumsily crawling from the backseat, Ethan stood and tried to stretch the kinks from his body. His joints popped and cracked. Morgan stood in quiet awe of his massive size. He appeared to be well over six feet of pure muscle. She knew that he was extremely uncomfortable the entire drive but he just smiled and did not complain. His knees had been folded up around his ears for the entire ride. Luckily, the diner was only a couple of blocks from the school; any longer and he probably would have required a chiropractor!

Ethan caught her staring at him and before she had a chance to turn away, he extended his hand to her. "Shall we?" he asked, as his face spread into a heart-stopping smile that made Morgan blush straight through to her toes.

Ignoring his outstretched hand, she walked past him and headed for the diner's entrance. Ethan ran ahead and pulled the door open for her like a perfect gentleman.

She paused. A boy had never opened a door for her before. She hesitantly stepped forward, realizing that Ethan was so tall she was able to walk right under his arm and into the diner.

As they stood in line waiting for service, Morgan watched Ethan's face turn serious. "Are you always this intense? Is this like a Canadian thing?" she asked as she searched the busy diner for her conveniently missing friends.

He didn't answer as he grinned then placed his hand on the small of her back.

A zap of electricity surged through her body where he was touching her. She pulled away. "I guess that's a yes!" she yelped.

She gathered her strength and faced Ethan straight on. "I don't know what you want from me, but you should know that I have a boyfriend. Well, kind of. I'm just not available. So...So, you need to keep your hands to yourself!" she spoke in a low growl, trying to get her point across without making a scene.

"Your booth is ready," the middle-aged server bellowed across the restaurant, as she pointed to a booth for two.

"No, we need a table for eight!" Morgan argued.

The waitress shrugged her shoulders as she smacked on her gum impatiently. "The big booths are all taken and we are real busy. Do you kids want this table or not?"

"That table will work just fine, thank you." Ethan answered politely as he followed the waitress and slid himself into one end of the two-person booth.

Morgan sighed as she took the seat opposite him.

"We would like vanilla shakes and a plate of fries please," Ethan ordered.

The forty-something waitress blushed when he spoke to her. Morgan smirked; at least the service would be good today.

She turned her attention back to Ethan, his eyes fixed on hers. "Don't," she whispered lowering her head to break their stare as she fidgeted with the salt shaker.

"Don't what?" he asked as he reached his hand across the table and placed his fingers beneath her chin, gently tilting her face up to meet his.

Morgan let out the breath of tension she had been holding in all day. She figured she might as well tell this guy everything she was thinking. What did she have to lose? "There is something strange about you. I don't know what it is exactly, but you are unlike anyone I have ever met. When you look at me it's like you're gazing into my very soul...You...This... " She flapped her arm wildly gesturing to the two of them, "Kinda freaks me out! I mean, don't get me wrong, you're a super-hot guy and I sense that I'm safe around you, you saved my life, but when you're close to me crazy things start happening. This morning I could have sworn I saw a blue cloud surrounding your body, like an aura or something. And I think I have lost my mind because when you touch me there are sparks, and not 'oh he's so dreamy sparks' but like real freaking sparks!"

Ethan sat across from Morgan, silent and void of expression. She waited patiently for him to call her a complete nut-ball and walk out of the diner planning to never talk to her again. Instead he said nothing. He just sat there with his head down, twisting his napkin.

The waitress arrived with their milkshakes and fries and sloughed them on the table. Stealthily, she dropped a tiny paper on Ethan's lap and gave him a cougar-like wink before she walked away.

Morgan stared in disbelief. "Okay, did she just slip you her number?"

Ethan reached down and crumpled up the note without ever taking his eyes away from Morgan's astonished face.

"You think I'm super-hot?" he asked.

"That's all you heard in my long spiel isn't it?" she asked, fuming with frustration. "I have a boyfriend, Ethan." she lied.

"No, you don't. He's a prop, nothing more than a friend and someone to fill a space while you wait."

Morgan looked at him in confusion. "Wait? Wait for what?"

"For me." He leaned back into his seat and confidently slurped the remainder of his vanilla milkshake.

Morgan realized arguing with this guy was pointless. "I gotta go. If you were really interested in me you wouldn't have blown me off at the pier. You had me sitting there at the entrance still shaking from the trauma I endured and waiting for you, like an idiot. " she said.

She was done playing Ethan's weird little games. How could he call Lucas her prop? He didn't even know her and for him to assume she was shallow enough to treat Lucas as a prop till something better comes along, really got under her skin. She rose from the table coming to the conclusion that he was even crazier than she was. She wasn't sure what was happening between them, but whatever it was she was done with it. She surveyed the diner for Nala and the crew.

The waitress saw her looking around and shouted over the crowd as she pointed to the empty parking spot outside. "Your friends left honey!"

Perfect! They are so dead tomorrow. Morgan fumed.

She slumped back down into the booth, ignoring Ethan's smug smile.

He pulled money from his pocket and threw it on the bill then stood and extended his hand to Morgan.

"Well, well, I guess your friends think you should be with me, too."

She ignored his hand and rose on her own. "I guess my friends don't actually think!" She grabbed the bill off the table and handed Ethan's his money. "I was supposed to buy you a shake," she said.

He accepted the money from her but then slipped it back on the table. "You will not provide for me. Buying you a milkshake is an honor."

She was about to retort but he cut her off. "This is one argument you won't win Morgan."

Morgan shook her head. Every once in a while this guy talked more like he was from a different century instead of a different country.

He ushered her out of the restaurant and she questioned their next move with a raised eyebrow.

"We can walk back to my car. It is only a few blocks away and it's a beautiful sunny day. I don't get to enjoy these much where I'm from."

"You don't have sun in Vancouver?" Morgan asked even more confused by the strange boy beside her.

"Come on," he tugged at her arm. "You just have to walk with me a little, then I promise to drive you straight home."

As they approached the sidewalk Morgan blurted the question that had been running through her head for days. "Why did you ditch me at the pier? Do you know how traumatized I was from the accident? Despite the trauma I had just gone through, I waited for the boy who saved my life because he asked me to. How could you ditch me like that?"

Ethan stopped and turned to her.

"I'm sorry Morgan. You need to know that I did everything in my power to get back to you. I went after the boys from the Ferris wheel, but they overpowered me. It's no excuse, though. I never should've gone after those boys. I should've stayed by your side and made sure you got home safely. I would never intentionally ditch you. I'm beyond sorry. Can you forgive me for being such an idiot?"

Morgan shrugged her shoulders, "Maybe."

Morgan stepped onto the sidewalk, not wanting to argue with Ethan any further, as it didn't seem very productive anyhow. Ethan reached down and grabbed her hand intertwining their fingers. Morgan's first reaction was to pull away, but Ethan held on firmly. She felt an inner warmth and comfort building inside her body when he touched her, persuading her to give in. She curled her fingers around his, allowing the wall between them to crumble slightly. They walked in silence along the vacant sidewalk. Morgan sensed more than their hands joining as they moved forward. She knew she should be alarmed, but she did not feel weakened or dizzy like the last time. This time it felt right, like her body had been waiting for this. The small tendrils of swirling light she had seen that morning began to flow. The bluish aura surrounding Ethan grew steadily as she watched it glisten in the sunlight.

"What is this? What are you doing to me?" she gasped

"Just walk with me and relax, you're safe with me. I think you know that right?" He slowed to a stop and faced her for her answer as the lights continued to dance around their joined hands.

Morgan looked into the eyes of the boy who saved her life and rescued her again this morning. Yes, she honestly knew she was safe with him.

She nodded then spoke, "I do trust you, but I need you to tell me what the strands of light are, and to tell me why you blew me off at the pier then show up at school acting all interested in me?"

"Not tonight, just keep walking and watch the lights with an open mind." He answered and began to walk again.

Ethan's magnificent blue aura reached out further, wrapping Morgan inside of it and filling her with indescribable happiness. Her skin felt bathed in warmth as all her worries and tension melted away. Small surges of heat and electricity were steadily flowing up her arm from where their hands met. She allowed the tiny strands of light to enter her body and enjoyed the rush of energy as they surged through her from head to toe. Morgan embraced the strange connection she had to the mysterious by she clung to as they continued to walk in silence.

Ethan stopped and turned to face her once again. Morgan was shocked to see that they had already reached the school parking lot. She had been so caught up in the sensations of simply holding his hand that she hadn't spoken a single word for the entire three blocks!

"Come on," he said, giving her a little shake to lift her out of her dreamlike state. "Let's get you home."

He opened the car door and she reluctantly let go of his hand. She slipped into her seat, longing to have her hand back in his. She placed her palm face up on her lap hoping he would reach for it when he got in, but he didn't.

Driving down the Santa Monica beach line, they were mostly silent. Morgan gave Ethan directions to her house, and they arrived quicker than she had hoped.

Ethan parked on the street in front of her small house. "I would like to take you to the beach tomorrow"

"I can't," she said.

He shifted backwards pressing his body against his door; she knew her refusal hurt him. "I thought maybe," he paused in search of the right words, "I thought maybe things changed for you on our walk. I thought you had seen enough to know you can trust me, trust this...trust us."

"I thought you knew that there is no 'us', because I am an 'us' with someone else."

Seeing the impact of her words on Ethan's face made her hate saying them, but she didn't trust anything that was happening. How could she trust something that was so incredibly strange? Things were moving way too fast for her to wrap her head around them. This morning her only worry was the fight between her and Lucas. Now she was wrapped up in some crazy, intense, visible connection with a complete stranger!

She tried to soften the blow a little. "It's not you, Ethan, I don't like the beach. I never have," she explained. "I can't swim and the thought of walking into an immense body of water full of sharks, weeds, sea monsters, and god knows what else, makes me panic." She looked down in embarrassment. A girl who lived by the ocean but was scared to go near it; he probably thought she was an idiot.

"Sea monsters?" he asked with a chuckle. She was not amused. "We will change that, my sweet Morgan. Don't be embarrassed. I completely understand why you would be scared to return to the ocean."

"Return to the ocean? What do you mean?" she asked, puzzled by his statement.

Instead of answering he leaned in toward her. She closed her eyes in anticipation, eagerly turning her body in his direction. His breathing quickened, echoing through the silence. Her seatbelt clicked as he undid the buckle, his arm grazing her chest as he guided the belt back into the seat. His breath lingered on her cheek as she clenched her eyelids and desperately awaited the touch of his full lips. She had never desired a kiss more in her life. Keeping her eyes closed tight, she tried to control her breathing. The distracting click of the door brought her back to her senses. Ethan was getting out of the car! He walked around the front and then opened the door for her.

Her face reddened and she prayed that Ethan hadn't noticed how eager she had been to kiss him.

What the hell is wrong with me? Pull what's left of your dignity together and smile politely, you idiot, she chastised herself.

Ethan reached in to help her from her seat.

"My, my, you really are old fashioned," she said with a double meaning she hoped he would not catch.

Taking his large hand, she awkwardly crawled from his Jeep.. She was surprised by her disappointment over his lack of advances, yet furious and confused at herself for wanting that.

What was she thinking? She had to deal with her "Lucas issues" before getting involved with some other guy. If Lucas heard she'd kissed someone days after he confessed his love for her, their friendship would never recover and he would probably hate her forever.

She blushed yet again when she realized she was standing deep in thought still holding the hand Ethan used to help her out of the car. Trying to get as much distance as possible between her and this handsome stranger, she pulled away and bolted up the sidewalk as fast as her legs would walk without running. How did this strange boy send her world spinning with a simple touch? She needed this night to end and be forgotten before she got herself into more trouble. Ethan began to follow after her.

"No need to walk me to the door; it is right there. Thanks for the ride home!" She hurried up the front steps trying to get away from him and all the unexplainable events of the day while trying not to scuttle off like a complete lunatic.

"Morgan, wait!"

She opened the door to her house and pretended not to hear.

"Morgan, stop!"

She turned in the doorway and found his handsome face gazing up at her from the bottom step. He climbed the wooden porch stairs and approached her; his voice was low and intense.

"I wanted to kiss you in the car, but I resisted. You're unsure of me still. I will kiss you one day soon, my sweet, and believe me Morgan, when I do kiss you, there won't be an ounce of doubt in your mind."

He was standing inches away. Her name on his lips was all she could comprehend as she focused most of her attention on keeping her knees from buckling under the intensity of his stare.

"Please come to the beach with me tomorrow. You won't regret it," he said, as he gently ran his hand along her arm.

Weak with emotion, she couldn't refuse him any longer. She nodded her head, yielding to his request.

He leaned in and brushed his lips against her neck.

Not wanting to resist, she lifted her arms to embrace him but he had already pulled away and was headed down the stairs.

"See you tomorrow then!" he shouted behind him as he strode toward his car.

God he's good, Morgan smiled, as she rolled her eyes and walked into her house.

I bet I would have said 'yes' to jumping off a bridge if he had asked me! she thought as she walked into the kitchen, rubbing her neck where Ethan's lips still lingered on her skin.

Lucas! You can't do this to Lucas, the little voice in her head scolded.

"Who's the boy?" Mom's voice echoed from the living room.

Her mom was standing in the living room, her hands on the pulled-back curtains, peering out of the front bay window. Morgan smiled at her mother's overprotective nature. They had always been a two-person team since Morgan was adopted as an infant.

Throughout the years, her mom had assumed not only the role of doting mother but that of overprotective father as well.

"He's just a friend, Mom," Morgan answered, attempting to be aloof.

"A friend who walks you to the door? What about Lucas? Won't he be upset that you found another 'friend' while he was away?"

"Last time I checked a person could have as many friends as they like, Mom," Morgan said. "I'm going to my room." She quickly headed upstairs to avoid further interrogation, not finding the overprotective father act quite as endearing as she had a moment earlier.

Chapter 4

Morgan rummaged through her closet until she spotted the bag of last year's birthday presents crumpled up in the back corner. She dumped the tattered pink gift bag onto her bed and grabbed the jean miniskirt and rhinestone tank top out of the pile of girly clothes her friends insisted on buying her every year. They knew their trendy outfits would never see daylight again, but they were persistent in trying to break Morgan of her Plain Jane dressing habits.

Morgan and the girls became quick friends when they all made the grade seven Junior pom squad but when cheerleading got serious in grade ten Morgan was the only one to get cut from the team. She was worried that her friendships with the girls would crumble or fade away but they surprised her with their loyalty. They always sought her out at lunch or after cheer practice and made a continued effort to keep her in the fold.

Morgan slid into the admittedly cute ensemble and snapped the tags off as she eyed herself in the mirror. Her straight blonde hair was down for once and it flowed smoothly over her shoulders to her mid-back. She finished the look with a pair of simple silver dangle earrings and black strappy sandals. *WOW!* she thought, barely recognizing the girl in the mirror in front of her. She took a deep breath and headed downstairs before she lost her nerve.

"Here goes nothin'," she whispered.

Morgan moved stealthily through the kitchen managing to grab a handful of breakfast as she avoided her mother. "I'm late, so I gotta run, see you later Mom!" she yelled toward the laundry room. She felt a little guilty about sneaking anything past her mom; they had a really great relationship but she was already unsure of this "look at me" outfit and didn't want to have to explain the change in style, or lose her nerve.

She wasn't sure why she felt the need to dress up today. At least that was what she kept telling herself.

She grabbed her backpack then paused before opening the front door. What was she doing? She couldn't go out like this. She turned around and headed toward the stairs as the door opened behind her.

"Oh...My...God! Morgan?!"

Morgan felt her entire body blush with embarrassment as she turned to face a dumfounded Nala standing in the entranceway.

"I came to see what was taking you so long. Now I know. You were being abducted by aliens! Where did frumpy t-shirt girl go?" she asked, not waiting for, or wanting an answer. "Come on, let's go. I can't wait for the crew to see you!" Nala chirped, way too happy about a little wardrobe change in Morgan's opinion.

"I made a mistake, I just need to run up and change. Give me a couple of minutes and..."

"Oh, no you don't!" Nala grabbed Morgan's arm and pulled her toward the door. "I don't know what brought on this change, but you are going to stick with it, at least for today. I bet you just took the tags off that outfit!"

Morgan hung her head in defeat; she knew there was no point in arguing. Nala had never been one to mince words; she was straightforward and as stubborn as they came. So, like it or not, she was now stuck with the attire she had on.

In preparation for all the hooting and hollering she knew was coming her way, Morgan took a deep breath as she opened the car door to the fashion divas inside.

They didn't disappoint.

Now that Morgan was part of the "fashion world," Ava and Jen prattled the whole way to school about the latest in makeup and clothes, talking to her like she had just awoken from a style coma. They had avoided such things before since they knew Morgan didn't care and would always change the subject. Morgan still didn't care, but they seemed so happy with the idea that they had finally converted her to the world of fashion "now," that she couldn't bear to burst their bubbles.

When Nala turned into the school parking lot, Morgan found herself scanning for Ethan's vehicle. It wasn't there.

To Morgan's surprise, maneuvering her body out of Nala's car while not exposing her underwear to the entire high school, was much harder than she realized. She wondered why the hell girls wore such awkward things. After another quick scan of the parking lot, she headed for the school entrance trying to hide her obvious disappointment from Nala. She didn't think that she was dressing up for Ethan but it was hard to lie to herself. She just wasn't sure why she felt the need to impress a guy she didn't even know. How could he make such an impression on her after one day? He was frustrating, arrogant, and extremely forward. The absolute opposite of what she looked for in a guy, but for some crazy, unexplainable reason she could not stop thinking about him.

During the morning classes, Morgan found herself moping around, incapable of concentrating on anything but Ethan. All the extra attention she'd gotten from almost every boy in the school didn't even seem cheer her up. Morgan knew she was getting the extra attention because of the way she was dressed, which was why she never dressed this way, ever. She had always been a "blender," not a stand-out-in-the-crowd type of gal, and she hated being noticed by every single person she walked by. She could almost feel the extra energy they were directing at her.

When first period was over Morgan stepped outside of Mr. Goldam's math class and into the hall. The more people that shuffled around her, the more disoriented she felt. She could see thin wisps of whitish clouds forming around each of the kids in the hallway. She tried to move forward but even the simple act of walking was becoming difficult. The clouds grew and became dense. A streak of dizzying jolts began hitting her body as one-by-one the wispy formations blasted toward her. As each cloud hit, her body surged with what felt like pure energy. What was going on? Was she sick? She felt light-headed and was unable to focus as the crowd's faces whizzed by her in a tornado of noise, colors, and energy. Her knees weakened, sending her crashing against the locker behind her. She stumbled forward, frantically forcing her legs to move. She had to get out of the school and away from the chaos or she would end up fainting like she had yesterday.

The entrance doors flew open as Morgan shoved them with excessive force. She let out a little cry as she tumbled forwards and skidded out, onto the cement entranceway on her bare knees. She lifted herself up, brushing the grit from her scrapes and limped toward the side wall of the school where she always went with Nala when they needed a little privacy.

She pressed her back against the rough, stucco wall and closed her eyes. Taking deep breaths of the fresh morning air, she tried to stop the uncontrollable shaking that consumed her body. She was thankful nobody had followed her outside or witnessed her crazy exit. After a few minutes of regrouping, she felt a hand on her shoulder. She did not need to open her eyes to know who it was. She felt a warm surge of energy flow down her arm and spread through her body, calming her completely.

"You weren't in school this morning," she said.

Morgan opened her eyes as Ethan stepped in front of her, his face enveloped in a silken smile as the sun shone through his golden blonde hair.

"You noticed?" he smiled.

"I am not feeling well; I think I should go home. Could you give me a ride?" Morgan asked, not wanting to wait for Nala.

He nodded his head and slid his arm into the small of her back as he led her to his Jeep.

Before Morgan could reach for the door Ethan scooped her off her feet and into his arms. "Allow me." He smiled and gently slid her over the door of the convertible and down into her seat.

He reached across her, leaning intentionally close as he attempted to fasten her seatbelt. Morgan grabbed the belt away from him. "I'm not that sick."

"Forgive me," Ethan nodded as he backed off.

He walked around the vehicle and hopped into the seat beside her, staring at her. Morgan could tell he was noticing her choice of outfit for the first time as an ear-to-ear grin suddenly spread across his face.

She suddenly felt self-conscious, but also a little powerful. She crossed her lean, ivory legs toward him. Ethan's eyes locked on her exposed skin, and she could hear his breathing slow as he closed his eyes.

The blue cloud she had seen around Ethan yesterday began to swirl around his body. A jolt of panic flushed through her as she waited for the dizzying weakness, but this time was different. As the dizziness resurfaced it transformed. Instead of frailty, she felt strength and power building within her. For the first time she felt in control of herself and the clouds of energy between them. She allowed the wisps of blue to wrap around her, gliding across her skin in long curious tendrils as she welcomed the soothing sensation. It felt good and it felt right. She took a deep breath pulling the tendrils in through her nostrils, drawing even more of them into her body as they muffled the sounds around her. She reveled in the pure joy the blue cloud was giving her and she wanted more. She leaned in to Ethan, trying to draw more of the intoxicating energy from him. His eyes remained closed as he let out a quiet moan. Blue shards of swirling light flowed freely from Ethan's chest and danced between them. Ethan's cloud of blue was not met by her own white swirl of energy—this time it all seemed to flow toward and into her. She felt her body grow stronger as it consumed all the energy between them. The wisps of light had changed into a steady glowing stream, filtering straight into her body.

Ethan's energy came to her as the streak of light grew larger and more forceful. She breathed it in, her body absorbing it more and more rapidly. She felt a rush of pure energy from her head to her toes. The power surged through her body making her feel so alive and so unbelievably happy. She felt in control of it, and her body was calling on it, demanding more as an inner strength built up inside her.

Ethan lifted his hand limply toward her. His lips opened to speak but the sounds he made were inaudible. She put her ear closer to his mouth. Then the words he muttered finally reached her.

"STOP, please Morgan, STOP, you're killing me."

What? Killing Him!

She didn't know how to stop, and her body didn't want it to stop. She wanted more, so much more. The color drained from Ethan's face and somehow she knew his soul was fading. But why was he asking her to stop? He was doing this, not her. Wasn't he?

Morgan pushed herself away from Ethan, chopping at the cloud between them with her hands in a desperate attempt to stop the flow of energy between them but she couldn't stop it. She didn't even know what it was. Ethan's energy had now become no more than thin wisps of light flowing from his chest. His head slumped backwards as his body went limp against the dark leather seat.

He is going to die, she panicked. *I have to find a way to stop this, NOW!*

Fighting the intense pull the energy had over her; she reached for the door handle and gave one big push. She threw herself from the Jeep, spilling onto the pavement below and scraping her already-skinned knees even worse. She felt the break between them as she fell, and the energy flow had stopped. Paying no attention to her bleeding knee, she lifted herself off the ground and ran around to Ethan's side of the vehicle. She flung his door open. His body was pale and unresponsive.

"Ethan, Ethan!" she screamed, shaking his still body.

She put her ear to his chest to listen for a heartbeat. It was there, but weak. She lifted her ear to his mouth and listened for breathing. A rush of air grazed her face and Ethan began to gasp and choke a few times as color slowly returned to his face. Morgan realized that she was still awkwardly close to his face and began to take a step back but Ethan pulled her back in toward him.

"You shouldn't have worn that outfit today," he growled in her ear.

She couldn't help but smile an evil seductive smile.

Ethan let out another small growl. "You are a little minx, aren't you?"

"Are you okay?" she asked, their faces so close their lips almost grazed one another's.

"Yes," he whispered.

"What happened? Did I do that to you? Do you know what is happening to me?" She stared at him demanding an answer.

He lowered his eyes and she pulled her face away. She stood, towering over him, waiting for a response.

He did not turn to look at her and she knew he had the answers to her questions but he was reluctant to tell her the truth.

She shut his door gently, then walked around and slid back into her seat. She took a chance and placed her hand on his knee, leaving thoughts of everything else in the world behind her, including thoughts of Lucas. She focused solely on the indescribable connection she felt to this boy she had known for only two days. He didn't pull away but he did not look at her either; he just started the car and put it in reverse.

"Will you tell me everything?" she asked, softly breaking their silence.

Ethan backed the Jeep out of its stall before he finally stopped to look at her. "Yes, I will explain everything."

Chapter 5

The vehicle turned south along the scenic ocean drive, which was not in the direction of Morgan's house.

"Where are we going?" she asked.

"You're feeling better, right?" Ethan asked waiting for her nod. "Good, then we're going to go have a little fun."

"Not the beach, not today," she argued. She hated going anywhere near the ocean, it seemed to make her recurring nightmares that much more vivid. They would start with her fighting for air beneath the water's surface as she sank further and further into the watery darkness. The cold saltwater burned her throat as it forced itself in through her gasping mouth. Her eyes and nostrils stung as the salty water shows no mercy. Something grabs her, something dark and flowing that radiates the heavy feeling of death across her body. It forms a glass-like wall of water behind her, preventing her escape. Morgan tries to make out the face of her attacker, but it is clouded by the darkness that surrounds it. Each night it rips the flesh from her throat and she would lie on the ocean floor helplessly waiting for her heart to take its final beat. People always told her it was impossible to watch yourself die in a dream. They were wrong. She had watched herself die twenty seven times before Lucas became her savior.

"No beach, I promise." He took her hand in his and gave it a gentle squeeze. "Just relax and enjoy the ride. Feel the wind on your face and breathe in some of this beautiful ocean air."

He accelerated down Ocean Boulevard and then turned onto the Pacific Coast Highway.

Trying to relax, Morgan pressed her back firmly into the seat and closed her eyes. She drew long deep breaths letting them calm her body as the wind whipped her hair against the leather headrest. Ethan turned up the radio.

"You're not kidnapping me or smuggling me across the Mexican border are you?" she asked playfully.

"No, I think we'll stay in the U.S. for the time being. Maybe we'll try the Mexico kidnapping idea tomorrow." He laughed.

"Pleeease tell me where we're going?" she asked, flashing him her best attempt at puppy dog eyes.

He held his hand up. "All right I surrender! I'll talk; just put the puppy dog eyes away." He chuckled. "We're going to a cool aquarium Nala told me about."

She rolled her eyes. "What's with you and ocean-related activities?"

He looked at her, the smile falling from his face. "I'm sorry. I didn't think an aquarium amusement park, qualified as 'the ocean.' You don't hate sea creatures do you?"

She squeezed his hand. "I'm just giving you a hard time. I love the aquarium. My mom has taken me there twice a year since I was a toddler. This will be fun. I had better call home and tell Mom I'm hanging at Nala's house for the afternoon so she doesn't freak."

The trip went quickly as they argued over music and movies. The conversation flowed easily between them, as if they had known each other their entire lives.

They pulled into the tourist stuffed parking lot at the aquarium and Ethan parked. He opened his door but Morgan grabbed his arm before he could get out. "Are you going to give me answers about earlier today? I need to know what's happening to me."

He gave a warm smile of reassurance. "I'm going to tell you, but not today. Today we're going to have fun. When I take you out again tomorrow, I will tell you everything. Deal?" he bargained.

"What makes you think you're getting a second date tomorrow?" she teased.

"What makes you think this is a 'first' date?" he replied.

Embarrassed by her assumption she turned, trying to hide her reddened face.

Taking her hand softly into his, Ethan tugged gently so that she would face him. He looked at the ground as he kicked at the pavement. "Actually, I count this as our second date. I know you have unresolved issues with... Lucas is it?" she nodded and he continued. "But, I like you Morgan. From the moment we met there has been this connection between us and I hope you're willing to give us a chance because you're all I think about. We've been through so much in such a short amount of time. I feel a strong connection to you it goes beyond the energy you can physically see between us."

Morgan noticed small worry lines forming above Ethan's thick blonde brows as his full lips tightened to a thin line. A feeling of disbelief washed over her as she realized the amazing guy in front of her looked worried that she would reject him! She thought about what he said. Energy. That was what the streams of light were. She could suddenly see energy, but why? She thought maybe it was some sort of post-traumatic stress disorder but then why did Ethan see it too? And what's really crazy is she felt like she was actually briefly in control of the energy between them this afternoon.

He took her silence as a sign of hesitation.

"Just relax and enjoy the day with me. I promise to explain everything that has been going on with you, tomorrow. Deal?" he negotiated.

Laughter and cheers echoed from the park, and like a small child visiting for the first time, she felt the anticipation of fun building inside her. Ethan's explanation could wait a little longer. "Deal," she answered.

They passed through the tourist-filled gates and headed to the Tower-Riser ride. Ethan maneuvered himself through the crowded glass elevator ride, till he found a comfortable spot behind Morgan and they rode the vessel skyward. From their high vantage point, they could see the whole park and out across the ocean. "I love this ride," she whispered behind her. Ethan wrapped his arms around her, pulling her against his chest. They silently stared out toward the ocean, soaking in its beauty.

After the Tower-Riser they headed to the dolphin show. The sleek grey animals danced through the water with precision and grace. Morgan loved watching them perform. "Do you think they are as smart as people think they are?" she asked, not taking her eyes from the performance.

"What do you think?" he asked, his eyes glued to her and not the show.

"I think they are smarter than we could ever imagine."

"I agree," he said and stole a quick kiss on her cheek.

She turned her face to him and blushed.

When the dolphin show ended, Morgan pulled Ethan toward the Sea Lions and Seal habitat. "These are my favorites! Well, second favorites," she stated. "I like the shark tank the best, but I always save that for last."

As she and Ethan strolled hand in hand, Morgan thought of her first visit to the park. She remembered weaving through the crowds of screaming children, till she heard the grunting of sea lions. Her heart raced. The smell of salt water wafted through her nostrils and she remembered her mother gently holding her hand so long ago.

"Those are sea lions, sweetie," her mother had said.

Morgan looked at the slippery animals. She felt a strong desire to jump in the water, to swim, to touch their glistening skin. One of the baby sea lion pups poked his head out of the water and swam up to the glass, bobbing up and down. Morgan placed her tiny hand to the glass – she could almost touch his whiskers. His beady eyes held hers for a brief but memorable moment and a feeling of calm passed through her.

She looked up at her mother. "I love him," she whispered.

The grunting and barking of the large brown animals grew louder as Morgan and Ethan approached. They stood and watched through the clear tank walls as the seals played. One large brown seal swam up to where they stood and laid its head on the glass ledge beside Morgan. She knew she shouldn't, but she reached over to pet its smooth wet head.

"Aren't you adorable?" she cooed, admiring the seal's large chocolate eyes. More seals were now jumping into the water and heading toward them. More than ten seals had their heads resting along the top of the glass, barking loudly as they pushed and slapped each other out of the way to get closer to Morgan.

Morgan looked at Ethan, confused by the seals' behavior and then she noticed a crowd starting to gather. "This must be a new trick," she said.

"I think we should get away from here," Ethan said, tugging at her shirt. The seals began to bash and crawl over one another, becoming more and more aggressive as they seemed to battle for Morgan's attention.

Morgan cautiously stepped away. The group of seals pushed their heads out further across the ledge, reaching for her the best they could. Noticing the alarmed look on her face, Ethan grabbed Morgan's hand, quickly pulling her out of the seals' sight before a seal riot broke out. The crowd that was building behind them began to clap and cheer, thinking that they were a part of a routine show. Morgan's anxiety over the strange seal behavior quickly passed and they both burst into an uncomfortable laughter over the strange experience.

"What the heck was that?" she asked, trying to catch her breath.

"Not a clue. Has this ever happened before?" he asked with a serious look across his face.

"Nope, that was a first."

Ethan just shrugged his shoulders, but Morgan could tell that there was something more he wanted to say. He led her to the nearby bench and then ran across to the concession. Morgan giggled when she spotted him returning minutes later overloaded with nothing that resembled real food. He carried bags of pink and blue cotton candy, caramel apples, popcorn, pop, and a gift bag.

She laughed at him sweetly. "Holy cow! Who is going to eat all that food?"

"Me. Why? Did you want me to get you something, too?" he joked. Morgan thought it was nice to finally see a lighter, less intense side of Ethan.

"This is for you," He said and pulled an adorable, plush, fuzzy brown stuffed seal with large brown glass eyes, from the red paper gift bag.

"Ahhh, he's so cute. Thank you. I love it." She smiled as she nuzzled the plush little creature. "This is probably the only type of seal I should be around from now on."

They sat and snacked for a while, filling their selves until they both moaned and groaned with belly aches from junk food overload.

"Where to next?" Ethan asked as he tossed the remaining wrappers in the garbage.

"Sharks?" She pointed to the exhibits entrance.

"Sure, why not," Ethan answered as he pulled her to her feet.

They entered the acrylic tube that went right through the shark tank and watched as the sharks swam overhead.

"Isn't this amazing? They are so close you can almost touch them," she awed.

"You're afraid of the ocean, but not one of the most dangerous predators that swim in it?" he mused.

"Well, I'm sure I would be afraid of them in the ocean, but in here I'm safe so I can enjoy them for what they are. Which is sleek, fast, and beautiful!" she answered, as she ran her hands along the tube.

The sharks began swimming overhead more rapidly. Agitation showed in their bodies as they brushed up against the tubes. The crowd jumped back and cheered every time a shark's body careened against the tube. All of the sharks now seemed focused on the tube of humans in their tank, and with a frenzied swoosh of fins, the entire group of sharp-toothed creatures charged toward the tube. The massive shark bodies assaulted and shook the tube. Two bolts sprung free from one of the tubes connections, releasing a small trickle of water. The crowd's joy instantly turned to terror as they rushed for an exit.

"Come on Morgan. We have to get out of here." Ethan pulled at Morgan's arm. Another shark struck the tube, turning the trickle of water into a steady stream.

"We have to go now!" Ethan screamed.

The shark hit the wall so hard, its dead body sank to the bottom of the tank floor and Morgan realized this was more than just a feeding frenzy. That shark had killed himself trying to break into the tube! Another shark came straight toward them with teeth bared as it slammed into the tube where they stood.

Morgan screamed. Ethan pulled her body toward him protectively and they ran from the tube as the Aquarium staff ushered them out.

The crowds were still in hysterics outside the exhibit. Ethan diligently led Morgan through the chaos to an empty piece of sidewalk.

"Quick, get sedatives!" a maintenance worker screamed.

A short aquarium attendant was yelling at another attendant as they ran back into the building fighting through the crowd of curious tourists.

Ethan grabbed Morgan's hand and swiftly pulled her to the park entrance before they finally stopped. "I think it's time to get you home," he said, panting from the 'power' walk they had just made across the entire park.

"What the heck was going on in there? It seemed like they were trying to attack us!" Morgan gasped. "Wasn't that the craziest thing you've ever seen?"

"Yeah, it definitely rates in the top ten of my most bizarre moments," he answered, as they headed for the vehicle.

On the way home, Morgan didn't say much. She couldn't stop thinking of the entire day's bizarre events as she tried to make sense of it all.

"My seal! I think I dropped it in the tube," she blurted, as she felt a preschooler pout welling up inside her. She had planned on keeping that adorable stuffed seal forever.

"I'm sorry Morgan. I didn't even notice it was gone or we could have gotten you a new one before we left. We'll go back one day and I'll buy you a new stuffed seal. Maybe even a walrus to go with it," he promised as he pulled into her driveway.

She doubted there would be a next time after the 'Aquarium Animals Gone Wild' episode they had just witnessed, but she smiled at his effort to cheer her up. She reached for her door handle. "Thank you, it was a little weird, which seems to be the norm for me lately but, I like being around you Ethan. So thank you for today."

Morgan felt a surge of bravery and used it to ask the question that had been bothering her for days "I just have one question I need you to answer." She blurted before she lost her nerve.

Ethan waited, the smile dropping from his lips.

Morgan continued, "Why did you ditch me at the pier?"

Ethan let out a deep breath. "The boys on the Ferris wheel were not my friends, but I know who they are and they are bad, real bad. They were following me after I got off the ride so I led them away from the pier---away from you. I wanted to wring their necks for the crap they said to you that day but I wasn't sure if I could beat both of them. So, I did the next best thing and made sure they wouldn't bother you. I wanted to meet up with you so badly it hurt, but I couldn't do that at the risk of endangering you. I'm so sorry you thought I ditched you. Believe me when I say that I would never intentionally hurt your feelings like that. I really like you Morgan."

Ethan's hand shot out, grabbing hers on the door handle. "Can I pick you up tomorrow after school? We'll go to the beach."

"I don't know if the beach is such a good idea. God, the aquarium was weird enough! How do you think the open water is going to turn out?" she argued.

"You'll be safe with me. I think today was just one of those days when everything goes haywire. Maybe it's a full moon or something. I'm really looking forward to spending the day at the beach with you."

"I know I just..."

"You just... promised." He finished her sentence as he took his hand off hers and pulled her cheek to his lips, planting a soft kiss before backing away.

"I will pick you up tomorrow after school," he said, as he turned the key in the ignition.

She crawled out of the Jeep, desperately trying to think of an excuse that would get her out of tomorrow's beach trip, but none came to mind so she simply said "goodbye" and shut the door.

"By the way!" she heard him yell after her as she headed for the house. She paused and turned to face him.

"Nice outfit today."

She did a small curtsy as her face turned red, then bolted toward the house. Tomorrow, she was definitely going back to plain old jeans and T-shirts.

Morgan lightly rubbed the cheek where Ethan had kissed her. Her belly twisted and fluttered like a fury of butterflies lay beneath her skin. She didn't want to have feelings for this strange new boy who ploughed his way into her life. She didn't want to have feelings for any boy, for that matter but she felt a strange connection and familiarity with Ethan that she couldn't explain. She craved his presence, and not just because he held answers to the crazy energy thing happening between them or because he was consuming her every thought, but because against her better judgment, she was falling for him, utterly and completely.

Chapter 6

The rusted blue pickup hummed impatiently behind her as the boy inside slapped at his steering wheel and laid on the horn. Morgan stepped out of the way and scanned the parking lot one last time for Ethan's Jeep. She had searched the halls for him between classes but he hadn't shown.

Nala offered her a ride home after school. When they pulled onto her street, the red Jeep she had been seeking all day was sitting in her driveway. The handsome blonde boy she couldn't quit thinking about was leaning against his bumper wearing a white button-up shirt that hung loosely over dark blue board shorts. She hurried out of Nala's car, mumbling a quick goodbye to her friend.

Wow, he is the hottest guy I have ever seen, she thought as she threw her book bag on the front porch.

"Are you ready for the beach?" he asked with a deviously handsome smile that spread from his lips to sparkle in his eyes.

"No, do we have to? Why don't you come in and hang out here?" she offered.

"Come on. Just for a little while. You promised," he said as he walked around the Jeep to open the door for her.

She knew there was no point in arguing, so she slid into the passenger's seat. "I don't swim and I'm not going in the water," she huffed as he shut the door behind her.

Ethan turned the vehicle in the direction of the beach and Morgan grumbled under her breath.

"You promised," Ethan reminded her.

They walked along the Santa Monica Boulevard, heading toward the beach in complete silence. Morgan felt the fear she knew so well creeping up inside—the fear she'd had of the water since childhood. Whenever she was near the ocean an unexplainable terror would swell in the base of her stomach. They were about 20 feet from the water now, and Morgan slowed to a stop. She remembered all the horrifically vivid nightmares she endured, all of them about the ocean. Lucas had stayed with her almost every night since the nightmares had started, selflessly protecting her from her own overactive imagination. Now here she was with some guy she had only known a few days, allowing him to bring her to the origin of the childhood nightmares that Lucas had tried so hard to protect her from. Ethan turned once he realized she no longer trailed him.

He took her hand. "It's okay. Trust me, Morgan," he reassured her.

She stood in place unable to force her body into motion.

"Let's just walk here on the sidewalk for a while. You don't have to even put your feet in the sand. Okay?" He pleaded, tugging at her arm like an impatient child.

"You'll tell me everything?" she bargained.

"I promise," he replied.

Her legs gave into reason and they walked hand-in-hand down the sidewalk.

They walked for over an hour, heading north of the Santa Monica Pier, away from the hustle and bustle of tourists and people playing hooky from work and school. Morgan glanced at the crowd and caught sight of a few naughty Santa Monica High students but there was no one she knew well enough to wave at.

They walked in silence until they could barely see the pier. Morgan was becoming impatient, tired of waiting for the explanation she had been promised but not wanting to press Ethan.

Finally, as they reached the end of the sidewalk, Ethan spoke. "Wait here. I will be right back," he muttered.

Before Morgan could argue he jumped off the sidewalk and over the meridian to dart across the street. He quickly disappeared into a small convenience store on the corner.

Feeling silly just standing there alone on the sidewalk, she looked around for a bench to sit on, but there were none. She pulled off her shoes and pushed her toes into the warm welcoming sand; it wasn't so bad.

She spied a group of large rocks a few feet away and decided it wouldn't hurt to go a little ways onto the beach, as the rocks were still far enough away from the water for her to feel safe. She took a step towards the beach, then another, before she knew she was standing in front of the rocks

She sat on the lowest, flattest rock and leaned back against the other. She watched the waves gently washing against the shore. She breathed in the warm salty air and closed her eyes, listening to the repetitive calm of the waves along the sandy shore. The chirps of seagulls circled above her. Surprisingly, she felt completely relaxed. Her own heartbeat seemed to be in rhythm with the lapping waves. How could she have thought that this place was horrible for all these years? She lay back further onto the rock and let her body absorb the warmth of the late afternoon sun as she closed her eyes and replayed the craziness of the last couple of days in her head.

"Morgan," Ethan whispered while nudging her shoulder.

Her eyes were heavy as she opened them. She looked around quickly remembering where she was.

"You were asleep when I got back, so I just let you sleep for a little bit. Are you hungry?" he asked, pushing a hotdog toward her.

"You went to get food?" she asked, knowing the answer.

"I love these things," he said, while stuffing half of one in his mouth in a single bite.

Morgan noticed four other empty wrappers beside him. "It looks like it." She smiled. "I can't believe I fell asleep. How long have I been out?"

"About an hour, I didn't want to wake you. You looked so peaceful."

Hmm, that was a first, Morgan thought. She pictured herself sprawled out drooling and possibly snoring on the rock while

Ethan sat there watching her and eating hotdogs. "Gee thanks," she grumbled, wiping the residual drool from the corner of her mouth.

He smiled.

She took a bite of her less-than-warm hotdog while Ethan unwrapped another for himself.

"Why do they call these hotdogs?" he asked her curiously.

She looked at him in amazement. "You've never heard of a hotdog before?" she questioned, realizing this was one of the many, many things she did not know about this guy.

"No, we don't have them where I'm from. In fact, I would be in big trouble if they knew I was eating meat of any kind."

"Your family is vegan?" she asked in amazement.

"We don't eat or take from anything warm blooded," he stated, popping the last hotdog in his mouth. "Except today," he added, with a boyish grin as he chewed.

She eyed his muscular body, which was almost bursting from his shirt. "Wow. You certainly don't fit the mold of a vegan." She giggled. "You may want to lay off the hotdogs though slugger, or you'll be sick tomorrow."

He furrowed his brow. "You're right, what have I done? What if you need me, I could fail you over something as foolish as eating meat."

She was confused. What was he talking about? "What? Relax, it's just a hotdog, there probably isn't anything resembling meat in it anyway."

"We are weakened when we have meat in our system. We are 'pure' beings. Our bodies' energy is blocked when we consume other warm-blooded beings."

"We?" she asked.

She could feel the barrier between them begin to fall.

Finally, some answers!

He pulled himself up onto the rock alongside her, laying out his body to face her as he propped his head up on an elbow. He fiddled with the cuff of her t-shirt and she could tell he was searching for the right words. He pulled the necklace he wore out from beneath his shirt, then lifted it over his head. He held his hand out, dangling the shimmering chain between his fingers. "This is my family pendant. It is supposed to protect the one who wears it. It is like an amulet, worn to protect you from evil." He placed it in her hand.

"I want you to have it, and when you are ready, I would like you to wear it."

Morgan lifted her hand and studied the elegant gold chain. There was an upside down teardrop-shaped pendant hanging from the end. Lifting it to the light of the setting sun, she could see silver symbols intricately carved along the pendant's edges. It was beautiful.

"I can't take this," she answered, handing it back to him.

"It's yours." He cupped his hand over hers. "It's always been yours," he said, then took it out of her hand and stuffed it in her pocket.

Ethan leaned in, and Morgan turned her face toward him expecting another peck on the cheek, but this time it was what she had been waiting for. His full lips pressed against hers and her breath froze in her chest as he kissed her. It was a slow, warm, and loving kiss that melted her heart and found her soul. A shiver of pleasure crashed through her body as he wrapped his large arms around her and continued to kiss her awaiting lips. She felt surges of pleasure and excitement shoot through her body from his mere touch as she allowed her inhibitions to fall away and just enjoy the moment between them.

"Your lips are amazing, so soft and sweet. I never dreamt my first kiss- our first kiss, would be so perfect." Ethan whispered, moving his mouth down along her chin then bathing her neck in light, playful kisses. Morgan pulled away.

"Are you telling me you've never kissed a girl before?" Morgan gasped. Ethan pulled away and locked his eyes on the small space of rock between them as he bashfully shrugged his shoulders.

"I've just never connected with anyone." He confessed quietly.

Morgan couldn't believe her ears. She found it hard to believe that the gorgeous boy in front of her could make it through the better part of high school without a single kiss. It's not like she had a huge track record, but she had definitely kissed a boy or two. There was still space between them, as Ethan lay rigidly in front of her, quietly vulnerable from his confession. Morgan twisted her fingers around his collar and pulled his lips back to hers.

"If this is what a kiss is supposed to feel like, I have definitely never been truly kissed before either. You're amazing." she whispered with a new found confidence, brushing her lips against his as she spoke. He crushed her to him and kissed her slowly, his breath warm and sweet as his tongue entered her mouth. Butterflies surged through Morgan's belly as her mind numbed to everything but Ethan's immediate touch. She could see the blue cloud around him and then she felt the sparks of light return and pass smoothly between them. She felt energy shards begin to rage between them. She pulled away quickly, afraid that she might hurt Ethan again but he drew her back towards him.

"It's okay, you just caught me off guard last time, I didn't realize how powerful you would already be," he whispered into her hair then began kissing her neck.

She shoved him away, breaking the moment. "How powerful I would already be? What does that mean?"

Realizing the romantic moment between them had passed; Ethan climbed off the rock and held his hand out to help Morgan down.

She shook her head.

"This is as close to the water as I get," she said stubbornly.

His hand hovered in the air. "Trust me...Please."

Morgan took in the vision of the sun setting behind the beautiful boy in front of her. The wonderful, mysterious boy, who just wanted to stroll on the beach with her. She nervously took his hand. She didn't know why she always felt so much anxiety about the ocean, but she knew she had to get over it sooner or later. He pulled her to a stand then put his hands on either side of her waist as he lifted her off the rock. She fell against him and could feel the energy surge between them. The blue cloud around Ethan was beginning to form again.

He dropped his arms away and released her.

"You really are almost too powerful for me already, my sweet." He smiled, stroking his thumb against her cheek.

"What are you?" she whispered, scared to breathe.

"I am, as you are," he replied.

She looked at him in confusion, trying to understand.

"I'll show you." He took her hand gently and guided her to the ocean. The sun had now set and she could see a glow around him in the moonlight, his blue aura shimmering brightly around him.

He faced her and lifted his shirt over his head, exposing his bare chest. Morgan gasped.

His chest glowed like the moon; his skin was almost translucent beneath the moon's soft light.

He let go of her hand and stepped backwards until his ankles were immersed in the lapping shore. He raised his arms straight out from his glowing body with his palms down. The water began to move in an unnatural swirl around him. Long spindles of water emerged like puppets alongside him. They rose and divided until there was one touching each of his fingertips. He swayed his hands back and forth orchestrating the water as it water danced before them. He turned his hands toward her now, reaching for her as the small swirling spindles of water twirled around him. He approached the shore, then stopped and reached out his arms.

"Come now, Morgan. Join me" he commanded in a godlike tone. She shook her head like a toddler in trouble.

He took a step closer and muttered just one word.

"Please."

"What are you?" she asked, knowing she should be way more scared of a glowing, water-controlling guy than she was right now, and that she should be running away screaming, instead of questioning, but she knew she was somehow connected to this and she needed answers..

Although her mind felt connected to what was going on, her body was frozen with fear, and even if she had wanted to, she couldn't move a step closer.

"The question, Morgan, is what are you? Can you feel it? Feel your lineage, your calling, your destiny?"

Ethan raised his arms and the water rose on either side of him, completely parting to reveal a clear dry path leading to him.

Morgan remained frozen.

The water moved toward her in fast flowing narrow streams, circling around her, forming a wall behind her and a path forward. Just like her nightmares. Morgan didn't like this. She was scared now, and the water around her was making her feel trapped. She did not run to Ethan as she knew he wanted; she stood frozen and afraid. Feeling forced against her will, anger surged inside her like she'd never felt before. The cloud of energy that surrounded her earlier that day, returned, and this time with force.

"Stop it now...STOP IT!" she warned Ethan, unsure of what was about to happen.

"Just take a few steps to me, love. It's safe. I promise you. You just have to trust me Morgan" He coaxed her calmly, oblivious to her warning.

She was furious. She did not like this; she was trapped in a wall of ocean water.

She knew that her legs would not walk toward him even if she tried. She was too scared to move even an inch. She could feel the water pushing at the backs of her heels trying to force her forward as it slowly pooled at her feet. The water was growing deeper around her ankles with every beat of her quickened heart.

"Please, Ethan!" she cried out, as the water climbed to her calves. She was terrified now and knew she had to stop this.

"Nooo!" she pleaded. The water grew and pushed harder.

"Stop!" she yelled, throwing her hands up and feeling all the fear and anxiety rush through her body as it visibly balled at her fingertips, forming a sphere of swirling white light. The sphere instantaneously flew from her outstretched hand and struck Ethan squarely in the chest.

The water dropped away and so did Ethan.

"Ethan!" she screamed, finally able to move her legs.

Ethan's motionless body was eerily floating face down. Without thinking, Morgan dove into the water.

The glow of his skin was becoming fainter and fainter, as she approached. She grabbed his large shoulders and with strength she never thought she had, she pulled his water-logged body to shore.

She pounded on Ethan's lifeless chest, hysterically trying to get the water out.

"Come on, Ethan! Wake up, please!"

She pushed him onto his side to drain his lungs as she slammed his back with her tiny fists.

After what felt like an eternity, his arm suddenly shot up and grabbed her fist before she could strike him again. "Jeez, are you trying to finish me off!" Ethan smirked.

Morgan felt the tears of relief stream down her cheeks. "I thought you were...I thought you died, I thought I'd killed you. I'm so sorry, I don't know what happened." She sobbed apologetically.

"No, I'm sorry," he corrected her. "I shouldn't have pushed you when I know how little control you have right now." He patted the dry beach sand beside him. "How did I get here? You pulled me out of the ocean? You went *into* the ocean?" he asked.

She nodded.

"Well, well, if I knew that was all it took, we could have just started with that."

She struck him, knocking him back into the sand. "That's not funny," she muttered, wiping the tears from her cheeks as she rose to her feet. "I want to go home," she said, keeping her eyes locked on the sand, fighting the tears that were building beneath her eyelids once again.

Ethan had not yet answered a single one of her million questions, but she was not about to risk another episode involving the ocean.

Ethan nodded, not having the strength to argue.

She helped him up and Ethan put his long sleeve shirt back over his glowing body. The glow of his face began to fade until it was almost a normal hue in the moonlight.

Morgan raised an eyebrow in question.

"In time, we learn to dim ourselves and blend, the face glow is the easiest to control," he stated with nonchalance, like he was just discussing a typical, everyday subject, like glowing.

Hand in hand, they started to walk back to the vehicle.

"Why were you forcing me into the water?" she asked feeling much stronger than Ethan at the moment. She figured this was probably her only chance for answers, especially since she had almost killed the guy twice in two days. She decided now, was her only chance for answers since he probably wouldn't be back for a fourth date.

"It is needed for you to start your transformation." He spoke simply, walking with his eyes to the ground. Then he added quietly, "I was trying to gently coax you in. I didn't realize you were feeling forced."

"What are you?" she continued.

He stopped and faced her then whispered one life-changing word.

"Atlantean."

"WE are Atlantean." He corrected himself. He pulled her body against his as he looked deep into her eyes.

She looked away and with as much indifference as she could gather she quipped, "So you're NOT from Vancouver then?"

Ethan chuckled, shaking his head as they started up the path. "You aren't like anyone I have ever met before, Morgan. They will love you in Atlantis."

Morgan looked at Ethan, the glow still slightly visible beneath his cheeks. His eyes were shining and almost fully dilated. She wondered if he could see better in the dark like that. She wanted to argue with him, to tell him that he was playing a trick on her, or just straight out lying but nothing she had seen tonight made any sense, and try as she might, she couldn't come up with a reasonable explanation for any of it. She realized she was going to have to accept any explanation given, even if it included some madman saying he was from Atlantis. What she had seen tonight was too incredible for any normal explanation, so she was willing to listen to any answers Ethan offered.

"Why me? Why are you doing this to me? Are you turning me into one of you?" she asked.

"I'm not turning you into anything. You are Atlantean. You were born Atlantean. Seventeen years ago, the Atlantean Council reached their year of Nine hundred. That was the year they had to produce the royal heirs. Their knowledge and power was at its greatest at that time and could easily pass on to an unborn child. The Council's children were born within the same year or two so that they may be raised together and learn all the ways of Atlantis as a team, right from birth."

"So, seventeen years ago, the Councilmen produced six healthy, beautiful children and all was as it should be. That was until a seventh child was born, not from the Council, but from King Nariedon's closest friend and confidant, Thavan. Thavan was the only one of his kind residing in Atlantis. He is a Triton. Our King found him on the ocean floor banished from his own people and took pity on him. They soon became good friends and King

Nariedon allowed Thavan and his family to live in Atlantis, but they were forbidden to have children or to consort in that manner with Atlanteans. Thavan disobeyed the King, and had the first Triton child to be born in Atlantis since the cataclysm. The Council ruled that the child was to be removed from Atlantis immediately. The guards took the baby from its parents and hid it on land, never to return. This angered Thavan, and he sought revenge by stealing the six Council children from Atlantis. He hid them on land, too, subjecting them to the same fate as his own stolen child.

"You are one of the six royal children stolen from Atlantis seventeen years ago, Morgan. We resemble humans until we reach seventeen or eighteen. Then we begin to change- on the inside. Atlanteans have the ability to see and control their body's energy. Each one of us learns to wield the energy in our own way but all of us have to spend a lot of time learning to control it or we can hurt others. I am here to bring you home before that happens."

Morgan swallowed the lump in her throat. A million thoughts raced through her head, and before she could process anything she spewed, "What if I say no?" She stopped and pulled him to sit on the bench beside her.

"There is no choice. You're too powerful for humans right now. Atlanteans and humans don't mix once we start to form our powers and begin our change."

Ethan ran his hand through his hair and searched for the right words as he continued. "Your change has already begun. The way you pulled energy from me without even trying in the car would happen to a human ten times easier and faster, and they would die from the effects. You don't have enough control yet to stop from hurting them and they are defenseless against you. Plus, the energy inside you will soon start to glow and that might be hard for you to explain."

Morgan felt the tears she was trying desperately to contain trickle down her cheeks. "I can't leave. What about my Mom? I'm all she's got. I can't just leave her behind. I won't!" she argued.

"I know this is hard, but you can't stay with her—you could hurt or possibly kill her. That would be worse than missing her, right? You have to come with me Morgan, it's the only option." He stroked her back, trying to offer some comfort.

She pulled away. "Don't touch me!" she snapped.

Ethan winced and withdrew. "There may be a time before she passes that you can return, once you are trained to control your powers."

"How long do you live?" she asked.

"We live for about a thousand years, give or take. We have learned how to control cell degeneration; we have learned and evolved far more than the human race. We use sixty- to- seventy percent of both sides of our brains simultaneously, and we have unlocked our minds to many possibilities. We can control and manipulate energy. Some of us have more ability than others, but all of us manipulate energy to some extent."

"So, were you humans once?"

"All life, including humans began in the ocean. Humans chose land and evolved through the years to live there. Atlanteans chose both, and we adapted and evolved, too. We were always truly water people, but for a few short years we lived among humans on land when King Poseidon ruled."

"I thought Poseidon was a god?" she asked.

"He thought so too, but he was not. He was a king and an Atlantean. He had dreams of ruling the world. He brought his followers, the Atlanteans, to a bountiful island he had discovered in the center of the Atlantic Ocean. It was lush and beautiful and at the center of the worlds trade route. They soon grew wealthy and knowledgeable from the many walks of life that passed through their land. They created a great city, a beautiful city, and they became very powerful. They had humans as slaves and trained animals of every type. The city was futuristic for its time, with irrigation and even power! But Poseidon became greedy in his wealth and wanted more. He married the powerful and magical

Goddess, Ashmana, who they say was Mother Nature herself. She heard his cries for more power so she built him a great army. She took his greatest warrior and dear friend Ulysses and she blended his DNA with the fiercest animals on land and sea. That was when the King's new Triton army was born. The Triton did all of Poseidon's bidding. They destroyed human villages, stealing all the riches and enslaving any humans who were unfortunate enough to cross their path. They lured in and then destroyed ships of traveling humans before they left the Atlantis port, pirating all of their possessions for King Poseidon's trust.

"Ulysses, the Triton leader, realized the power he possessed and he turned on Poseidon. But the Council and Poseidon himself could not be killed. Ashmana had gifted each member of the Council with a protective crystal. It was a large crystal in the shape of a skull and it radiated the power of protection. When the six skulls were combined in the Council chambers the power of protection was strong enough to keep the entire city of Atlantis safe from the Tritons.

"The skulls were a curse to the Tritons and would kill any Triton who came within their area of protection-instantly. So, their leader Ulysses made a deal with the humans. He guaranteed their freedom from the Atlanteans and King Poseidon's terror if they stole the six skulls from the Atlantean Council and tossed them into the dormant volcano some miles from the city. The humans agreed, and when they tossed the skulls into the volcano, the world experienced such a disturbance it had never seen before. The volcano erupted, shaking the earth to its very core, causing the continental plates to abruptly shift and swallow the entire city of Atlantis in a single gulp. The people of Atlantis were buried alive under volcanic debris. Millions were killed. Atlantis broke off from land quickly and it sank so fast and with so much force, an air pocket formed as the volcanic lava hit the pounding waves.

"It formed protective tunnels and caverns and somehow most of the city stayed intact as it slid to the ocean floor. The skulls possessed a power even greater than anyone could have imagined, and when the dust settled, there was a protective crystal-like dome around the entire sunken city. That is where the few hundred survivors remained and rebuilt what they could of the city, creating the Atlantis I live in today."

"You aren't seriously telling me that there is a whole civilized community living under water?" she asked in disbelief.

"The earth is two thirds water. Is it really that hard to believe that a civilized species wouldn't evolve and adapt to life there?"

"Yes!...No! I don't know. God, this is just so much to take in." Morgan felt like her head would explode. Ethan stood, indicating that they should head back.

As they approached the Jeep, Ethan turned to her, careful not to touch her again. He took a deep exhausted breath. "I'm supposed to bring you home, to Atlantis... tonight. But..." he paused, seeing her defenses rise.

"Is that why you brought me out there? To kidnap me?"

"Yes." He watched her eyes turn to panic, "but I couldn't. I'm going to take you to your Mom for one last night if you promise to come with me tomorrow...into the water."

For the first time in all her seventeen years, Morgan was speechless.

"The Tritons are here on land, and they are looking for the Council's children. They are planning an uprising and they want to take Atlantis for their own. They were forbidden entrance to Atlantis after the fall and they have been doing everything in their power to gain the throne ever since. My point is...they are looking for you and they will do everything in their power to make sure you never make it back to Atlantis."

Reality hit her with a thud "The boys from the Ferris wheel, they're Triton aren't they?"

Ethan nodded confirmation.

"Did they make the safety bar open? The flash I seen and thought was lightening was them wasn't it? They were really trying to kill me." Morgan felt sick to her stomach.

She nodded in exhaustion. She wanted to yell, to call him a liar and run for help but something inside her knew, something had always known that what he said was the truth. Without further protest she slipped into the passenger side of the Jeep. All she wanted right now was to go home and see her Mom, to hug her, and to tell her she loved her.

On the drive home, Morgan thought about the stories her mom used to tell her about her adoption. She would make up all these fantastic bedtime stories of seals and mermaids delivering her in a small fishing boat. Morgan wondered now if these childhood stories had a small truth to them. "I know this is hard Morgan," Ethan said looking at her with true compassion and concern as they passed the pier.

She could see the pain in his eyes and she actually began to feel sorry for HIM! She wondered how he got elected as the messenger of bad news. She felt the anger of being ripped from her family and friends rise inside her, and she knew there was no one else to direct it at but the man sitting next to her.

"So, are you like their messenger boy? Is this what you do? Go around pulling teens away from their friends and family and crushing their hopes and dreams?" she spat angrily. Tears were swelling in her eyes from the shame she felt for being so evil to the man she knew was trying to help her.

They slowly pulled into her driveway. Ethan turned the car off and shifted his body to face her. "No," he said flatly.

Morgan stared at Ethan, how his lip quivered. He seemed vulnerable, as if he would break at any moment.

"I am one of the stolen six. I am Ethanius, the king's only son. When we were all stolen, the Council decided it would be in our best interests to remain on land until things were sorted out in Atlantis and until they were sure we were out of danger. The King agreed, but then he became depressed and worried about me to the point that he could not rule efficiently. The King's advisors pleaded with the Council to let them find me and return me to Atlantis. They rationalized that at least one of the six should be raised in the traditional Atlantean way. The Council agreed, and after a couple months of searching, they found me. I had washed up on the shore in Vancouver."

Morgan couldn't help but smile at how she thought Ethan was just some crazy Canadian.

He reached for her hand, holding it lightly as he fiddled with her fingers. "I was told of the stolen children from a young age; I was educated and raised to rule Atlantis once our circle of six is reunited." He paused again perfectly still and looked into her eyes.

Morgan turned her face away. She was not ready for this. Not yet. She was seventeen for god sake! Not a powerful Council person from some crazy, mythical place!

She'd imagined, like most adopted children, how it would feel if her birth parents showed up at the door. They would stand there in their crowns and announce that a terrible mistake had been made and that she was their daughter; the long lost Princess of England and her adoption had been a terrible mistake. She would then take her adoptive mom and go home to England with her birth parents and rule England and eat scones and stuff, but she never quite imagined the whole Atlantean thing. She had a great imagination but Atlantean parents were a stretch even for her.

Ethan continued, trying to make eye contact, but she would not raise her eyes to him. "I am no delivery boy, Morgan. I came to find you. Only you. You're my destiny."

She felt herself melt under his gaze as she let everything sink in. "I feel like I've known you my whole life. Is that because I'm Atlantean? Will this happen with all of them?" she asked.

"No, it is because you're my soul mate. It's easier for Atlanteans to know who we are meant to be with. It's called a 'Sharing of Souls' when energies mix as ours do. When you touch me, it's like I can feel your very soul. I knew the second I saw you that you were the one I was meant to be with. I think I knew even before that. I know this is hard for you to understand, but I hope you can see what is between us. There is a bond already formed that will last forever, and I know this will sound weird to someone raised as a human, but I am already in love with you. I would give my life for you."

He kissed her before she could say anything in return, with the passion and urgency of a man searching for acceptance.

She held back and could sense his pain and anguish as he held his warm lips to hers. This was all too much. She knew there were crazy irrational feelings between them, but love? They had spent three days together; was it possible for anyone to be in love after three days? She didn't want this; all she wanted was to go home and to be a normal teenage girl as she had thought she was up until yesterday.

She gently pushed him away holding him at an arm's length. "I don't think that love is possible so soon, for any species. I need time to think. I don't want to leave my family. I don't want any of this."

She looked at the crushing pain her words caused him as his body crumbled backwards. She could not endure the pain her rejection caused on his face any longer. Her body melted toward him, accepting his soft kisses as tears fell from her eyes.

He kissed her wet cheeks and murmured softly, "Don't cry my sweet princess, please." He stroked her hair from her face and found her lips once more. She felt the energy flowing between them. This time, neither side was taking or giving—it just mixed and flowed together as it danced around them.

Chapter 7

"If I only have one day left, I need to spend it with my mom," Morgan said as she opened the door.

"I'll be out here if you need me," Ethan comforted.

"All night?" she asked.

He nodded and she already knew there was no point in arguing. She closed the Jeep door and headed into the house. Her mother was curled up on the sofa enjoying her usual Friday night ritual of chai tea and Nicolas Cage movies. Morgan stared at her mother's finely featured face, framed by the long, smooth dark hairstyle she had worn for as long as Morgan could remember. Raven black strands had given way to a few grays recently. Morgan wanted to drink in every second of their final evening together. She wanted to tell her mom what was going on so badly it caused her heart physical pain. She had never kept any real secrets from her before. She knew that if she told her what was going on, her mother would do everything within her power to force her to stay, and that would put both of their lives in danger. Morgan stroked the back of her mother's hair lightly and breathed in her simple, familiar scent of vanilla fabric softener. She forced a smile through her despair and rounded the couch.

This was it, the last time they would be together, and she intended to soak in every second of it.

"Mom! What are you doing sitting there watching movies?"

Her mom turned to her in confusion. "What do you mean? It's Friday night. I always have a date with Nicolas Cage on Friday night." She smiled devilishly.

"That's what I mean. You're always here. You should be out meeting people and doing things. Not wasting away in front of a television set!"

"Okay, who died and made you the parent?" Lynn joked.

Morgan knew this was a battle she was never going to win, so she took a seat on the couch beside her mom. "I'm serious, Mom.

It's not healthy for you to stay home all the time. Promise me you will try and get out more?"

"All right," Lynn agreed as she shifted closer to the screen. "Now be quiet, he's about to take off his shirt!"

"Oh puke!" Morgan laughed as she mocked her mom's fantasy husband. Morgan had accepted the fact that her mother would probably never marry. She once told Morgan that her heart was so full of love for Morgan, that she didn't think there was room for anyone else. She said she had always dreamed of being a mother one day but never felt the need to be someone's wife. Morgan prayed this wasn't true. She didn't want to imagine her mom spending the rest of her life alone.

Morgan grabbed a throw blanket and curled up beside her. They watched Nicolas Cage movies and snacked on junk food until the wee hours of the morning.

***

The first bit of sunrise pushed a warning of light through the curtains. Morgan hadn't slept a wink. She had watched over her mom the entire night wanting to absorb and prolong every detail of their last evening together. Neither of them had wanted the night to end. Her mom took her hand halfway through the movie, just like she'd done so many times when Morgan was small. She held it for the rest of the night. It was as if her mother somehow knew that this would be the last time she saw her.

Morgan kissed her mother on the forehead. She felt the energy pulling from her mother's body, and realized that touching her had already become dangerous. She took a step back and watched her mother sleep—breathing in and out—how peaceful she looked. She blinked back tears, swallowed a lump in her throat, and quietly left the room.

As she slowly ascended the stairs, she stared at the pictures in the hallway, pictures of her and her mother. Her hand glided over the railing. This would be the last time she stepped foot in this house, in this hallway. She paused, caught her breath and tried to absorb every memory-filled nook and cranny of her childhood home.

She threw on a clean pair of capri jeans and a T-shirt with her favorite soft, black hoodie. She grabbed the necklace Ethan gave her and stuffed it in her pocket. She picked up her cell and tried to call Lucas one last time since her texts had all gone unanswered, but was not surprised when she reached his full mailbox for the hundredth time. She typed, "I love you mom" on her phone, then threw it on her bed—she knew it wouldn't do her much good underwater.

She took one final glance around her room. It was quite ordinary, with cream-colored walls and beige carpeted floors, but she had added just the right touches of warmth. Her mom made her a quilt from their extensive collection of souvenir t-shirts and it filled the room with memories of all their cheesy "daycations" they had taken through the years. Morgan ran her hand along the patch from Dan's Croc Farm, which read *What's up Croc?* in large neon green letters. She remembered how horrified her mom had been when SuperDan the Crock Man stuck his entire head into the crocodile's mouth. Her mom marched over to SuperDan's wife and stated that, showing children to stick their heads into the mouths of wild animals, was completely inappropriate. She demanded a full refund, and they left before Morgan got to see the second half of the show. Morgan was ten at the time, and she poked fun at her mom for weeks after that trip. When Sally, the neighbor's gentle Labrador Retriever, trotted over to their porch, Morgan would yell for her mother to come and see. She would then open Sally's mouth and nudge her head toward the obedient dog's open jaw. "Look Mom, my head almost fits!" Morgan remembered her mom's face going so pale she looked as if she were about pass out.

Above her bed hung an array of wacky posters Lucas had given her, each one displayed the two of their heads on various kinds of bodies. Her favorite was the one of their smiling faces atop bikini-clad gorilla bodies. She left her room and walked hesitantly down the stairs, taking one last look at everything around her. And after she watched her mom sleep for a minute or two, she whispered, "I love you," as she walked out the front door.

Ethan was still parked across the street, when she crawled in the empty seat beside him. She took in a deep breath but did not say a word.

Finally she asked, "So, how do we do this?"

"It's an amazing journey, really, and I'll help you so don't be afraid. I know you're sad, but that will fade. You'll soon love Atlantis as much as I do, I promise." he said and pulled away from the curb and away from the only life Morgan has ever known. She watched her house grow smaller in the rearview mirror and sobbed profusely.

On the way to the beach, they passed Lucas's house and thoughts of him flooded her racing mind. He should have been back from vacation yesterday. *Why didn't he call me? What's he going to think when I'm just gone, poor Lucas, for things to end between us like this is just wrong.* She rested her head in her hands, trying to block the fear and sorrow that welled up inside her.

She searched the Jeep's console for a tissue; her eyes were blurred and swollen from the tears. She lifted her head and raised her eyes to the windshield. She had just enough time to spot the vehicle speeding towards them and to let out a blood-curdling scream.

Chapter 8

"ETHAN!" Morgan shrieked as the headlights of a large dark van ploughed into their Jeep, t-boning Ethan's side of the vehicle and sending them in a sideways spin.

Morgan could feel the warm trickle of blood on her cheek. The glass from the windshield sprayed around them as the Jeep shook to an abrupt stop across the intersection.

Ethan reached out, assessing her quickly. "Are you okay?" he asked frantically.

Morgan looked at Ethan, then at the van that hit them. Everything seemed to be happening in slow motion. The shiny black, now damaged, van that hit them was knocked sideways as well and was now sitting idly atop the curb adjacent to them. It backed up slightly, its front bumper now dragging along the pavement and creating a shower of sparks as it began to speed ahead. Like a one eyed creature back from battle its demolished front headlight hung to one side. The van wobbled off the curb then turned towards them!

Morgan screamed when she realized that the van was accelerating and headed straight for their Jeep, again! It wasn't an accident. Whoever was driving that death machine, was trying to kill them!

"Hold on!" Ethan yelled, stomping the gas pedal to the floor. Morgan felt some relief when the Jeep was still drivable until she looked up and saw where they were. Passing overhead was the greeting sign for the Santa Monica Pier and they were headed straight toward it!

Ethan swerved and skidded around the vending carts and obstacles set along the wooden attraction. It was like a bad episode of *Miami Vice* as they sped ahead, carts of clothes and trinkets sprayed out around them.

The end of the pier was approaching quickly. Ethan turned to her with tears in his eyes, undid her seatbelt and uttered, "It's the

Triton, they've found us. I'm so sorry Morgan, it wasn't supposed to be like this." The Jeep ripped through the pier railing like butter and sent them crashing into the salty water below.

Morgan's body flew from the open-top Jeep as the vehicle dove toward the ocean. Her body plunged into the deep, murky water, breaking through the surface with so much force it felt like her skin was being ripped from her body—her flesh felt like it was on fire as she was sucked deeper into the tide. The salt water stung her eyes until she couldn't see and burned her nostrils as she breathed it in through. She panicked and flailed around as she fought the downward pull of the undertow; she was going to die just like in her nightmares. The force of the Jeep's impact was sucking her further and further down into the icy water, but she tried to fight the current as best she could. When the Jeep hit bottom, it sent a wave upwards and she felt herself rising upwards. She struggled for air and thought for a moment that maybe she would make it to the surface. She flapped her arms like a bird trying to work with the upward current to reach the surface, but time was running short. The current fizzled out too quickly and Morgan began to sink back down into the frosty darkness. Her body thrashed about as she let out her last bit of air. *This is it*, she thought, *this is the end.*

She felt Ethan behind her grabbing her waist. *He's alive*, she celebrated briefly.

She turned to him, and he grabbed her head pulling it toward his. He gently put his lips to hers and she could feel air passing through his mouth.

You can breathe, just stay calm, we breathe through our skin, just stay calm and it will happen. Morgan could hear Ethan's voice in her head while his lips were still pressed against hers.

I am going to pull away now. I need you to try and breathe on your own, he said telepathically.

She held him with a vice-like grip not wanting to let go. What if he was wrong? What if she was wrong about him? He flicked his tongue into her mouth turning his rescue into a kiss, then pulled away.

Morgan gulped a deep breath of ocean water. The cold liquid blasted through her lungs and she felt herself suffocating as it stuck in her throat. Her body convulsed uncontrollably as it fought for air—she could not breathe and she was drowning. Her defeated body began to crumple to the ocean floor, unable to endure the stabbing pain in her chest any longer. Ethan was wrong about her and now she was going to die…

She felt Ethan tugging at her.

Come on Morgan, we have to get out of here. Please, Morgan!

He pulled her to her feet and she opened her eyes slowly—scared of the sting from the salt water—but her eyes did not hurt and she could see Ethan in front of her. Then it hit her—she was still alive. Alive and standing under 20ft of water! She looked at Ethan in wonder.

"*How?*" she thought back to him, hoping he could hear her voice in his head the way she had heard his. Before he could answer, a surge of water crashed up from behind them. Something pulled her body backwards, smashing her into the pier's footing. She thrashed her arms and legs in a blind frenzy trying to strike whatever was attacking her, and then she froze.

Morgan blinked hard, trying to focus through the murky water. A man was standing in front of her holding her arms against her sides. It wasn't some vicious sea monster dragging her to her death. It was a tall muscular man, who was maybe twenty years old, staring directly at her. His hair was as black as coal and scruffy enough to sway against the current. His eyes were as green as emeralds and his face was oval with a thin nose. He was breathing under the water too! He looked familiar but she couldn't place where she had seen him before.

It's okay, Lady Morgan, Just relax, you're safe now, he soothed.

Something didn't feel right, but her body was washed over with a strange sense of calm. A trickle of warmth slid through her limbs and she closed her eyes, falling against the mysterious stranger.

Morgan, NOOOO! Ethan's voice shot through her groggy mind waking her out of a strange trance. The dark hair and green eyes suddenly dawned on her—Triton! She fought the pull of her own eyelids and managed to open her eyes just in time to see the man in front of her for what he really is.

His mouth was opened wide, extremely wide, displaying a row of serrated, shark-like teeth that were plunging toward her neck! She watched the arms that held her transform as hard black fins protruded through her attackers flesh. Their steely sharpness pushed against her stomach and threatened to slash through her skin at any moment. She could not pull away. She was defenseless against him.

Locked in the monster's grip, Morgan watched as Ethan fought desperately to get to her. He managed to evade the Triton who was holding him, long enough to grab Morgan's attacker. In one swift motion, Ethan had his arms wrapped around the creature's head, and with what seemed to be little effort, he broke its neck. The limp body slumped against Morgan, pinning her against the leg of the pier. She screamed in terror and shoved her attacker's limp, lifeless body to the seabed. The fins disappeared back into the dead Triton's arms and the teeth were no longer noticeable. She shuddered at how human the body in front of her now looked.

Morgan recognized the second attacker who rushed at Ethan, slamming him against the pier. It was Trenton, one of the jerks from the Ferris wheel. *He's a Triton!* Ethan struck the cement buffers so hard that a cloud of silt rose through the water. Morgan was blinded by the silt and struggled to see what was happening, which made her all the more terrified.

She saw someone approaching through the muddy cloud.

Did you get him? Is he gone? She asked with her mind, hoping Ethan would hear her.

Oh yeah, I got him, he's gone, and you're next! Trenton growled as he charged toward her with jagged shark-like teeth shooting from his mouth and onyx-colored fins shooting from his forearms. His eyes turned from a mesmerizing green to deadly black, and his long black hair flowed around him like a cape. He grabbed Morgan by her hair and yanked her to him like a rag doll, yanking her head to one side.

You should have let my brother do this while you were in the trance, cause this time it's gonna hurt! Trenton thrust his head forward ripping his teeth into the flesh of her neck.

The pain was excruciating as his teeth cut through her skin. A cloud of her blood filled the water and Morgan felt her body growing weaker by the second.

This is it! She thought, as the blood flowed freely from her neck and the man continued to eat her alive.

She spotted Ethan approaching them from behind and tried to avert her eyes so as to not alert her attacker. It worked. Ethan was on him now with the same quick assault he had used on her other attacker. Morgan heard the cracking of the monster's neck and watched him fall to the ground before she fell too. She knew she would be dead soon, in fact, she could feel it. Her body was numb and unable to move.

Ethan dropped beside her. She could tell he was badly hurt but his attention was focused only on her.

Just hold on, please my love, just hold on, he pleaded.

I'm glad I met you, Ethan, she thought, offering a weak smile.

I'm glad I met you, too, he answered as he pulled her wilted body to his chest.

She felt the warmth of their connection as Ethan's energy surrounded her, then entered her body passing through his chest and into hers. She felt the numbness of her looming death disappear as life poured back into her through Ethan's wonderful, healing flow of energy. Once she gained enough strength, she turned to face Ethan. Panic surged through her veins when she realized how grave his situation had become.

Stop Ethan! Stop! He was giving her his life, but she knew it was killing him. She could feel what little strength he had disappearing, yet he did not stop. He held her tightly in his arms as all the energy he had left, seeped into her resistant body.

We will always be connected now Morgan. Part of my soul now lives inside you. He said and then his body went completely still.

Ethan no! Please hang on, please fight this! Don't leave me! Mustering as much strength as she could find, Morgan hit him square in the chest. He did not respond, instead his body simply fell away from her. Ethan was unresponsive and lifeless. Morgan knew she had to give him back some of his. But she didn't know how! She tried to concentrated and envision the energy streaming through her body. She imagined it flowing to her hands and was excited to see it slowly starting to form at her fingertips. She pulled herself closer to Ethan and placed her hand on his chest. The energy she held in her hand was small, but it was worth a try. She pushed the meager zap of energy into chest.

Even though it was a small zap, she felt an insurmountable loss of energy and before she could see if it had even helped Ethan, her world went dark.

Chapter 9

"Morgan, come on, Morgan, wake up," she felt the soft whisper against her ear.

"Ethan?" she muttered, still groggy.

"What? No! Lucas. Who's Ethan?"

Morgan's eyes flew open, her body jilting to a sitting position and almost knocking heads with Lucas. She looked around quickly. The room was unfamiliar. Tattered chunks of old wallpaper covered the slat-boarded walls. She struggled to breathe in the musty air.

"Lucas...Where am I?" she asked rubbing her neck, feeling for the wound where the creature had bitten her, but nothing was there.

Lucas sat across from her, a worried look in his eyes. "Oh, the nightmares I had when you left...I'm so sorry for everything Lucas, please don't leave like that again. You wouldn't believe what I dreamed about. It was so real." She shook her head as if she were able to physically shake the nightmares from her memory.

Lucas clenched his teeth but remained silent.

"Can we please go back to the way we were, Lucas? I need you in my life," she sobbed.

"I don't know," Lucas said, averting his eyes.

"What? What do you mean you don't know?" she asked, forgetting the question she had asked him in the first place.

"Where we are..." he said slowly. "I don't know where we are."

Morgan looked around in terror. If it had been just another one of her horrid nightmares, she hadn't woken up from it just yet. Ethan's lifeless body was lying on the cot across from her.

"Why are you here?" she asked, confused.

"Jeez, don't act so happy to see me," Lucas said, his handsome face turning to a pout.

Morgan looked at him closely. His usually clean-cut preppy blonde hair was longer and disheveled, his face was scattered with stubble, and his normally confident muscular body was slouched and defeated. His sparkling blue eyes were grey with fatigue. She could tell that wherever they were, Lucas had been there for a while.

Lucas spoke calmly. "I don't know where we are. I woke up here four days ago. I was in Hawaii with my parents, and I was trying to surf when something grabbed me, something big. I remember struggling and thinking that I was being eaten by sharks or something, then everything went black. And I woke up here. We are on an old houseboat of some kind. I'm so glad you're here, Morgan. I'm so sorry for what happened between us, too. I'm okay with just being friends, I promise. I will never ask more from you again. You have my word." As he spoke, he lightly kissed the top of her head.

Morgan searched his big blue eyes for the truth. She wanted to believe that he had switched back to friend mode, but it had only been a little over a week since his declaration of love. Could anyone get over their feelings that quickly? She cared for him so deeply she did not want to hurt him by questioning his apology; she would take his word at face value and hope for the best.

"There are six of us now, including that guy over there. He hasn't woken up yet. He arrived around the same time as you, but he's still sleeping it off. Is his name Ethan?"

She nodded as she looked at Ethan's large crumpled body lying comatose on the bed across the room. She wanted to run to him and try wake him but thought it would be best to wait until Lucas left the room.

Ethan? she probed with her mind a little.

Nothing.

She looked back to Lucas. "You must have seen who brought us here. The boat? The people?" She tried to piece together what was going on. Things were happening so fast—one minute she is lying at the bottom of an ocean with Ethan, the next minute she was on a boat with Lucas. Her mind whirled.

He shook his head. "No, I was the second to arrive and I still haven't got a frigging clue as to what's going on. Tia was the first. She's real nice, but she doesn't know anything about what's going on either."

Morgan could tell that Lucas felt something more than he was saying for this Tia girl. His eyes twinkled when he said her name the same way they did when he was crushing on Sadie Rickshaw in the tenth grade. She did not push the matter, nor did she care if Lucas had moved on. In fact, she hoped he had. It would at least make one part of her life a little easier. She never felt like he was more than a best friend, and she was glad he claimed he didn't want to be her boyfriend anymore. She wanted things to go back to the way they were so badly that she was willing to believe him. They always acted as a couple of convenience, pairing up on group dates with friends and stuff. That was happening a lot lately, and that must have sent Lucas off course somewhere. They were friends, best friends, and that was all. But no matter how complicated things had gotten between them, Morgan was glad he was there now, beside her.

"Nobody's seen what brought us here. Well, not all of it anyway. We were all taken when we were in the water, by something very big and very fast," he said, shaking his head in disbelief at the memory of it.

"So you never saw it bring me?" Morgan asked as she still tried to piece everything together.

"All we ever see is a large wave of water approaching with a body on it, this time your body and it just kind of nudged you up on the deck and then it was gone. It looks kind of like… I know this sounds stupid but..." He paused carefully selecting his wording, "like a Waterhorse, or freakin' Ogopogo, or whatever you call it. It has a long neck and a large dinosaur-like body, but

I've never gotten a chance to see it long enough to describe it. It's just too fast."

He stared at her, leaning forward, as if he was waiting for her to laugh or call him crazy, but Morgan knew anything was possible and she was open to any explanations.

"You know what the funny thing is?" Lucas continued. "We think this thing is actually saving us from something, not hurting us. It brings us crates of food and supplies all the time."

He slid his hand onto hers and smiled.

Morgan smiled back, thinking how much she needed that. She inhaled his warm musky familiar scent. With him by her side, she felt safe.

"I can't believe you're here," she began to cry. "I didn't think I would ever see you again. I didn't think I would ever see anyone again. I was attacked in the ocean and the last thing I remember was becoming so weak I thought I was going to die. There is so much I have to tell you, Lucas."

She choked back tears. Lucas waited patiently for her to continue, still holding her hand.

"This is going to sound crazy but there are underwater beings trying to kill me, well, us," she gestured to Ethan. "They're called Triton. They look human but they can change into horrible monsters! They drove us off the pier and then came into the water after us. They're so scary Lucas, they're pure evil, I swear. They had this inner row of teeth like a shark or a vampire or something. The first guy that grabbed me almost hypnotized me and then a second one attacked me and ripped a chunk out of my neck. I thought I was going to die when I collapsed onto the ocean floor."

Morgan knew the question Lucas would ask next.

"Who is he? How did you meet him?" Then he added, shaking his head, "I've only been gone a week and you show up here with some stranger for God's sake." He stopped himself.

"I know this is hard for you, but Ethan is a good guy Lucas. He has literally saved my life twice since you've been gone."

Morgan carried on telling Lucas everything Ethan had told her about Atlantis and the six lost Council children. She left out some of the finer details of her and Ethan's encounters, not sure how he would react. Morgan listened to and tried to answer Lucas's hundred and one questions, but a wave of exhaustion rolled over her. As much as she fought to stay awake, she couldn't keep her eyes open any longer. She drifted off to sleep on her lumpy little cot, across from Ethan.

When Morgan woke it was dark, she kept her eyes closed for a while, allowing the gentle rock of the houseboat to soothe her as she tried to go back to sleep. She heard a rustle in the corner and opened her eyes, straining to see.

"Who's there?" she called out.

The large form approached her. A man with dark ebony unkempt hair stood over her. His piercing green eyes almost shone in the darkness as he came into focus. His perfectly-chiseled facial features glowed in the bright moonlight. She stared at the stranger in front of her, and he was breathtaking. Suddenly, the scene from the bottom of the ocean came rushing back to her and she thought of the monsters that had attacked her. She looked at the man in front of her and gasped. The Triton had found her!

"LUCAS! LUCAS!" Morgan screamed in terror.

The stranger's eyes looked startled and he stumbled backwards until he was pressed against the farthest wall in her room. Lucas burst through the door wildly and flicked on the light.

"What the hell's going on here?" he asked, panting from the run.

"They found us! Look out, Lucas! He's behind you!" she yelled hysterically and then jumped from the bed to pull Lucas away from the fierce monster. The Triton monster was looking around in confusion too.

"Where?" Lucas asked quickly, pushing her behind him for protection. Then Lucas spotted the figure pressed up against the wall. "Him?" he asked, relaxing as he walked up and set his hand on the man's shoulder.

"No, Morgan, it's okay, this is Larrance. He was the third one to arrive. He's one of us. He's from um..."

"San Diego," the boy offered, taking a step closer, then stopping when he saw Morgan stumble backward in fear.

"He is a Triton, Lucas! Get him out of here!" she yelled.

"I'm sorry," Larrance said, "I didn't mean to scare you. I just offered to check on you so Lucas could get some rest. He has been by your side since you got here. I know I probably should have turned on a light but I didn't want to wake you. I will leave," he said with his head bowed.

Morgan stepped closer to the monster, eyeing him suspiciously. "Open your mouth and show me your forearms!" she yelled as she maintained a safe distance between them. She studied his arms in search of black fins like the Triton who had attacked her at the pier.

Larrance lifted a quizzical eyebrow. "Okaaay..." he said. He opened his mouth to reveal a full set of normal pearly white human teeth. Then he held out his forearms, which bore nothing but a small tribal tattoo.

"Is there anything else of mine you'd like to see?" he asked sarcastically.

"I'm sorry, I...I was sure you were a monster, you look just like one," she mumbled. She could see the disgust in his face, so she walked toward Larrance with her hand outstretched. "I mean..."

He shrank back against the wall, avoiding her touch. "You think I look like a monster?" he asked with disgust. His green eyes sparkled and swirled the way Ethan's blue eyes often did, but Larrance's eyes didn't possess the power that Ethan's did. Larrance's eyes radiated a deep sorrow and sadness.

Before Morgan had a chance to defend her actions, Larrance turned on his heels and stormed from the room.

"That's not what I meant, you just..."

The door shut and he was gone.

Morgan stood there trying to figure out what had just happened.

"He's a good guy, Morgan. He has kept us all from falling apart around here. He's been our leader, of sorts." Lucas noticed Morgan was still resistant. "Does he really look that much like those guys from the ocean?"

"Like they could be brothers," she griped, and sat on the edge of Ethan's bed, trying to change her focus.

"Well, I'm going to go check on Larrance, he looked more scared of you then you did of him. Come to the living room when you pull yourself together. I think you should meet everyone so this doesn't happen again." Before he left the room he added, "Don't worry about Larrance. I'm sure that once he gets to know you he'll see that you aren't usually such a lunatic. If you want, I can talk to him and explain that you are usually more of a borderline nut job than a raging psycho."

Morgan threw her pillow at him as he ducked out the door.

She knew it was wrong to wish this unpredictable fate on anyone, but she couldn't help feeling glad that Lucas was with her.

She sat on a small wooden chair beside Ethan's bed for the rest of the evening, concerned that he had not woken yet. He was so badly hurt by the Triton's and then he foolishly gave up what remained of his energy to save her! He tried to give his life for hers. What was he thinking? She fumed. How could she live with herself if he did not survive this?

She placed her hands on his chest and tried to envision her energy flowing into him. It happened a lot easier this time. The energy she envisioned quickly appeared and passed through her fingertips. She could tell small amounts were making their way through the internal shell she felt surrounding Ethan. She prayed it was enough to heal him.

"Please wake up Ethan," she whispered. But there was no response.

Chapter 10

Morgan fished the necklace Ethan had given her on the beach, from her front pant pocket. She was relieved to discover it hadn't fallen out during all the chaos. She fastened it around her neck, and slipped it beneath her shirt feeling the cool metal as it dangled against her skin. She walked over to Ethan's small bed and looked at his body cramped up on top of it. She leaned over him and ran her fingers through his beautiful golden hair. She hadn't slept much. Being so worried about Ethan, she kept waking to check on him. They had been on the boat two days and he still did not even stir in his bed.

Wake up, Ethan. Please wake up. She gently kissed his forehead as she tried to probe his mind. Still nothing. She wound her fingers into his, hoping for a surge of energy between them. Nothing.

Come on Ethan! I don't know what the hell is going on here. I need your help. I need you.

"Aahhemm." She heard a throat clear behind her. "We are having a group meeting, and I think you should be present." Came the deep icy voice behind her.

She turned and seen Larrance in the doorway but he walked off before she could respond.

She kissed Ethan's forehead one more time before heading to the living room.

Morgan entered the musty, tattered, dust covered living room. She could feel the houseboat shifting back and forth under her feet. The only lighting came from a cracked window in one wall and the kerosene lamps, which she thought must be fastened somehow to the mantle since they didn't seem to move when the boat rocked. The boats walls creaked with every sway, revealing its age with every creak and moan of its timbers.

Lucas was sitting on a worn yellow love seat, and beside him sat a beautiful petite girl with long flowing blonde curls. She had the petal pink cheeks and small, rosy, pout lips to match. Morgan watched Lucas quickly remove his arm from around the girl's shoulders and she knew right away that the girl was Tia. In an old, velvet, blue chair across the room, sat a stunning, super-model-sized blonde-haired girl. She had bright pink streaks adorning her straight, platinum locks. She introduced herself as Cleo. Morgan looked at all of them—all blue eyed, and blonde haired, even Ethan. They're bone structures were even similar. So much so, Morgan thought they could definitely, all pass for relatives. All of them, except—Larrance.

She spotted another tattered yellow love seat in the corner. It was vacant so she walked over to it and sat down. She groaned when she realized that the only empty spot left to sit was beside her, and the only one left without a seat was Larrance.

Crap! She thought.

She could tell that Larrance was not comfortable with the seating arrangements either, since he stood for as long as possible. He shifted his weight with the movement of the boat and held onto the crumbling brick façade on the mantle behind him. They all listened to Lucas recite the stories of Atlantis that Morgan had told him earlier, all of them turning to look at her for a nod of confirmation here and there.

A large wave hit the houseboat almost tossing Larrance into the fireplace.

"Oh for Gods' sake, just sit down beside me before you end up in the bloody fireplace. I don't bite!" she blurted.

"No, that's what I do, remember? I think I'll take my chances with the fireplace," he said in annoyance. He did not sit.

She sat back, holding her neck, remembering the vicious Triton attack; as she listened to Lucas recite her story word-for-word. She could feel Larrance watching her the whole time. She turned to meet his eyes, but he looked away, and if Morgan didn't know better she would have thought she saw him blush.

After Lucas finished speaking, the Q & A portion of the evening began.

Cleo, the most brazen of the bunch started. "Sooo...We have powers?" she asked, obviously taking nothing else from the conversation.

"Yes," Morgan nodded. All eyes and ears were hanging on her answers. "Well, most of us should, but it may be years before we know what they will be. They will vary with each of us, I think, but they will all be powers of the mind, like telepathy, telekinesis, empaths, and stuff like that. Atlanteans have unlocked the powers of the mind and they can manipulate energy."

Cleo nodded her head in approval. "Cool," she said, plugging her iPod headphones back into her ears, no longer interested in the conversation.

Tia spoke up this time. "Why did an Atlantean come for you but not the rest of us? They just pulled us into the ocean?"

Morgan shook her head. "I don't know, maybe because I never go near the ocean," she whispered.

Lucas chuckled. "That's right our newfound mermaid is afraid of water."

Morgan felt humiliation storming into her face. "Shut up, Lucas! Besides, if I'm a mermaid, what does that make you? I wonder how your football buddies will react to a Merman on the team?"

Lucas became extremely silent and she knew he wouldn't be teasing her any further. They pushed each other's buttons sometimes, but they always got over it and remained good friends. She noticed a twinge of pain on his face though and wondered if she went too far. She dropped her eyes to the floor.

Larrance took his turn at the questions. "Do you think you absorbed too much of Ethan's life force?"

She looked at them. She had never thought of the energy between her and Ethan as their life forces, but when Larrance phrased it like that it made sense. She thought of how they had kissed and she felt his energy inside her. How he had pleaded for her to stop because she was taking too much from him. She could have killed him then without even knowing, without even trying. Was that her power? Sucking the life from others? Was she some kind of Atlantean succubus? Had she taken Ethan's life from him on the ocean floor? Was he just a shell now? That would explain why she was healed and he was...not.

She felt sick to her stomach and could feel the color drain from her face. She suddenly felt like the monster in the room.

She rose from the couch wanting to get out of there and clear her head. She hurried to the entrance door, bursting through it, not stopping till she hit the railing surrounding the houseboat's small back deck. She looked out desperately searching for land, but there was nothing but water as far the eye could see. The water taunted her as it washed around the boat. The water was her only way out, and she refused to be afraid of it. Nothing else was going to frighten her today.

She thought of Ethan—his kind blue eyes, the way that he looked at her, the feeling of his touch…

She took a deep breath of courage and jumped.

She didn't know where she was going and she didn't care if she made it there or not. She just swam and swam as fast as her body would take her. Tears streamed down her face, escaping to the salty water beneath her. She had never swum in anything but a kiddie pool before, but somehow she was swimming effortlessly now. The water embraced her as one of its own and she felt free. Free from burden, free from ridicule and free from her thoughts.

She was swimming away from Ethan, from Lucas — from everything. She swam as fast and as far away as her limbs would take her, frantically trying to escape everyone and everything.

All sight of the houseboat soon disappeared. She was happy for a brief moment until she realized what she had done. She didn't know how to get back. There was no sight of her boat and no way of knowing what direction to head to get back to it. There was only water, everywhere.

She felt something rise from beneath the water and smack into her side. *Oh god, it's sharks!* She panicked.

She tried swimming in the opposite direction of whatever bumped her, but it was too fast. Another large bump in the ribs sent her sideways. She squeezed her eyes shut as she turned to face her attacker. She was prepared to scream at the bloodthirsty beast. Why hadn't she thought of the possibility of shark-infested waters a little sooner?

She slowly opened her eyes to meet her fate but the face of her vicious attacker was not quite what she had expected. Peering curiously into her face looking almost as scared as she felt, was a young seal pup. Its big brown innocent eyes were framed by long eyelashes, and it gazed at her curiously, as it tilted its head from side to side. The seal's nose moved in toward her, sniffing a greeting as it set its front flipper on her shoulder.

"Hey, little guy! You scared me half to death. I thought you were something that wanted to eat me. What are you doing out here by yourself?" she said, barely finishing her sentence when a rumble of waves began to bubble up around her.

Brown heads poked up all around until she was surrounded by a herd of seals. They roared and slapped the water.

Morgan spun around treading the water beneath her. They had her completely trapped. She looked for the houseboat but it was still out of sight. *Damn, I can be such an idiot! What the hell was I thinking! How could I be so stupid!* She reprimanded herself.

"My thoughts exactly," Larrance said as he swam toward her. The seals parted, allowing him through.

He grabbed her in a lifeguard rescue position before she could even argue and began to swim with her in tow. They passed the circle of barking seals and headed back toward the houseboat that she could now see about 80 feet away.

The seals followed behind them, almost pushing them back toward the house.

"I was fine. I knew what I was doing!" she argued, as the seals still roared behind them.

"Do you think none of us tried to get away before? Do you think we're that stupid that we'd all just sit and wait in this house for whatever's coming next?" He yelled over the seals, still holding her helpless body against his chest and swimming forward as if she were nothing more than a buoy tucked under his arm.

"Let me go. I can swim," she argued. He continued without saying a word. "Let me go!" she screeched, way too aware of his half-naked body pulling her to safety.

"Fine, we're here," he replied with a triumphant smirk, as he pushed her up onto the deck like she was a wet rag doll.

"You didn't have to come after me. I was fine," she yelled over the boom of barking seals. They had become so loud she couldn't hear herself think.

Arf, arf, arf, they continued, louder and louder as water splashed and sprayed around them, circling the boat.

Larrance pulled himself onto the deck beside her.

Morgan thought her head would burst from the sound. She couldn't take it anymore. "SHUT UP!" she yelled across the water to the large mob of mammals.

Instant silence fell across the ocean. The seals obediently dipped their heads beneath the water's surface and swam off without another sound.

Larrance shrugged and shook his head in disbelief. "Hmm, I never thought of trying that," he said in amusement.

She looked at him closely, as the golden hues of sunset gleamed across his muscled body. Wow, he was beautiful. He was big, too, at least 6'6" she guessed. Way bigger than Ethan and Lucas in height and mass. She looked in awe at the sheer size of his arms. He leaned in toward her so she could feel his breath hot against her cheek.

"I'm cuter, too," he whispered, and walked past her into the house.

Morgan wanted to drown herself then and there. Larrance could read her mind, just like Ethan had! And he just eavesdropped on her mind while she was checking him out!

She sat on the front deck a while and waited for everyone (Larrance in particular), to go to bed.

She thought about the evening's events. She did not trust Larrance because he was not one of them, she was sure, and he had powers already, like Ethan, like her. She wondered why the seals just let him through the circle to retrieve her like that. She could hear him walking by the door of the houseboat, so she lay on the deck and covered herself with an old tarp she had found in the corner.

Morgan was surprised when she opened her eyes again.

Larrance was standing over her as she lay crumpled up on the deck floor still covered with the tarp from last night.

"Are you planning on sleeping out here all night?" he asked gruffly.

Morgan combed down her bed-head with her fingers and wiped the drool from her lips. She looked at him innocently. "I guess so, yeah," she said. She was surprised that she could have slept out there at all and not had a single nightmare.

"Are you some kind of idiot?" he barked.

"Excuse me?" she asked quickly, not sure if she heard him right.

"I asked if you were some kind of freaking idiot? You've been out here all night. You know how easily you could have rolled off into the water? Or how easy it would have been for those seals or one of those Triton-whatever's to grab you?" he fumed.

She looked at Larrance closely, noticing his bloodshot eyes and tired face. She realized that the real reason she hadn't had a nightmare last night was because he must have stayed by her side.

"You should've just woken me, I would have gone inside. You didn't have to keep watch over me. I don't require any special treatment."

"Yeah… right," he snorted. "Can you imagine what would happen if I, 'the monster,' leaned over you to wake you up? God, you just about brought the house down last time I startled you. I had no choice but to stand here keeping guard until you opened your stupid eyes!" he yelled.

"You had a choice. You should have just minded your own business. I am awake now, so why don't you leave me the hell alone," she snarled as she stood up to face him head-on.

He spun around and stomped into the houseboat, slamming the door behind him and leaving her to fume alone on the deck. She looked at the boxes Larrance had slid in front of the deck entrance to protect her from rolling off in her sleep. She kicked them as hard as she could, and then slumped against them, shaking her head in disbelief. *God! He is such a jerk!* She realized he probably heard that and a smile came to her lips.

A good amount of time had passed and she figured it was safe to slip back into the house and check on Ethan.

She slinked through what she assumed was the kitchen and headed toward her and Ethan's bedroom. A door opened across from her and bumped her side. In the doorway stood Larrance, his hair disheveled and his eyes filled with sleep and innocence.

"Oh sorry, I was just grabbing a water bottle," he said, obviously caught completely off-guard.

Morgan said nothing. Instead, she just opened her door and slipped inside thinking that the hallway was way too small to fit two people. Especially the two of them.

She turned back towards Larrance as she held her bedroom door. She knew she should just go to bed but she wanted some answers and she knew she wouldn't sleep well without them. "How did you know where to find me in the water yesterday? How did you know where I was?" she asked curiously.

"You were 100 feet away Morgan. I knew where you were 'cause I could see you."

"But I couldn't see the houseboat anywhere," she argued.

"You were panicked and surrounded by seals; what more do you want me to say? I suppose you think I followed you or something?" He let out a defeated breath then stepped toward her. He was so close she could feel the heat radiating from his chest. "When you are done convincing yourself that I'm such a terrible monster, let me know Morgan. Until then I'll just stay out of your way."

He took a step back into his doorway and shut the door, not bothering to get his water and not bothering to hide his annoyance with Morgan any longer.

Morgan went to the kitchen and opened the fridge. She couldn't believe how well stocked it was. She made a note to ask Lucas about that later. She grabbed two water bottles and headed back down the hall. She gently opened Larrance's door and reached in as she set one water bottle on the floor for him, then closed his door again and quickly retreated to her own room.

Ethan's body was still lying lifeless on the bed across from hers. She was so sad, and so tired, and so confused. She grabbed the blanket from her bed and curled up beside Ethan sending energy into him like she'd done every evening since they arrived. For once she was thankful to be Atlantean and have her ability. Without her energy, she knew Ethan would not have survived so long without food or water. But she worried that soon even her energy would not be enough to keep him alive.

Chapter 11

A couple of days passed without incident. Morgan stayed in her room most of the time, other than playing a few games of cards with Lucas and Tia. She was amused at how easily Lucas seemed to have moved on—his eyes locked on Tia the entire time they played rummy, so much so, that Morgan was beginning to feel like a third wheel. She was happy nevertheless that she did not have that issue to deal with any longer. Ethan had not changed much, but he was starting to regain some color in his face and his heartbeat had grown much stronger in his chest. Morgan knew that he was healing, although slowly.

Morgan woke early and thought she would try sunning on the roof deck of the houseboat. She had tried a couple times in the last couple of days, but Larrance was always outside, and she was doing her best to avoid him at all costs. Sure enough, when she opened the door he was out there, but he did not see her. She crept up the side ladder and managed to get to the top deck unnoticed. She laid out her towel and removed her clothes down to her bra and underwear—she felt safe since no one ever came up there.

She could see the top of Larrance's head down below, but she was sure he could not see her. He was always too busy swimming and doing all the hunting and gathering stuff for the group. She marveled at how amazing he was—he went out with nothing but a simple spear and mesh bag and would come back with a feast of fish. No matter how much she despised him, he truly was a beneficial addition to the group. No wonder he had that awesome body with all the exercise he did.

Morgan lay against her fluffy towel with her eyes closed, enjoying the warm morning sun. She wanted to lie there and forget all that had happened and just pretend. Pretend she was home with her Mom laying out on their back deck, sun tanning and laughing over some silly unimportant thing.

You miss her a lot, don't you? She felt Larrance's mind intruding on hers.

She jumped up and rapidly covered herself with her clothes as she looked around for him in a panic.

Relax, I can't see you. I'm on the deck. I just heard your thoughts, your sadness. I'm sorry this is so hard for you.

She snatched up her towel and headed for the stairs.

There he stood at the bottom, looking up at her with a devilish grin. "So, you think I have an awesome body?" he teased, trying to embarrass her.

"Were you up here?" she demanded furiously. "Did you see anything?"

"No," he answered to her relief. "...and yes," he added.

"You are such an ass!" she yelled, shoving him out of the way as she crawled down the ladder. He reached out to help her, wrapping his large hands around her hips and pulling her to the deck floor. She kicked him in the shin.

I was just trying to help! He yelled in her head as he hopped backward on one foot. She felt the energy build inside her. The anger balled into a large sphere in her mind, and she sent it to him, slamming a mental door in his face. He winced as he fell on his butt and grabbed at the sides of his head.

"Owww!" he yelped.

It worked! She felt joy in the fact that she could now block him and she vowed to practice putting walls around her thoughts from now on.

She walked back into the house, leaving Larrance clenching his head in pain with a dumbfounded look spread across his face.

Good Girl! She felt him in her mind again! She was about to slam him for the second time when she realized it wasn't Larrance. It was Ethan!

She ran to their room, threw the door open and kneeled by his bed. She looked into Ethan's eyes. He still seemed to be comatose, but she could see a small grin at the corner of his lips.

"Oh Ethan, I was so scared you were going to die. I truly thought I'd lost you." She kissed his still lips, crying tears of joy onto his face.

Careful, sweetheart, I'm still very weak. She heard a deep, earthy moan rumble across his chest.

"Can you open your eyes?" she asked, hopefully.

No response.

She felt his mind slip back into the abyss.

She kissed him lightly. "Rest, you'll be better soon," she whispered, as she lovingly brushed the hair from his brow.

Lucas walked in and lowered his head as if he were intruding.

She looked at him in excitement. "He woke for a minute! He talked to me."

"He spoke?" Lucas asked, looking at the still body beside her.

"Well, not physically spoke, but he can talk to me in my head. He spoke in my head!" she exclaimed.

Lucas raised his eyebrows, unsure of how to respond to the crazy girl claiming she had just heard voices in her head. "Oookaaay," he said, "you mean you have some sort of telepathic connection with this guy?"

"Yes, we can speak to each other through our thoughts somehow. Larrance can hear and speak to me through thought too, but it's different with him because he can hear all of my thoughts, not just the ones I send to him. Strange right?"

"Well, it explains the intense connection I see between you and the two of them. How can a regular, old, boy like me, compete with that?" Lucas winked. He left before Morgan had the chance to argue that he was hardly just a regular boy in her eyes.

Morgan wasn't sure what Lucas meant by "you and the two of them." Larrance was nothing more than a huge pain in her butt. But at that moment she didn't care; she was just happy that Ethan was going to be all right and that was all that mattered.

Cleo appeared in the doorway next. She leaned her tall slender body against the frame. "Breakfast is ready," she said in an uninterested manner. She stood there with an annoyed expression waiting for Morgan to leave Ethan's side, which she did, reluctantly.

Morgan found them all sitting in the living room, swallowing down spoonful's of overcooked porridge in silence.

Lucas broke the silence. "So, Larrance said you scared the seals away the other night?"

Morgan turned to Larrance, who stared intentionally into his porridge bowl and did not acknowledge her existence.

"Yeah, Lucas, thanks for being the one to come after me the other night. I mean, you're my best friend, right? So why not send Larrance? That makes perfect sense!" she snarled.

"I..I..Larrance…" Lucas stuttered as he struggled for words. "Larrance was out the door before I could stop him. I knew he would look after you, Morgan. He is the strongest and fastest one here. You showed up here heartbroken over some comatose guy, and you have barely given me the time of day or even talked to me since you got here. Forgive me if I assumed I was no longer your best friend. All you do is sit and mope by coma guy's bedside, all day. You don't seem to want anything to do with anyone else—including me." She could feel the anger he directed at her, but she kept her eyes on her bowl.

"Drama," Cleo chimed.

Tia's small body curled up even smaller as she leaned in to Lucas's side.

Larrance got up, put his bowl in the sink and walked out to the deck without saying a word.

Morgan rose and headed back to her room. She didn't care about these people—they could all just 'suck it' as far as she was concerned. She would just stay in her room from here on in and sit by Ethan's side until his eyes opened.

Ethan will fix everything, when he wakes up, he'll make everything right, she told herself.

When she entered the room, Morgan's heart nearly stopped.

Ethan's bed was empty.

Chapter 12

"Ethan? Ethan!" Morgan yelled as she rushed to the empty bed.

"I'm right here, my love," came a warm voice behind her.

She turned to face the man she now realized, she loved, since the day she met him. His eyes were warm pools of blue desire. She heard Larrance come running down the hall knowing that he must have sensed something was wrong. She quickly shut the bedroom door, leaving her and Ethan in privacy.

"Is everything okay?" Larrance asked as he banged a fist on the door.

"Everything's fine! Just go away Larrance, I don't need you anymore!" she yelled back. She heard him walk away and swore she physically felt the pain in his heart from the double meaning he heard in her sentence. She wished she'd chosen her words a little differently.

She didn't care, Ethan was awake now and that's all that mattered. She removed all thoughts of Larrance from her head and stared warmly at the beautiful boy in front of her.

"I can't believe you're actually awake and standing here."

He grabbed her face and kissed her softly. His aura was strong and full around him. He was desperate for her touch as he crushed her body against his. She felt his tongue gently flicking at her lips and shoved him away from her. The last thing she wanted to do was take any energy from him.

She pulled him over to the chair beside the bed. "Please sit. You don't want to do too much. You're still weak."

He looked at the chair then sat beside her on the bed. He pulled at the chain around her neck lifting the pendant out from beneath her shirt. His eyes brightened at the sight of it.

"You put it on. You know what this means?" he whispered, gently kissing the neck that held his pendant.

"It means you and me, forever."

She kissed him back, letting go of all her worries and pain as she embraced the warmth of his love, the warmth she didn't think she would ever experience again.

She dutifully pulled away, not wanting the moment to end, but not wanting to weaken Ethan either. He understood and didn't fight her on the matter. They sat in silence for a short while just enjoying each other's presence.

"Where are we?" Ethan asked, breaking the silence.

"I don't know. We're on an old houseboat in the middle of the ocean. We're anchored here and no one comes or goes, other than the large water animal that brought us here. I tried to swim out, but there's nothing out there, nothing at all" she answered.

"It's the House of Azores. It's an Atlantean safe house. The Water-runners must have brought us here. That's what the Atlanteans will use to bring the other kids as well."

"There are six of us here already. Are the Water-runners big?" she asked.

"They're prehistoric. Humans have seen them a few times and call them things like the Loch Ness Monster and Ogopogo, but the water runners aren't too fond of those names. They're our messengers and retrievers, and on occasion they will allow one of us as a rider. There are only four Water runners left in the world. They're truly magical creatures. Today's Atlantis couldn't survive without their help." Ethan explained. "Did you say all six kids are here already?"

"Yes, assuming you're part of the six. You are, aren't you? Why haven't they come for us yet?" she asked.

"I don't know." She saw that he was trying to hide the concern in his face.

He turned his body toward her, holding her small pale hands in his. "Tomorrow I will lead the group to Atlantis. I know where we are and the entrance is only two days or so, away from here."

He then held his hand out with his palm toward her. "Your powers are growing stronger, I can feel it," he said. "I want to show you something. Here, put your palm close to mine without actually touching me." He spoke with boyish excitement.

Morgan raised her hand up in front of Ethan's.

"Okay, now I want you to feel the energy inside you. Feel yourself gathering it throughout your body and sending it to your fingertips."

She closed her eyes and envisioned the energy moving through her.

"Good, now picture yourself holding that energy in your hand," he coaxed.

She opened her eyes to see little strands of white light like tiny lightning flashes dancing between their outstretched hands. She pushed the energy further, allowing it to rush from her fingertips and form a globe in her hand. Ethan slowly pulled his hand away so she was holding the glowing orb of light in her hand alone.

"Wow, this is amazing!" she exclaimed, as she teetered the ball in her hand back and forth.

"Okay, now I want you to focus on the energy ball again, but feel your body absorbing it this time. Feel your fingers taking it into your body and spreading it out to every limb. You have the ability to give and take energy, you just have to concentrate and control it. Pull it inwards and visualize it flowing beneath your skin."

She watched as the ball slowly grew smaller and she could feel it spreading through her fingertips and back into her body. She felt pure joy as it poured into her and flowed beneath her skin. Soon, the glowing sphere of energy vanished from her hand and she looked up happily at Ethan.

"That was amazing," she beamed.

"**You** are amazing;" he smiled lovingly. "It took me years to learn how to control energy like that."

"Is that what I shot at you on the beach?" she asked guiltily.

"Yeah, that's why I figured you would be able to do this. You're very gifted already. I can't even imagine the powers you'll possess one day."

A shudder of fear rippled down her spine for reasons she did not know.

Ethan took her hands in his proudly and squeezed them. "Everything's going to be good from here on in. I promise."

Ethan backed away from her and fidgeted with his clothes. "I need to go for a swim. I need to feel the ocean on my skin and absorb the energy from it. That way I can hold you and kiss you all night without you having to pull away from me again," he whispered as he kissed her cheek. She felt an army of butterflies gush through her stomach as the bliss of his kiss radiated across her body. She had almost forgotten how much his touch affected her. She held his hands a moment longer, not wanting to let him go, anywhere.

He looked at her and smiled. "It's okay, everything's okay now, Love. It'll only take an hour or so and I'll stay close to the boat." He cupped her chin and tilted her head up until their eyes locked. "Thank you for sitting by my bedside and sending energy into me each day. You saved my life. I love you, Morgan." He headed for the door. She walked out behind Ethan and saw Larrance's door shutting as they entered the hall.

I suppose you heard everything? She sent her thoughts to Larrance.

I couldn't hear anything! What the hell's going on? he interrogated.

Ethan's awake. She curtly responded to Larrance's direct question, and then built a wall in her mind as high as it could go so no one could intrude.

She sat on the deck of the boat as Ethan disrobed down to his boxers. She tried not to stare at his beautiful bare chest and broad, muscled shoulders. The elastic on his boxers read Joe Boxer. Ethan turned his head, and she realized that he'd just caught her staring at his goods.

"Sooo, they have name brand boxer shorts in Atlantis?" she asked, stupidly.

"They have a lot of things in Atlantis," he said coyly, giving her a wink as he dived into the welcoming waters.

She watched as he swam, the water sprayed and circled, working with him as he glided through its surface. It was like a perfectly orchestrated dance between him and the water. He moved with the speed and grace of a dolphin.

She was so engulfed by Ethan's water skills that she startled when she finally noticed Lucas standing on the on the deck.

"May I?" he asked gesturing to the empty spot beside her.

She nodded and moved over so he could sit.

"So coma guy finally woke up?"

She nodded, still watching her magnificent man. "Ethan. His name is Ethan."

"Sorry. Ethan." Lucas said almost choking on the name. He sat beside her, shuffling so close to her, their legs touched as they hung over the boat.

"I get it Morgan; I feel the connection between you and him and I'm happy for you. Truly. It's just hard you know? It's always just been you and I against the world. I was foolish to act the way I did the day I left for Hawaii. I guess I just felt that if we were such good friends we would be great lovers. I know better than that now. It's my biggest regret. I know you've accepted my apology, but I still feel the tension between us. I screwed up royally, I know that and now I'm scared the friendship we had, the real, true bond we had, is gone, lost forever." His sparkling blue eyes were filling with tears.

She placed her hand to his cheek. "It will come back Lucas. Our bond is still strong, and you'll always be my best friend. I'm sorry I didn't sit and talk with you about this sooner. I just didn't know what to say. It's weird, isn't it? That you and I, two kids who grew up together on the same block in the suburbs, both end up being from Atlantis. There are only six like us in the world and we're two of the six. I don't know what to make of it. But, I'm glad that you're with me through all of this. It's like having a little bit of home with me out here," she answered, leaning her head against his bulky shoulder.

She turned her attention back to Ethan but she couldn't see him. The water in front of them began to stir and bubble. Morgan could sense something bad was about to happen and quickly stood pulling her feet away from the edge of the boat. Suddenly, a large greyish-green tentacle burst up from beneath the water's surface, slamming onto the boat deck and wrapping itself around Lucas's leg before he had a chance to scramble away.

"Holy shit!" he yelled, trying to pry his fingers beneath the giant hostile limb and free himself but with every movement it just tightened further around his calf. He grabbed the railing of the deck to keep the tentacle from pulling him into the water.

Morgan heard Ethan scream. She saw him now, twisted in another tentacle, fighting the grip of whatever this monster was. The army of seals helplessly swam at the beast trying to protect Ethan, but their innocent bodies were being thrown effortlessly through the air by the many other limbs of the enormous squid-like sea monster. The squid's large, black, emotionless eyes scanned the water for prey. Its loose grey skin shivered around its head as it pulled its tentacles upwards revealing a large mouth of jagged teeth in the heart of the appendages. It roared a deafening sound that rippled across the water's surface, and then angrily slammed its tentacles against the waves.

"The axe, Morgan! Grab the axe!" Lucas screamed.

She ran to the emergency fire axe strapped to the side wall and ripped it from its bindings. She turned back to Lucas and without out a second to spare, she slammed the axe down into the grotesquely oversized tentacle. Dark red blood oozed from its rubbery flesh but it did not let go. Lucas still held to the railing, his body being stretched as the squid-like monster pulled at him.

"Again!" he screamed. "Hit him again!"

She gripped the axe, and with as much strength as she could muster, she slammed the blade down again, this time cutting right through the beast's appendage.

Lucas scrambled back against the house, limping on his one good leg, the other one streaming blood from the large circular wound the tentacle had left behind.

He grabbed Morgan and pulled her toward him, grabbing the axe from her hands. "Come on, we have to get inside!" he yelled over the splashing turmoil.

"I can't! It has Ethan! I have to help him!"

"Get in the house!" Ethan screamed from the squid's grip.

"Come on!" Lucas yelled, shoving her into the house against her will and hobbling in behind her armed with the fire axe. They stood in the kitchen and watched as the large greyish tentacles slithered through the living room in search of them.

They heard screaming from the living room and ran toward it. A tentacle was wrapped tightly around Larrance's chest and he appeared to be unconscious. Morgan felt her knees weaken as she saw Larrance's body being slammed back and forth against the living room walls like a rag doll. The tentacles had smashed through the window leaving a gaping hole in the side of the houseboat.

Not both of them. I can't lose both of them. The thought rushed through her head, surprising her.

She saw what looked like silvery webbing burst from Tia's back forming a dome of safety around her and Cleo in the corner of the demolished living room.

"Come on!" Lucas yelled again, pulling her toward the cocoon-like shield as it opened before them.

She followed Lucas into the opening. "What is this?" she asked, poking at the membrane surrounding them.

"It's Tia," Lucas said, as if that should clear up everything.

Through the safety of Tia's energy dome, Morgan watched the squid finally drop Larrance's wounded body with a "thwomp" leaving it lying bloodied and motionless on the wooden, boat floor. Another tentacle picked wrapped itself around Larrance and began thrashing on him once again. The sight made Morgan feel physically sick. She had to help him! She pushed against the energy wall, but it held her in as effectively as it kept the tentacles out.

"We can't just stay in here, we have to help Larrance…and Ethan," she cried.

"No shit, Sherlock!" Cleo snapped. "I was just waiting for the right moment. I have a plan to save him, but you're staying here princess. I fight alone."

"Open up, Tia, I want out NOW!" Cleo ordered the small girl huddled on the floor.

A tiny hole appeared beside Cleo and she jumped through. Morgan dashed forward following Cleo, but Tia closed the hole too quickly. "Open the shield. I want out too, Tia!" Morgan hollered at the petite balled-up figure that glowed with energy, ignoring Cleo's orders.

Lucas turned to Morgan as he stroked Tia's back. "No, you're staying put. You can't help him. You're just going to get yourself killed! Have faith in Cleo. She can do this."

Morgan helplessly watched Cleo through the protective shield. The pink-haired diva yanked the ornamental swords that hung innocently over the fireplace, from their worn perch. She pulled them from their sheaths simultaneously as she jumped through the air toward the squid. She moved with the speed and viciousness of a crazed animal. The swords swung over her head with deadly precision and then she brought them down on the squid with the fury of a true warrior. The sword sliced through the tentacle holding Larrance, severing it completely. The detached appendage fell to the floor still wrapped grotesquely around Larrance's crumpled body.

"Tia, let me out! NOW!" Morgan screamed furiously at her captor.

The shield opened slightly and Morgan rushed toward Larrance.

Cleo was still flying around the room with swords spinning in a deadly dance. She moved with amazing strength and agility, her blonde and pink hair flying behind her as she maneuvered strategically against the probing tentacles. She cut another tentacle from the beast and the freed appendage whipped wildly across the room.

Morgan grabbed Larrance and pulled the severed tentacle off of him. His eyes opened but he was incoherent. "Come on, Larrance, you have to help me get you to the shield."

He did not move and she felt the tears streaming down her face. "Larrance, please! You have to help me. I can't lift you!" she panicked.

His arm rose and he wiped a tear from her cheek in silence. He pulled himself up slowly, bracing his body against hers as they limped and crawled towards safety.

The shield opened, and with all her might, Morgan slid Larrance through the opening until he was safely inside the protective walls.

"Close the shield, Tia," Morgan said as she pulled away from them and ran back across the room to help Cleo.

Cleo managed to keep the beast's remaining slimy tentacles from re-entering the living room, but the squid monster was now focusing on bigger things, like destroying the entire boat.

Morgan stood where the living room wall used to be and waited, calmly gathering all the energy in her body. Cleo stood behind her, and she could feel Cleo's energy pouring into her, giving her more power than she ever thought possible. It felt like she had the power of the world at her fingertips, and as the beast from the ocean bobbed its large grotesque head above the water,

Morgan sent every ounce of power she possessed toward the beast in a large fiery white ball of energy.

The squid's massive, clammy, grey-skinned body shot up and out of the ocean, its remaining tentacles flying wildly through the air as water sprayed everywhere. It soared backwards skidding across the water like a giant skipping stone before it sunk beneath the surface in defeat. The water instantly turned calm and blue, just as it had been an hour earlier.

She felt a hand on her shoulder. "It's gone," she turned to see Larrance standing beside her, holding his bloody, wounded chest with his free hand.

Morgan felt weakened from the loss of energy and overwhelmed by everything that had just happened. Her body trembled uncontrollably. She gasped for air. Ethan was gone too, and she could feel his presence missing.

"Ethan!" she yelled, pulling away from Larrance. "I can't see him! We have to find him!" she ordered the group.

They all just stood there frozen and shell-shocked like useless lumps. She pushed through them and ran to the boat deck.

"ETHAN!" she wailed into the vast, empty ocean.

She ran from one end of the boat deck to the other. Nothing. She dove into the ocean and swam in every direction. She desperately searched for Ethan, not caring if the monster or squid or whatever the hell it was, came back and devoured her whole. At this point, she didn't care if the ocean itself swallowed her alive. She only cared about finding the boy she loved. The boy who had just came back to her today.

How could he be taken away again? How was this possible?

She finally spotted him in the distance! She rubbed her eyes to make sure he was real. He was there, swimming just past where the squid had been thrown by the blast.

"Ethan!" she cried out with joy and began to swim toward him.

Their eyes locked for a split second and then he turned, without a word and swam off in the other direction. He soared up and above the water and then plunged beneath the small waves that formed around him.

"Ethan, wait!" she yelled. "Wait!"

He never resurfaced. He was gone.

The group sat there in a bleeding, injured heap, watching her helplessly from the deck. Morgan was sure they had all seen Ethan swim off too. She ignored their calls to come back, swimming away wildly as she sobbed. She swam furiously until her arms and legs were so tired they could barely move.

She returned to the boat in defeat and was too tired to refuse even Larrance's help. He reached in and gently pulled her exhausted body from the water. She stood there, dripping and dazed. Her body was numb with grief.

Larrance gently and cautiously wrapped his arms around her, catching her just in time. Her limp body fell against him and she sobbed into his wounded chest, he lifted her into his arms and silently carried her into the house. He was severely injured and carrying her must have been excruciatingly painful but he didn't show it. He placed her on a loveseat in the living room and the others gathered around them.

She looked at poor Lucas who was sitting next to Tia on the other loveseat. The flesh on his leg was torn and oozing blood through the tattered shirt he had wrapped around it. She walked over and kneeled in front of him.

"It's okay Morgan, I'll be fine. I'm so sorry for about Ethan, I really am sweetie," he said as he stroked her hair lovingly. She smiled at him with as much sincerity as she could force her lips to show, then she gently unwrapped the shirt from his leg and placed her hands on each side of his gaping wound. She pushed her energy into his leg, drawing strength from the ocean that stole her love and her life away from her. She wanted to take from it now. The ocean was no longer in control. She channeled the energy of the small waves that lapped mockingly at the side of the boat and from all the creatures within its watery depths. She watched as Lucas's leg slowly healed in her hands. She felt the energy whirling inside her, guiding her to a higher purpose. Her body instinctively took over and projected just the right amount of healing energy into Lucas. She felt a rush of calm as the power passed through her and she did not want it to stop. She turned to Cleo who had cuts across her arms from the claws that were tucked inside the suckers of each tentacle. She reached up to touch Cleo's arm but Cleo snatched it away.

"Don't even think of it," Cleo snarled, making it very clear that although they fought side-by-side they were still not friends.

The group remained silent as she moved to Larrance. She pulled the remains of his torn shirt from his chest and placed her hands near his heart, where the worst of his injuries seemed to be. He let out a quiet gasp. She called to the ocean again pulling its energy through her and pushing it into Larrance's bare, bloodied torso. She felt her energy streaming into his chest and across his body. She could actually feel the graveness of his injuries—his crushed lung, his broken ribs—and she felt the sheer pain of the million bumps and bruises that racked his body. She pulled more and more energy from herself and pushed it into his broken body.

"Stop now," he whispered into her ear as he leaned into her.

She kept on, still feeling the immense pain inside him.

"Please Morgan, you're weakened, you have to stop now."

She pushed on, healing even the surface cuts on his body, pushing herself harder and harder. The tears and misery of all that had happened was now breaking through her numb surface. She couldn't hold on much longer and was beginning to feel the loss of energy within herself. She pushed more, healing him as best she could until his arms came up to hers. She felt the world spinning around her and her body collapsed against him.

Larrance scooped her up and carried her to her room, sitting down on the bed with her in his lap. She looked at Ethan's empty bed and felt the last bit of energy escape her body.

Everything went black.

Chapter 13

Opening her eyes brought the world back into focus, but it was a world of pain and darkness. Her chest and body ached with despair.

"Ethan..." she sobbed.

"Shhh," Larrance soothed as he brushed his hand along her cheekbone.

She realized that he was still holding her from when she had fainted! She frantically tried to get her bearings. The room was dark. It was night. *This meant that Larrance had been sitting there holding her for hours! What else had he done while she was lying in his arms?*

He shot up from the bed in anger, dropping her body crudely onto the mattress. "Don't flatter yourself," he grumbled.

"I'm sorry, I didn't mean to," she said quietly. "I hate that you do that, you know. You need to stay out of my head."

"Do you think I like hearing your thoughts? I don't know how to stop it or I would, believe me. That mind slam knocked me on my ass," he griped.

"Can you hear everyone's thoughts?" she asked, intentionally changing the subject.

"No, just yours, and not all the time either, only when you're alone and in thought. I think. Can you always hear my thoughts?"

"No, I only seem to hear you when you're *trying* to speak to me. Same as with Ethan," she added.

"Hmm," he mumbled, his anger subsiding. He sat back down on the bed beside her. "How can you feel so intensely for a guy you've only known a week or two? I mean, you were out of your mind out there," he stated softly.

"I don't know. It's like we fused somehow. When we touched there were sparks," she saw his eyes roll, and continued. "No, like real sparks, and I can see his aura, feel it, touch it. I can feel his presence and his absence."

"I get it," he said gruffly, then looked at her. "Lucas swam out as far as the seals, but there was no sign of him. I'm sorry Morgan. I wish there was something I could say. There must be a good reason for him to abandon you... I mean," he paused not knowing how to change what he had just said, and knowing "abandoned" was not what he wanted her to feel, but he had nothing, so he just leaned sideways so his shoulder rested against hers.

She pulled away. "I just need to be alone, Larrance," she said, lying down in her bed carefully so she wouldn't accidentally touch him.

He let out a deep breath, running his hands through his hair in frustration, wanting to stay but having heard the hurt in her words and felt it in her heart he knew how much she wanted him to leave.

"All right," he said as he rose from the bed and headed for the door. "I'll be right outside if you need me."

He stopped mid stride and turned back toward her, his eyes brimming with compassion. "Thank you for what you did out there." He cleared his throat and looked away. "You saved my life Morgan....I owe you my life. A week ago, I think you probably would've personally fed me to that squid, so thank you." He then shut the door.

Morgan pushed her face into her pillow and cried and cried and cried. Night turned to morning and she found herself in a restless sleep. She woke once to see someone had brought her a sandwich and had placed it by her bed. She began to sob again.

Please don't cry anymore, Morgan, you are killing me out here.

Stay out of my head! She mentally yelled back, and then mind slammed the intruder.

"Ouch! Damnit! I can't help it!" she heard him yell from behind the door.

Morgan ignored him. She rose from her bed just long enough to crawl over to Ethan's bed and throw herself down again in despair. She slept there all through another night. She woke in the morning not wanting to leave the bed. She tossed and turned not knowing what to do with herself. She wanted to scream, run, cry, yell, and fight all at the same time. She grabbed her pillow in frustration and threw it against the wall beside her. *Why would he leave? Why would he work so hard to bring me here and then just leave?* She couldn't wrap her head around it; it just didn't make sense. She knew he felt for her, the way she felt for him. He had given a part of his very soul to save her life at the pier for god's sake. So how could he just swim away? Why? The questions ran through her head on a steady loop.

She tried to cry again but her tears had run dry. She couldn't believe he was gone. She held the necklace he had given her, rubbing the gold symbol between her fingers and thought sadly of their short time together.

She replayed the moment over and over in her head. When she called his name he turned and stared at her for a moment. They made eye contact. He had to have seen her, hadn't he? Maybe he didn't see her, maybe she imagined it. And then he deliberately turned away and dove, headfirst, into the water without as much as a goodbye. That was what she saw, but there was so much going on…maybe she only thought she saw him dive into the water and disappear forever.

She rolled over and night slowly came again. Larrance had not bothered her but she knew he was not far away. She could see his feet continually pacing outside her door and since she had poured so much of her energy into healing him she could sense his presence and his worries even easier than usual. She wished he would just leave her alone.

Morgan hated venturing out of her room and did her best to hide away in it most of the week, other than helping Lucas tarp in the hole in the living room wall and dutifully joining the group for meals each day. The others politely kept the conversation light when they saw her. Even Larrance was perfectly distant and cordial. Morgan knew that with their strange connection--- her intense mix of emotions would be banging around in Larrance's head too. Thankfully, he did his best to pretend otherwise. She thought guilty of the powerful feelings of sadness and despair she must have projected onto the poor guy. She wished she could stop but she couldn't help it any more than he could. She didn't know how to break their connection, and she could only keep a wall up between them for short amounts of time.

Her door burst open and she was about to mind slam Larrance for intruding again, when she saw Lucas in the doorway.

"We have a new arrival! Get out here quickly!" he yelled running past her door toward the deck.

When Morgan reached the deck she saw a teenage boy lying unconscious on the floor. He looked like the rest of them with the same golden blonde hair, and Morgan guessed that his eyes would also be ocean blue. This boy was not muscular like the other boys, though; he was softer looking and slightly pudgy.

On the deck beside him was a crate of food. Morgan nodded, realizing that was how they kept the cupboards full. She had forgotten to ask Lucas.

"How long will it take him to wake up?" she asked.

Tia answered this time, her voice warm and friendly. "It takes about an hour usually. You and Ethan were different, though, you took much longer."

"No friggin' kidding," Morgan retorted dryly.

Tia lowered her head and cowered from Morgan. Morgan caught the glare Lucas sent her way. *Great! Now he's going to be mad at me for bruising his little Tia's feelings. Oh well,* she thought. *Put it on your long list of grievances and mail it to someone who cares.*

She heard the muffled laugh behind her. "Don't even start, Larrance," she ordered.

"I wouldn't dare," he quipped, brushing past her and gathering the boy in his arms like he was nothing more than a 10lb bag of potatoes.

Larrance carried the boy to his room and laid him in his tiny bed. He pulled his arm from beneath the boy's head and Cleo gasped.

"You're bleeding!" she yelled, as she ran to his arm and pulled up his sleeve.

"It's not me, Cleo. It must be the boy." He barked, yanking his arm away from her worried hands. His face blushed with embarrassment.

Morgan saw the picture a little clearer. The four of them must have paired off before she got there. Lucas and Tia, Larrance and Cleo. She had thought Cleo was just an uninterested self-involved teen who hated the world, but it turns out that she just hated Morgan for stealing some of her man's attention.

As Morgan knelt beside the boy to examine him, she turned his head and gasped, "Oh God!" She felt queasy at the sight.

The boy's throat had been torn open. He was bleeding heavily and with every beat of his heart more blood shot from the gaping wound.

Larrance grabbed the boy's neck, pressing his hand against the wound. "It's his carotid artery!" he yelled. "There's no way we can save him."

Morgan leaned on the boy's bare chest, her hands on his cheeks. "Come on buddy, please don't die. Come on, sweetie, open your eyes," she urged.

"Morgan, he won't open his eyes. He's too badly hurt," Larrance preached.

She lay against the boy and began to cry the tears she had thought she had run out of days ago. She refused to let this boy die. She couldn't handle any more tragedy. She wanted him to live, willed him to live, — commanded him to live. She could feel energy flow from her fingers and seep into and across the boy's body. The energy crept in a smoky mist over the boy's body as it searched diligently for the wound; it swiftly pooled at the boy's gouged neck. Morgan concentrated on gathering and pushing all of her energy into healing the boy.

"Don't stop Morgan," Larrance whispered. "It's working."

She could hear the others gasping behind her as the wound began closing before their eyes.

Morgan felt herself weakening as her energy surged inside the boy's wound. She was already feeling dizzy and knew she would faint again soon since she didn't have her full strength back yet. She had to pull her hands away, but the boys wound were still fatal.

"Not yet," Larrance whispered. He placed his hand on hers, pushing his fingers between hers.

She felt him. Larrance's energy was feeding back into her. She could see a pale light that joined between them and flowed into the boy. Larrance's aura was glowing a bright white and wrapping itself around her. She squeezed his fingers between hers and he sighed as the light danced around them and through them. Morgan felt her energy pushing past Larrance's bad boy exterior and exposing the kind heart he so desperately tried to hide from the world. She pushed further and was surprised at how easily and naturally their energy combined into one beautiful flowing stream of healing. They moved their hands together over the boy like they were being controlled by a single mind. Morgan drank in the warm feeling of healing energy as it passed through her and into the boy. She allowed Larrance's energy to circulate through her body as it gathered momentum, and she yearned for it to soothe her. She let Larrance's energy in further, and for the first time in a week, she felt her broken heart beginning to mend. She felt the pain and hurt inside her, slowly melt away as their energy's combined in an intimate dance. Seconds later, the reality of what she had just absent-mindedly done hit her like a ton of bricks. She had just allowed Larrance's energy to flow straight into her very heart and soul!

"Okay!" Cleo bellowed behind them. "I think the guy's gonna live now," she snapped angrily and stomped from the room.

Morgan pulled her hands away from the boy and Larrance, and stuffed them behind her back. She kept her eyes lowered, knowing that Larrance's eyes were still fixed on her as he tried to process what had just happened.

Lucas came up beside her and placed his hand on her shoulder. "Holy crap, Morgan! That was unbelievable, look at his neck, there isn't even a mark," he said patting her on the shoulder, and then adding, "I always knew you were special, and not just in the short-bus kind of way." He winked.

Morgan rolled her eyes at Lucas. She leaned over the boy to see his perfectly-healed neck. The only remaining traces of the wound, was the blood on his collar and on Larrance's hands. She held her hands out in front of her; they were covered in the blood from Larrance's hands too. The sight of the blood on her skin sent a surge of queasiness rocking her body. She sat on the chair by the bed before her knees gave way.

Larrance had been watching her closely the whole time and when he saw her reaction to her bloodied hands, he jumped across the bed and grabbed her. He yelled at Lucas to bring a towel and Larrance quickly began cleaning her fingers. She tried pulling her hands away as he kneeled in front of her cleaning them meticulously.

"Its fine, I'm fine. It just caught me off guard, that's all. I'm still just a little weak from before," she murmured, still trying to pull her hands from his vice-like grip.

He paid her no attention as he finished wiping her hands clean, and then he helped her up. His arm beneath her elbow, he guided her across the hall to her room. They approached the doorway just in time to meet Cleo.

She sneered at Morgan. "Wow, Morgan, like to play the role of victim, much?" she snapped, then intentionally rubbed past Larrance and stomped down the hall, slamming her and Tia's bedroom door behind her.

Larrance grinned and Morgan shook her head.

He helped her to her bed, then to Morgan's horror, he walked over to the other bed, Ethan's bed, and lay down.

"What the hell are you doing?" she asked.

He turned to her calmly, as if already half asleep. "What? The new guy is in my bed. This is the only other open bed. You wouldn't want me to move an injured guy would you?" he asked. "And I know you're not uncomfortable sharing your bunk with a guy since 'comatose betrayal dude' was in here for days. So there shouldn't be a problem right?" he goaded.

"Ethan, his name was...*is* Ethan, and he didn't betray anyone. There's a reason he left. I know it, him and I are connected, for life. He wouldn't leave me without a good reason." she said weakly, feeling unsure if her words for her benefit or Larrance's.

"And I think I would rather risk moving the injured guy to that bed than have you in that bed, but I don't have the energy or strength to move him," she grumbled as she rolled over. Her feelings were raw and she felt extremely vulnerable now that she had accidentally given Larrance access to her very core. The last thing she wanted was to complicate things further by sharing a room with him, but she knew that if she snuck out and slept on the loveseat it would make the situation worse by involving the others. She conceded to the situation and closed her eyes, praying that he didn't snore.

Chapter 14

The sun's warm morning rays poked through the window as Morgan rolled over. Larrance was lying fully awake in Ethan's bed, gazing across the room at her. He yawned and gave his arms an over-exaggerated stretch.

"Mornin, sleep well?" he asked.

"Yes, thank you," Morgan answered. She rose from her bed and was about to scurry off to the kitchen.

"Morgan wait!" He blurted and she paused. "We didn't pair off."

"What?" she asked confused.

"Yesterday, you were thinking that Cleo and I 'paired-off' before you got here. I just wanted you to know, we didn't and I wouldn't," he answered.

"Whatever, I mean that's between you and her, it's really none of my business." She wanted to dart out the door before the conversation got even more awkward. She took another step and Larrance sat up.

"Wait, Morgan, can we talk?"

"I don't think that's a good idea Larrance. Besides, you already know everything in my head, what more could we possibly talk about?" she surprised herself with her abrupt and harsh answer.

"I don't know everything you're thinking Morgan. You block me better than you realize. Only the odd thoughts escape you these days. Please sit, just for a minute."

Morgan nodded and hesitantly plunked back down in her bed. She didn't like where this was going.

"Last night, when we healed the new boy, I felt something unexplainable happening between us. Like we briefly joined as one person. It felt like my soul actually connected with yours and I felt your heartbeat within my own chest. Is that crazy? I barely slept last night, I just couldn't quit playing it over in my head.

Something amazing happened when our energy connected, but afterwards you acted like you hadn't even noticed."

Morgan dropped her head and averted her eyes. She didn't know how to answer him. She knew something had happened between them, the way Larrance's energy had so easily flowed into her heart and soul scared her to death. She wasn't sure if she was ready to examine what happened last night when the wounds Ethan had left on her heart had not yet healed over.

Larrance walked across the room and sat on the bed beside her. "Please don't pull away Morgan. Every time I try to connect with you, you pull away from me. Am I really still that terrible in your eyes? Please talk to me. I don't understand what's going on here."

Morgan studied Larrance's big green eyes—they reflected so much vulnerability and need, they forced the wall she had built around herself crumble just enough to let him in.

"You're not crazy Larrance, I felt it too. Our energy is definitely combined now. I don't know if it's permanent or just a temporary thing that happens when Atlantean energy's connect. But the connection between us is unfortunately, there and I don't know how to get rid of it." Larrance gave a hurt little huff, so Morgan explained. "I'm not trying to be cruel Larrance. You just have to understand that I was abandoned by the boy I thought was my soul mate. I was sure I was meant to be with him because of the way we were connected. Now it happened again, with you. So I can't help but wonder if maybe it doesn't mean anything. Maybe it's just a normal thing that happens when two Atlanteans combine their powers and we're just reading too much into things."

"That's crap and you know it Morgan! You connected energy's with Cleo to fight that squid; do you have feelings for her now? The connection that happened between us last night isn't just a passing thing and you know it. I haven't felt anything this real in my entire life. There has been this explosive energy between us from the first night I walked in your room. Do you know how frustrating it is to feel an unworldly connection to someone who won't give you the time of day or even look you in the eye?" He cautiously laid his hand atop hers, which was on her lap.

Morgan instantly pulled away, but Larrance took her hand again and held it firmly. Energy swirled around their fingers joining in a spiral of white cloud that flowed up their arms.

"I can see the energy flowing between us when we touch, you know. This isn't just an Atlantean thing, and I don't care what happened between you and Ethan. This is about us, only us. We are connected through our minds and now our souls. I'm done avoiding you. I know you want me to disappear, Morgan. I'm not going anywhere any more. I don't care if this whole damn ocean is full of giant squids. There is nothing out there that would keep *me* away from you. I promise you that." Larrance let go of her hand and stood. "But, I know this is hard for you so I won't pressure you or push you any further today. I just needed you to know that when the time is right, I'm here." He reached his hand out to pull her off the bed. "Now, how about I make us some porridge and then maybe this afternoon I can teach you how to fish?"

Morgan studied the boy in front of her—her mind spinning in a hundred directions. He was right about so many things, including the undeniable connection between them that she had worked so hard to deny. She had tried to cover it with annoyance, frustration, and even anger but the covers have now fallen away, leaving only their strong undisputable connection remaining. She wasn't sure if her heart could trust another boy ever again, let alone so quickly after Ethan. But she didn't see the harm in having a bowl of porridge, so she took Larrance's hand and let him lead her to the kitchen.

After breakfast, Larrance surprised Morgan with a full snorkel set he had dug out of the closet in his old room. She knew she didn't really need it since she was Atlantean and could breathe and see in the salty water, but Morgan thought it was sweet that he took her fear of the water seriously. She strapped the flippers and mask on and accepted the laughter as her feet slapped by Lucas on her way to the deck. Larrance helped her off the boat and then dove in gracefully behind her. He swam a little, waited for her to catch up, and then he swam a little more. This became the theme since his swimming abilities far surpassed Morgan's.

He led her to a beautiful reef he had discovered a ways out from the boat. Fish of every color swam beneath their feet and through their legs, completely unaffected by their presence. Morgan had never seen anything so beautiful. She was watching a chubby clown fish dart in and out of an anemone when Larrance swam up with a tiny seahorse wrapped around his finger. She stroked the spine of the tiny creature as it blinked innocently and nudged its little nose against her finger. The seahorse unwrapped its tail from Larrance's finger and darted away. Larrance reached for Morgan's hand and led her around the reef, showing her where the puffer fish hung out. He pulled her through a school of small neon blue fish that swam alongside her, mimicking her every move. She kept her head beneath the water wanting to take it all in. It was like a beautiful photograph that was always changing scenes and she didn't want to miss a second of its beauty.

She was glad that Larrance decided not to bring his fishing spear; there was no way she could have harmed a single one of the beautiful finned creatures that swam around her, and she probably would have tackled Larrance to the ocean floor if he began spearing her new little friends. The fish radiated with such a natural beauty, she couldn't fathom eating one of them. She noticed Larrance's body shake a little as he chuckled and she realized he must have just read her thoughts. She smiled at him through the snorkel tube and mask, which made him laugh even harder. She pulled the mask and snorkel from her face and allowed them to fall to the ocean floor. She willed herself to breathe beneath the water and it happened much more naturally this time. Larrance gave her a smile of encouragement.

They swam around until nightfall and Morgan was surprised how much she hated returning to the boat. Her fear of the ocean hadn't even been a factor today, and with Larrance safely by her side, she could have stayed in the water forever.

***

The next morning came without sunshine. Morgan peered out her window at the clouds that lay like a thick and heavy along the skyline. It hardly seemed like a week and a half had passed since the giant squid had attacked them and Ethan had left.

She crept to the closet in their little room trying not to wake Larrance. She peered in, hoping for something, anything, clean that she could change into. She almost cheered when she spotted a pile of clothes abandoned in the far corner. She rifled through the random selection of male and female clothes the Atlantean's must have stashed away for emergencies. She found a black AC/DC t-shirt and size twenty-five Levi jeans! She laughed at the idea that this was the most excited she had been over clothes in her whole life. The jeans were boys but they would work. Then she saw a bikini folded in the corner and thought she had died and gone to heaven.

She looked at Larrance again to make sure he was sleeping.

She slipped out the door and headed for the shower. The water was from a large rain barrel strapped to the side of the boat, warmed slightly by the piping that ran alongside the solar panels on the roof. She found a cupboard with shampoo and scented soaps so she was happy. She washed her hair twice. She found lotion in the cabinet and rubbed it sparingly on her legs not wanting to hog it all and give Cleo a reason to yell at her again.

She slipped into the clean bikini, then wrapped the last unclaimed towel in the cupboard around her fresh body and went to her room to get fully dressed since Cleo was already banging on the bathroom door to get in. When she returned to her room, she was glad to find Larrance still sleeping.

She cast the towel aside and stood in her bikini as she quickly dressed. She zipped up her jeans and turned with a startle when she saw Larrance lying on his side, his elbow propped beneath him holding his head up with his hand.

"Wow, if I could be woken like this every morning, I would live life as a happy man."

She rolled her eyes at his mischievous smile and threw her towel at his head while she grabbed her t-shirt. "Oh come on, you wear less than that to the beach!" he grinned.

"I don't go to the beach!" she retorted.

"Wait!" he said.

She paid no attention to his teasing and began to pull on her shirt.

Larrance flew from the bed with unbelievable speed. He pushed her against the wall, his one arm over her head pinning both of her arms above her.

"Wait," he repeated.

He scooped the necklace from her chest and held it lightly in his palm. "Where did you get this?" he asked breathlessly, mesmerized by the pendant.

Morgan struggled for words, feeling him against her while her arms were vulnerably pinned above her body sent a shiver down her spine leaving her unable to answer his simple question. She was so painfully aware of her bare skin against his that it almost hurt.

"How did you move so fast?" she asked in no more than a whisper. She felt the energy building inside her and around her. She fought it back as hard as she could knowing that Larrance could see it when it left her body and it would give her feeling away completely.

His concentration on the necklace broke as he felt the energy she was fighting back. He raised his head to look into her eyes, holding his face inches from hers. His expression changed as he became fully aware of closely they were standing. The primal hunger that rose from his deep emerald gaze made Morgan's knees quiver.

Morgan could feel his breath hot against her lips. His breathing grew heavy as he leaned into her fully and whispered into her ear.

"We're meant to be together, our connection runs too deep to deny it. I know you feel it Morgan. Just forget everything and everyone for one moment and concentrate on right now, on right here, on you, on me. Nothing else matters. Just close your eyes and listen to your heart, your instincts and the energy I see you so desperately trying to hold back."

He brushed his cheek softly against hers and she closed her eyes as he had commanded. She felt his warm, soft lips gently graze her cheek while he continued to hold her firmly against the wall. His one hand was entwined with the both of hers overhead. She didn't struggle to get free, although she knew she should. What was she doing? She belonged to Ethan, not Larrance, but her body responded in ways she never imagined possible and she knew Larrance was right. They were connected on levels she hadn't even felt with Ethan. Larrance's touch sent a fire through her body that made her hairs stand on end. She wanted to embrace Larrance, to wrap her arms tight around him and pull him even closer, but he did not release her.

"No," he whispered, toying with her by running his lips to her earlobe and sucking it tenderly. She could not hold back any more, and the energy flew from her and met his mid-air. The light between them swirled and swayed around them seeping into each other's skin.

"My God," he whispered at the overwhelming pleasure of the sensation.

"I don't know why I'm faster and stronger than everyone else. I don't know why I'm dark haired and have different eyes or why I hear your thoughts and feel your feelings. I'm different, I agree, but I'm no monster," he groaned into her ear.

Finally, he kissed her lips. They kissed with an urgency and desperation neither of them could explain. There was a melding of passion, energy and need, which fused them together. Morgan felt a sensation like pure electricity swirling throughout her body as his tongue entered her mouth. She gave in to their connection and it was deeper and more electric than she could have ever of imagined. She let go of the remaining pieces of the mental wall she held between them and allowed their energies to form entirely as one. Everything between them felt right and the overwhelming wave of emotions she suddenly felt for this boy took her breath away. Her knees weakened as his kiss radiated across her body and she was now thankful he braced her up. His free arm moved up the bare skin of her stomach leaving goose bumps in its trail. She felt a sharp tearing within her chest, but she kissed him deeper. Larrance abruptly stopped kissing her and pulled away. He was staring at her, but his swirling passionate blue-green eyes seemed were now blank. She followed his stare to her chest. There was a large laceration across her skin and blood was beginning to ooze from it. She looked at Larrance in confusion. Then she saw his forearms. There were razor sharp onyx fins protruding from them.

"Oh my god! You're a Trit...."

"Don't! Please, don't say it, I didn't know," he stopped her. He stumbled backwards, sick with the realization of what he did and what he was.

The necklace around her neck sent warmth into her body as it glowed a pale blue light, healing her wounds in front of them.

"It's okay. It's just a little scratch. See? I barely felt it, Larrance. Please don't leave, let me help you." She reached out for him, wanting to soothe his fears. She was fine and she wasn't afraid of him. He shook his head and backed away and then darted out the door.

"Larrance!" she yelled.

But he did not stop.

Chapter 15

"Hey, looking good, Hollywood!" Lucas greeted her in the kitchen.

"Where's Larrance?" she asked impatiently.

"Wow, no good morning Lucas? It's like that is it?" he joked, then realized it wasn't the time.

"He went for a swim. He'll be back in a bit. I'm so glad to see you're doing better; I've been worried about you. Have a granola bar and some coffee, you've barely eaten all week."

He paused, then asked the question Morgan knew was coming next. "Is there something going on with you two? You and Larrance I mean? Cause man, the other night when you were healing the new guy it was getting a little intense in there."

She stood and chomped on her granola bar as Lucas happily carried on his one-way conversation.

"I'm not asking because I'm jealous or anything. Cleo on the other hand, oohh...weee, she don't like you. But I..." he paused to swallow his coffee as he looked around for listening ears. "I think I really like Tia," he confessed as he let out a deep breath. Morgan could see the relief on Lucas's face of having finally said the words aloud.

She reached out and touched his hand, then pulled him into a loving hug. "That's great, Lucas, I'm happy for you. Have you ever..." She looked up to see Tia standing at the doorway, her eyes glued on the two of them still in an embrace. She turned and walked out.

Lucas bolted after her. "Tia, wait!" he hollered as he rushed after her.

Morgan shook her head as she headed for the back deck. It was like she just had this natural ability for finding new ways to make people hate her. No matter what she did, she always seemed to find a way to bring out the worst in people.

She sat on the back deck staring out at the cloudy sky. A storm was definitely coming. The clouds rumbled and clustered in giant mounds of grey as they swirled angrily overhead. The winds and the waves were growing stronger and more intense too.

"Larrance!" she yelled out across the water. No answer.

At least not from Larrance she realized, as the seals moved toward the boat. She bent down to the one whose head rested against the boat.

"Hey, little guy, can you bring me Larrance?" she said patting it on the head, wishing it were that easy. She watched as they swam away. She paced the deck calling Larrance again and again. She could only imagine how horrifying it must be for him to suddenly take on the characteristics of the monster she now wished she hadn't accused him of being. Then she saw him. The seals were gathered around and nudging and pushing him toward the boat.

"Well, what do you know?" she said, wondering if they were acting on her orders.

Larrance approached the boat and she reached out to help him up since he was being beaten by the growing waves.

"Here, let me help you," she yelled over the wind.

He turned from her hand and grabbed the seal behind him. She watched him throw his head back revealing his second row of sharply serrated teeth, then rip viciously at the seal's neck. The seal yelped in pain. The other seals scattered and swam off in fear when they heard the young pup's screams. Morgan froze with fear as she watched Larrance lash out against the innocent seal. Everything seemed to happen in slow motion as she watched him bite the pup's neck in horror. Why was he doing this? The anger and pain that radiated from his eyes made her want to cry for him, not cower away from him like she knew he expected her to do. She bravely took a small step forward.

Larrance ignored her outstretched hand and pulled himself on board. He looked at her with an intensity that burned her eyes (and her heart) and then gave an evil leer as he wiped the seal's blood from his mouth.

"Now, why would a big bad monster like me need help from a pathetic, needy little girl like you? You were right about me all along; now stay the hell away from me, before you get hurt."

She just stared at him as his teeth and fins retracted and his eyes returned to their normal warm green color. Morgan wanted to shake the madness out of him as he pushed past her. Sure, he may have the outer appearance of a Triton with his finned forearms, large dilated black pupils and second row of jagged teeth, but he wasn't an ounce of Triton on the inside, and she knew that for a fact. She had seen into his heart and soul, and although he exuded a rough and tough exterior most times, he was genuinely good inside. His energy imprint was nothing like the Tritons she had encountered— it was remarkably similar to another Atlantean's energy whom she knew well...Ethan.

"Please, Larrance, I want to help you. I don't understand this; ten minutes ago you were kissing me and now you want me to get lost? This Triton stuff doesn't change anything. I know who you are on the inside Larrance and you're good. Not a monster. I'm not scared of you."

He leaned toward her and she welcomed him, thinking he had snapped out of his craziness.

He whispered, "Well, you should be scared, because I am monster. Look at me. Fins and fangs don't lie. You knew what I was from the start. I was a fool to think I was anything more. I hurt you and it will never happen again, in fact, 'we' will never happen again."

He walked into the houseboat and Morgan sunk against the back wall. She saw the injured seal pop its head up alongside the deck. She reached out, and it swam to her. She ran her hand down along the wound and was relieved to see that it was not deep like her Triton inflicted neck wounds had been. It was only a surface wound. She called on her energy and healed it.

"Go find shelter," she whispered to the frightened animal and it swam off.

When Morgan walked back into the house she found everyone gathered in the living room. Larrance was sitting on the loveseat with Cleo. She watched him smile as she walked in the room. She ignored him and plunked down in the vacant armchair. Undeterred, Larrance began kissing Cleo in front of her. She felt the sadness growing in her heart, and then she realized that Larrance was back in her head! He was hurting her because it would hurt him.

No more! she sent out to him. He did not respond.

She was about to slam him out of her mind when she thought of a better idea. While Larrance made out with Cleo, she sat back and thought of Ethan. She really pushed the images with her mind hoping to send Larrance more than just thoughts. She pictured Ethan and thought of the energy that flowed when their fingers intertwined. She watched Larrance pause, and then he pushed himself harder against Cleo. Morgan knew by the anguished look on his face that he was definitely receiving the visual images she sent him. Morgan continued. She thought of how much she missed Ethan and then she thought of the kiss. The earth-shattering kiss she and Ethan had shared. She watched as Larrance pulled away from Cleo this time, and his face was covered in hurt and disgust.

But Morgan kept on, as the memory of Ethan was just too warm and consoling. She thought of laying against him on the rock at the beach and rubbing her hand across his chest. She remembered holding his necklace and how he looked when he leaned down to kiss her again.

Larrance jumped from the couch and came at her in a fury as the boat crashed back and forth in the storm that was growing outside.

"He gave you that necklace?" he questioned.

"Why don't you just leave me alone? Go back and make out with your girlfriend," Morgan answered coldly.

He ignored her stab and continued. "I thought it was yours. Do you know what it means?" he asked, pulling a matching necklace from his pocket and holding it toward her.

"When I was found as a baby, this was with me," he gestured to the necklace. "I have always known that I would give it to the one I chose to spend my life with. That it would mean they belonged to me and I belonged to them. I thought that since you had one too, it meant that we were destined to be together. Now I find out that it's just some token to show you belong to another man! That ridiculous idiot who swam off and abandoned you!"

Morgan sat frozen.

"Take it off!" he spat.

She looked him straight in the eyes and coldly replied, "Never."

He clenched a fist around his necklace and threw it as hard as he could against the wall. It fell to the corner as he stomped out of the living room.

Morgan swallowed the lump in her throat, blinking back tears. Everyone's eyes were cast down and she could tell that they were all uncomfortable, having born witness to such a private conversation.

"Thanks for dragging me into your issues!" Cleo spat as she glared daggers at Morgan from across the room. Morgan rested her head against her arms and pretended not to hear the snide comment.

When Cleo realized Morgan had nothing to stay she stood with her arms crossed. "I'm going to go get the new kid. The storm is getting worse and we need to come up with a plan." She then huffed off down the hall.

The boat lifted and crashed from the waves again and again. The furniture was bolted so it did not move, but debris and water bottles rolled back and forth as water splashed in through the hole the squid had created. Plastic dishes flew from the cupboard as the kitchen chairs rammed back and forth.

"Cleo's right, it's getting worse," Lucas said to the group. "I don't think this old boat will survive this. We're probably going to have to jump ship," he said. He quickly grabbed onto the yellow love seat as the boat swung to the left so hard his feet were practically dangling in midair. Everyone was holding onto their chairs for dear life, riding the waves like a roller coaster.

"There are life jackets in the cupboard!" Cleo said when she returned with the new boy. She crossed the room and headed to the cupboard behind Morgan. She pulled out the dated big red life preservers and handed one to each of them.

"We have to tie ourselves together," Tia added, as they fought the crashing boat and hooked themselves to one another.

"Come on, Morgan," Tia urged, as she held her end of the rope out for Morgan to tie onto.

Morgan shook her head. "I have to get Larrance," she said as she stumbled to the corner and grabbed his discarded necklace.

She put it safely around her neck, tucking it inside her life jacket and grabbed another life jacket before she headed for Larrance's room.

She threw the bedroom door open and saw him sitting on the bed with his head in his hands. Defeated.

She stood above him holding out the life jacket. "Put this on, we have to get off the ship," she yelled over the crashing waves and cracking lumber of the old boat.

He did not budge or even look up to acknowledge her existence.

She stumbled forward as another large wave sent the boat sideways and Larrance responded in a flash, grabbing her hips to keep her from careening into the bedpost.

She placed a hand under his chin and raised his head so their eyes met. She winced at the pain and sorrow she saw there. She spoke quietly but with conviction. "You don't go, I don't go. I will not leave this ship without you."

Lucas stumbled into the doorway as he fought the sway of the boat. "We have to get off this ship now, she's going down!" he yelled as a surge of water slopped down the hallway and spilled into the room.

"Go! Get everyone off; we'll be right behind you," Morgan assured him.

He nodded. "Well, make it quick! You remember how the Titanic ended, don't you?" he said, as he hastily left them.

She chuckled. Even under the direst of circumstances Lucas had some dumb ass thing to say. She pushed the jacket toward Larrance again and he reluctantly put it on. She looked at the frazzled boy in front of her. How quickly her feelings had changed for him. Their energy flowed so easily together it was as if they were truly made for one another. Every time their eyes met she felt the traces of his energy that still whirled about inside her heart. She wished there was some way to let him see the same caring, protective, unquestionably good person that she saw sitting before her. They were so connected now, and seeing him hurting so deeply felt like knives piercing her own heart. She needed him to snap out of it, for both of their sakes.

Larrance nodded his head and Morgan guessed he must have been listening to her thoughts again. He rose from the bed stepping into the water that now flooded the floor and reached out to her. They waded hand-in-hand to the back of the boat.

The others were already off the ship and bobbing on the water a few feet away. "Wait." Morgan paused and tied their life jackets together then grabbed a circle buoy from the wall.

Larrance wrapped his large arms around her and they jumped, arm-in-arm, into the storm.

They swam toward the others as the water slammed down on them wave after wave. Morgan heard a large snap. Part of the housing had come loose and water was consuming the boat from the stern, where the most damage had occurred. As they fought to keep afloat on the increasing waves, Morgan heard the middle section of the boat give way, and the ocean made short work of the rest. Within seconds all traces of the ship were a nothing but a memory. There was no going back and no one knew which way was forward. Morgan felt doomed.

It's okay, we'll be okay, we just have to keep swimming, Larrance urged.

When they finally reached the others, they looked tortured and distressed as they fought the waves that hammered against them.

Morgan could do nothing but watch as poor petite Tia was pummeled by nature's wrath. Wave after wave mercilessly crashed down on her small back.

"Enough!" Tia yelled and a flash shot out. The next wave came crashing over but this time it fell around them.

A dome of energy burst from Tia's body and surrounded the group, protecting them from the wretched beatings they were taking. It was like going from night to day as the environment in the bubble turned instantly calm and serene.

"Well, well, looks like big things do come in small packages," Lucas said, as he gently rubbed Tia's back.

Tia smiled as she lay exhausted against her buoy. The storm had passed by nightfall. Tia released the protective dome and they floated quietly into the abyss. It was dark and the water felt much colder than usual. Morgan was scared. They could be miles from any form of land.

"I think we need to swim this way," Larrance said pointing to the single bright star in the sky. "We need to stay in one direction and hopefully we'll find land. We know that's the North Star so we'll follow it. We know the sun rises in the east and sets in the west, so we have that too."

"Thank God somebody paid attention in Boy Scouts," Lucas teased.

Larrance grabbed the rope that tied the group together and began to swim. He pulled the entire group faster than they could swim on their own.

As they crossed the water, the new boy extended his shivering hand toward Morgan. "My name's Donovan. I thought I should formally introduce myself, and thank you since you saved my life and all."

Morgan looked at his angelic face and boyish grin. He looked younger than the rest of them. She reached her hand out to shake his. "It wasn't just me who saved you, Larrance helped," she said humbly.

"But it was *you*, I felt inside me," he stumbled on his words as his cheeks turned red. "In my head, I mean. It was your soothing voice and your touch I felt on my skin."

Morgan heard a primal growl come from Larrance. She looked at Donovan and saw he heard it too.

"Anyway, thank you," he said and released her hand quickly.

Larrance slowed as exhaustion consumed him and dawn rapidly approached.

Lucas patted him on the back. "You did good, man. Real good."

Morgan watched as Larrance let out a sigh of disappointment. She knew he had hoped to find land before he tired. When she looked at him more closely she became frightened at how weakened he had become. He had used every last inch of his energy to pull them.

Morgan swam to him and rubbed his arm gently. "Let's rest, the sun is up and I'm not as cold, but I'm so tired. Could we please rest a bit, Larrance?" she asked.

She really wasn't tired at all, but she knew Larrance would not rest if she just told him he had to. He nodded and they laid their arms and heads on the floating buoys.

Larrance fell asleep quickly. Morgan placed her hand on his forearm and she could feel how weak his body really was. She knew she could at least help him. She leaned in closer to him, and as he slept she called energy to her fingertips. She felt it pass through her fingers and into him. It ran down to his feet and through his chest, down his arms and into his head. She felt him sigh with pleasure and she felt like a bit of an intruder, but Morgan was satisfied—she had healed him well, although now she realized perhaps that she healed him a little too well. She felt the dizzying weakness that came every time she used too much energy in the last few weeks. She tried to fight the rising weakness but there was no use —she passed out against the buoy.

Chapter 16

Morgan felt someone on top of her blowing into her mouth. She felt the grit of sand beneath her tenderized flesh.

"Come on Morgan, don't leave me," Larrance hollered as he drummed painfully against her chest.

She opened her eyes for the tattered boy as he leaned down to give CPR. "Wow, if I could be woken like this every morning, I would be a happy woman," she mocked. His lips hovered inches from her face.

His eyes flashed wide with surprise. "Oh God! I thought you'd drowned! I thought I lost you!" he pulled her body into his arms, crushing her against him. He kissed her neck and she could feel his hot tears against her face. "I'm so sorry, Morgan," he whispered. "I'm sorry for hurting you. I'm done pushing you away."

He raised his head to stare into her eyes. "I love you Morgan. I want to be with you in every possible way. Just tell me what I can do to make amends. Please tell me it's not too late," he whispered, cupping her face in his hands.

Morgan felt tears fall from her eyes. She searched for words to tell him how she felt, and then she found them. "I love you too," she whispered back.

He kissed her with such urgency and passion that afterwards she gasped for air.

"The others?" she worried.

"They're all fine. They're down at the beach on the other side of those rocks. We have...privacy," he said as he ran his hands slowly up her stomach.

She felt the waves lapping at her feet as his face buried into hers. He kissed her hard, crushing his lips desperately against hers as he flicked his tongue longingly into her mouth. She moaned, sending waves of excitement through him.

She felt his hands moving over her body. They were soft and warm and she leaned into them and this time he moaned. Then he froze.

"Get off her, you dirty Triton!!" A low angry voice came from above them.

Morgan saw a long steel blade pressed against Larrance's back. She followed the sword up to see Ethan on the other end of it. Ethan was alive?! Her mind reeled with a whirlwind of emotions as she stared at the face of the boy she thought had abandoned her close to two weeks ago.

Larrance was on his elbows hovering above her. She watched his eyes start to turn black and knew what was going to come next.

She put her hand to his face. "Larrance, don't!" she whispered.

"Ethan, no!" she yelled, as the sword pressed hard enough into Larrance's back to draw blood.

Larrance's forearms bore fins, and his second set of teeth shot from the roof of his mouth. With a quick twist of his body, Larrance blocked the sword with his fin sending it flying from Ethan's hands.

Larrance was on his feet in a heartbeat and lunging toward Ethan with his teeth bared.

"Stop!" Morgan screamed, but neither of them paid any attention.

Ethan grabbed Larrance by the throat and Larrance sliced him across his chest with his fin.

"Stop! Please!" Morgan sobbed.

Ethan had his other hand around Larrance's head and Morgan knew he was going to snap his neck like the Triton at the pier.

"Enough!" she yelled, as she threw herself between them with her hands out, shoving them apart. An involuntary jolt flew from her palms knocking both boys to the ground in opposite directions.

"He was on top of you, hurting you!" Ethan screamed.

"I was on top of her, golden boy, but believe me I was not hurting her." Larrance gloated with a deadly grin. "Besides, hurting her is your specialty," he added.

Morgan rolled her eyes at his unnecessary revelation.

"He's a monster, Morgan! Look at him, he's a filthy Triton monster!" Ethan yelled trying to make sense of her actions.

"He's not a monster, Ethan. He's not like them. He's one of us. I know he is. I feel it," she argued.

"He has you hypnotized; they do that," Ethan spat.

"No, it's different. I remember what it was like under the bridge when I was attacked. They tried to hypnotize me; they tried to convince me they were beautiful and perfect so I would fall under their spell. Which I didn't, by the way, and believe me I know that Larrance is far from perfect," she argued, wishing she hadn't added the last part.

"Thanks," Larrance grumbled.

She gave him a look of apology and turned back to Ethan. "You have to trust me, Ethan, I can touch his soul and feel his aura. He is good, like you," she added.

Ethan looked at her; his eyes were covered in layers of hurt and betrayal. "You felt his soul? His aura? You have shared your whole soul with him?" he shook his head, trying to let the information sink in.

Morgan felt guilt and regret for revealing what she had. It was not like she'd slept with Larrance, but by the look on Ethan's face this was worse.

She sat down on the sand beside Ethan. Larrance watched vigilantly from his spot.

"You left me, Ethan. Without a word, you swam off leaving me alone in the middle of the ocean. I honestly didn't think you were coming back. I thought you'd left me for real and for good. How was I to know you would return? You left my heart shattered and hurting so badly that I could barely pick up the pieces. Larrance was there and he helped me heal. If not for him, I would probably still be balled up in a corner mourning the boy who didn't care enough to even say goodbye! How was I to know anything other than that you left me without a second glance? You left me with nothing but your memory and your necklace. Do you know how hard that was for me?" she fumed.

She felt the tears well up in her eyes. Her stomach was in knots. Ethan just stared at her with a perplexed look on his face, as if he didn't understand the hurt she was describing, or how much his abandonment had ripped her heart in two. "Larrance was there for me, Ethan. He looked after me; he looked after all of us. You didn't," she stated.

"I'm sure he was there," Ethan sneered. Then his face drooped, his eyes glistening with tears. "Don't you think that if I could have come back for you I would have? Do you think so little of me? I didn't leave *you*; I just had no time to return to the boat. I had to follow the Giant Squid you injured. It led me back to its sender. It led me back to them," he said as he pointed to Larrance. "The Triton sent it. After the attack on the houseboat, they hit Atlantis itself. I had to go. I had no choice and I never wanted to leave you Morgan, but I had to protect Atlantis. I should have never left Atlantis—I think they knew I was gone and that's why they attacked. The Council was taken; the only one remaining is the King. We managed to fight them off, but I know they will return now that we are so badly weakened." He paused in sorrow then pulled her to him, wrapping her in his arms.

Morgan looked into Ethan's loving, crystal blue eyes as he spoke. She wanted to be angry at him for leaving her, but her heart did flop-flops against every word that came from his mouth. Her mind couldn't focus on anything but the fact that he was standing in front of her and he was truly alive! She wanted to wrap her arms around him and shower him with kisses, feeling every inch of him to make sure she wasn't dreaming. But she held back. She had told Larrance that she loved him mere minutes ago, and he was watching her every move like a wounded animal. She knew throwing herself against the guy who had just tried to kill him would definitely send Larrance over the edge.

"Never doubt that I love you, Morgan, I would do anything for you. You are my soul. That is why I left you my amulet. It is the sign of my father, my King, and a sign of my devotion and bonding to you. I know that nothing happened between you and that thing," he said, gesturing to Larrance, as if he were just a stray mutt sitting there on the sand. "I know because if you wear my pendant we are connected completely by a bond that can't be broken by anyone." He looked at her. "Where is it?" he asked, eyeing her curiously.

"I've never taken it off Ethan," she said truthfully. She pulled the chain up from beneath her wet t-shirt. The necklace fell forward tangled together with Larrance's. She had forgotten that she put Larrance's on for safe keeping before they had jumped ship.

Larrance and Ethan gasped in unison.

"Where did that come from?" Ethan asked, as he cupped the pendant in his hand. Morgan breathed in his sandalwood smell and let her fingers linger against his briefly as he took the chain from her. She could see his aura flare slightly as he stood before her. She felt her own aura of energy begin to stir, instinctively wanting to pull Ethan's familiar buzz of energy toward her, but she managed to fight against it and regain control. She took a deep breath and another look at Larrance who hadn't seemed to notice.

"It's your pendant and Larrance's," she whispered guiltily. She looked down at the two scribed teardrop necklaces and couldn't believe her eyes. They had changed. They had fused together, their pointy ends touching to form what looked like a figure eight.

"They were two separate, almost identical pendants when I put them on. Now they have formed what looks like an affinity symbol. How is this possible?" she asked, as she studied the merged pendants. She wasn't sure what was so bad about wearing a couple of necklaces but she had a feeling that she screwed up big time.

"My pendant was cast when I was born to mark the birth of the prince. It has great power and can only be worn by the one who shares my soul, my partner in life, my soul mate. If anyone else tried to wear it they would be poisoned by it and perish within days," Ethan said.

"Larrance's looked exactly like yours, but they have both changed," she said, now cupping Ethan's hand and examining the two pendants she wore.

"I know," he said.

"What does that mean?" she asked as Larrance came closer to them.

Ethan just shook his head afraid to answer.

"If this necklace can only be worn by your soul mate, how can I wear two of them?"

He studied her, his eyebrows low with concern. "I don't know, I don't understand any of this," he said more to himself. "This is all wrong. You can only intertwine your soul with one man. Your soul mate."

Without another word, Ethan let go of her hand and walked down the beach to join the group.

Morgan knew she had reveled and connected with the souls and light and energy of both Larrance and Ethan. She didn't try to do it, it had just happened.

Can one person have two soul mates? she thought to herself.

"NO," Larrance answered, as he laced his fingers into hers and led her down the beach to join the group.

Chapter 17

As Morgan and Larrance approached the beach, Morgan tried nonchalantly to pull her hand away but Larrance held it firmly. She cringed at the hurt she saw in Ethan's eyes as they approached. Ethan surprised her by grabbing her free hand.

"Wow, now that looks like an awkward situation," Lucas said, eyeing the three of them as he shook his head. Morgan looked away embarrassed.

She watched Lucas gather the courage and seize the moment as he wrapped his fingers around Tia's. Tia looked down and smiled, then looked at Lucas as he gave a shrug and flashed a loving grin.

"Wow!" Came the voice of the pudgy-faced new kid who nobody knew very well yet. "I guess if we're all holding hands that just leaves you and me," Donovan said in a desperate attempt for seduction as he stared up at Cleo.

"You come near me and I will punch you in the throat," Cleo sneered.

Donovan took a step backward taking her warning with as much seriousness as she delivered it. "Wow, vicious. I like it," he mumbled once he was sure he was safely out of throat-punching range. Cleo stomped over to the other side of the group's informal circle.

Morgan released both of the boy's hands and sat on the beach wood that someone had already pulled and arranged into a circular sitting area. Larrance, Ethan, and the rest of the group followed her lead.

As they gathered, Morgan looked at the faces of the six kids in front of her. She couldn't believe that this mismatch of teens was about to rule an entire underwater world!

"So, what's next? What do we do now?" she asked Ethan.

"We are on the Island of Garant, which is the safest way into Atlantis. It will be a day or two hike to the volcano, then a half day's walk inside of the volcano."

"You want us to walk inside a volcano? Are you short on brain cells? Isn't that how all you guys died in the first place?" Lucas asked in disbelief.

Ethan rolled his eyes, annoyed by Lucas's tendency to talk before thinking. "No, I don't you to walk into a volcano. You have to jump. It's safe, Atlanteans have been using this passage for the past 10,000 years, but if you're scared I guess you could let the women go first," Ethan shot back with a low blow. Lucas looked down, lost for words.

"Where is the volcano?" Donovan asked, joining the conversation.

"It's there," Ethan answered, pointing to the rocky mass behind them.

"That's a freakin' mountain, dude! You want us to climb a freakin' mountain in a day?" Donovan whined.

"No way in hell!" Lucas choked.

"I said a day or two; besides, it's not as high as it looks."

"Are you kidding me? I think I see snow at the top of that sucker. It's definitely as high as it looks," Donovan argued.

"Well, regardless, it's the only way in, so we better get started," Ethan snapped as he rose to his feet having had enough of the complaining.

Morgan rose too and the rest of the group followed. They started off down a small sandy trail that led them into the lush jungle ahead.

***

They walked for several hours down a well-worn path. The base of the volcano was close, and after they cut through yet another overgrown wall of heavy bush they stumbled into a picturesque clearing. There was a large inviting waterfall and pond with massive rocks set purposefully around it. There were beautiful plate-sized purple and red flowers that Morgan had never seen before, growing around the tree line. The whole area was so green and lush it created a dreamlike setting.

"Ooohhh yeah! That's what I'm talkin bout!" Lucas yelled as he excitedly began to strip his clothes off until he was down to his boxers. He ran and did a cannonball through the air before he splashed into the pond in front them.

"Wow, its warm! Come on, you guys!" he yelled.

"You don't have to ask me twice!" Donovan cheered as he pulled off his last sock and did a hopping run toward the water.

The girls were lucky enough to be wearing bikinis under their clothes. The morning they jumped ship, they had all gone for a swim. They followed the boys' lead, and soon everyone was splashing in the warm pond. Everyone — except Ethan, who sat on the shore impatiently.

The rest of the group splashed and played, letting the warm spring water heal and energize them. Morgan laughed as Donovan lifted her on his shoulders and they headed toward Tia who sat comfortably on top of Lucas's broad shoulders.

"Come on, let's play chicken!" Donovan exclaimed. "You're it!" he yelled to Lucas, as he darted away from him and Tia.

"Come on, Larrance!" Donovan yelled.

Larrance shrugged and reached an inviting hand out to Cleo. Cleo smiled slyly as she crawled on top of his shoulders. They rushed toward Morgan and Donovan. Cleo gave them a harder shove than necessary and knocked the pair underwater.

Morgan surfaced and Donovan was about to lift her back onto his shoulders. She looked at Cleo giggling on top of Larrance's shoulders as her big chest bounced around, slapping the top of his head.

"No, Donovan. I don't want to play anymore. I'm going to go sit on the shore with Ethan," she said as she wiped the wet hair from her forehead trying to act somewhat dignified as she stomped off toward the shore.

"Aww, no fair you guys, I don't have a partner!" Donovan whined to the group.

Larrance dipped down in the water pulling Cleo off his shoulders. "Here, Donovan. Cleo can be your partner."

Donovan's face lit up, but Cleo swam off annoyed. "Over my dead body," she grumbled.

Morgan did not look back as she crawled up the bank toward Ethan. She sat next to him and he rubbed her back lovingly as she snuggled in.

"I missed you," he whispered.

She thought his eyes looked so sad, so lost. "I'm sorry," she sighed.

"For what?" he asked, confused.

"For everything. For thinking you would abandon me, for not believing in you, for your losses in Atlantis and for... " she paused not knowing how to say it, "Larrance."

"I know you never meant for any of this to happen and now you're in an impossible situation. It's okay; when we get to Atlantis we'll sort it out." He gently kissed her head. "You're cold," he said, and pulled her closer as he began rubbing her arms for warmth but his words of understanding warmed more than he could possibly know.

"I'll make us a fire. Why don't you wash off in the waterfall, then throw your clothes back on," he said as he jumped up and began gathering sticks.

Morgan didn't want a fire; she just wanted to snuggle in Ethan's arms and have him reassure her that he was really there—alive and beside her. A lot had changed between them, and although she knew now that he had to leave, she couldn't help feeling a myriad of emotions over his return. Happiness—that he was alive and beside her, anger—that he left her, and guilt—for finding someone new so quickly. She was so confused, she loved Ethan, that hadn't changed, but she never expected to see him again, so she allowed Larrance into her heart. Now they were all caught in this complicated love triangle she wasn't sure how to break.

She didn't argue with his suggestion to get cleaned up. She rose and headed for the waterfall. She stood beneath the warm pouring water as it pounded on her skin. She felt it wash away her tensions, revitalizing her. She lifted her head, allowing the water to push her hair away from her face.

Suddenly she felt something grab her waist, tugging her further into the waterfall. She fought against it but couldn't see her attacker with the water coming down hard against her face. She thrashed her arms, and then something grabbed her hands as it pulled her all the way through the waterfall to a cavern on the other side.

"Stop, Morgan! Stop! It's me!" Came the voice of her attacker.

Then she dropped her hands as she embarrassedly looked up into Larrance's face. "What are you doing? You scared me half to death!" she said in a fluster. She leaned against the rocky cavern wall. The waterfall provided a wall to the outside world and Morgan quickly realized what Larrance was doing. They had complete privacy.

"I found this place and thought we could use a little alone time," he said in a voice heavy with desire. His body sloped toward her as he began to gently kiss the small of her neck.

"Don't you have the wrong girl? Where's Cleo? Did she just leave the cavern?" She was feeling guilty as each wretched word seeped from her lips. How could she be jealous when she was just cuddling with Ethan?

"Stop, Morgan, please, she's nothing to me, you know that," he muttered, "It's you and only you." He pushed himself against her slipping his arm behind her back so she wouldn't be scraped by the jagged rock wall. She stopped fighting him and stared into his eyes. She saw the hurt and anger that swirled around their surface and the deep longing and desire that burned deep inside him. She wrapped her arms around his neck and pulled him to her. She kissed him with love, need and desire. She couldn't stop, didn't want to stop. She held him tightly against her and felt the fins emerge from his forearms and his teeth transform beneath her tongue. She brushed their sharp edges with her tongue, teasing him as he tried to pull away.

Not this time, you don't get to leave this time, she whispered to his mind.

The atmosphere between them was pure energy. She could feel it flowing between them and joining together as he held her in his arms. He pulled away from her lips to kiss her neck and across her shoulders. He lowered her to the floor of the cave, careful not to graze her skin with his fins. She looked into his dark dilated eyes and at his silvery-black finned arms and thought how beautiful he was. She felt the heat between them burning into her soul. She cupped his cheek with her hand and as she laid back, their eyes locked in a gaze of mutual passion and love. He knelt in to kiss her again.

"Morgan, are you back here? Oh…I ….um!" a voice fumbled behind them.

Morgan shot up to a sitting position, knocking Larrance out of the way. Ethan stood in front of them with blank eyes, looking as if he were about to be sick.

"I will...um..." he paused as he studied the girl he loved flushed and panting on the ground in front of him. Morgan swore she could actually see his heart breaking as he stood there, sorting out the words. "I was just worried because you were gone so long, but it looks like Larrance has it covered." He gave a small awkward bow.

"Ethan wait don't go! I…" Morgan paused not knowing what explanation would be sufficient.

"I'm leaving before I kill him, Morgan. You thought I was dead or that I left you and you fell in love with someone else. It was a little fast, but Atlantean energy can be overpowering and intensify feelings, so I get it. And I thought we could work through it. But you are back here making out with that freaking Triton, Morgan! Really? All I could think of when I was gone was getting back to you. But if he is really what you want then carry on! I won't stop you." He turned his steel glare to Larrance and filtered his anger through clenched teeth. "Your days are numbered, Triton. When we return to Atlantis and sort out what the hell you are even doing here, this little love triangle is gonna end…badly." With his fists gripped tightly at his sides, Ethan spun on his heels and darted back out through the waterfall.

"Ethan, wait!" Morgan yelled, as she ran after him leaving Larrance alone in the cave.

She followed him past the group and felt a twinge of guilt as she passed the fire he had built especially for her. He marched on into the dark jungle.

"Ethan, wait! Please!" she begged as she stumbled over branches. The large leaves of the jungle trees swatted at her face as she blindly trampled on through the darkness. She stopped to find her bearings and tried to gather her senses enough to seek out his aura. She called to her new powers.

About ten feet north from where she stood she spotted a faint glow. She walked toward it and found Ethan sitting quietly on a fallen tree.

She sat beside him and they remained silent for a long while.

Finally Ethan spoke. "You need to go back to camp."

"That's it?" she almost shouted. "That's all you have to say to me?" She put her hand on his.

He pulled away in disgust. "Yes Morgan! That's all I have to say to you! What more do you want from me? Do you want me to go into detail on how seeing you with him is like having my heart torn out and shredded into pieces over and over again? Would that make you feel better?" He glared at her through tear-stained eyes. "Would you like me to tell you that I want to break all my vows to Atlantis and rip that Triton's head clean off his shoulders? Regardless of whether or not he plays a role on the future Council and despite your feelings for him?"

Morgan felt nauseous. She blinked back tears.

"I can't do this Morgan. Just go back to him. If he's your choice then I will try to endure it even though it kills my very soul. Go back!" he anguished.

Morgan reached out again putting her hand back onto his. "I have not chosen Larrance. I have not chosen anybody. I'm confused. I love you Ethan, to my very core, but when you left, I mourned your leaving and Larrance was there for me. Something happened between us that is beyond our control. I'm in love with him, too. I know it's not fair and don't think for a second that it doesn't hurt me. It feels like my heart has split and is being pulled in two different directions," she argued.

"Yeah, you really looked like you were hurting in the cave," he growled.

She had no words. Her heart just ached as tears began to fall from her eyes. She had screwed up bad this time.

"I love you, Ethan," she whispered in a final attempt to reach him. "Things are just so crazy and mixed up. I know this is hard for you, but it's hard for me too. Everything's happening so fast. Did you know I can heal now? I still faint all the time, but my powers are growing fast. Things are just so crazy, my head is spinning, and I don't know up from down anymore. Please give me time. I promise you won't find me and Larrance like that again."

He looked up at her and gently squeezed her hand. He pushed his fingers between hers, flattening her hand out. He moved his hand to the center of her chest slowly. "This is your center," he said softly, as he placed her hand against his.

He trailed his fingers down to below her belly button. "And here," he said softly, as he took her other hand and placed it just below her belly button where she could still feel his touch. The warmth of his touch seared through her. "These are your energy centers. When you feel your energy draining, hold your hands like this and your body will naturally recharge itself. No more fainting," he said as he leaned toward her.

She leaned in and pushed her lips to his.

Ethan jumped back and bolted up off the log.

"Stop it Morgan! What are you trying to do to me? I'm trying to help you by showing you this, yet you insist on hurting me!

"I'm sorry, Ethan, I thought..." she stammered, wanting to kick herself for misreading the situation as Ethan stormed off into the dark.

"Wait, Ethan!" she yelled after him but he kept walking. She didn't want Ethan to go. He couldn't just leave things like this. Despite how screwed up things were at the moment, she loved him and she wouldn't apologize for that. She needed him.

"Ethan!" she yelled, sending a surge of her anger and frustration toward him in a mass of energy. He stopped. She could feel her power over him as she drew his energy toward her. She wanted him to come back; they needed to talk this through. She could feel herself pulling at his energy until he began to stumble backwards.

"Morgan, stop it," he yelled.

She was drawing him in.

"Do not use your power on me. Morgan, stop, I'm warning you," he growled, his face clouding with anger. "Don't force me to do this," he begged. She pulled him closer not caring that it was against his will. He was being so pig-headed and he just needed to listen for one minute. So she demanded it. She pulled harder with her power as his body slid reluctantly toward her. He dug his feet into the ground in resistance and stopped four feet in front of her.

"I'm not letting you go until we finish talking," she said with an inner strength she did not know she possessed.

"I didn't want to do this, but you have left me no choice!" he said, shaking his head. A ball of energy suddenly shot from his fingertips.

Morgan felt the blast hit her and spread shards of pain across her stomach as her body fell backwards against the log on the ground.

He blasted me. How could he? I only wanted to talk. Her heart hurt worse than her stomach as she looked into his foreign eyes.

"You possess power now, Morgan, but with it comes responsibility. You can't just drag me across the jungle against my will because you want to. It's wrong."

"You left me no choice, we weren't finished talking, and you won't even listen," she sobbed as she clutched her stinging belly.

"We were finished talking, and as long as that Triton is with you, we are finished, entirely. I will do as I was meant to do and that is to retrieve you and teach you the ways of Atlantis. When you come to your senses, or when the Atlanteans throw that waste of fins out on his ass, then maybe we can finish talking. Until then I'm done." He spoke with so much hurt in his eyes, Morgan foolishly could think of nothing but how much she wanted to hold and comfort him.

There was a rustle in the bushes nearby and then the sound of quickened footsteps coming toward them. Larrance burst through the trees, lunging straight at Ethan. Fists were flying as their bodies toppled to the ground in battle.

"Stop it you damn idiots!" came another voice in the darkness.

"Lucas!" Morgan exclaimed, seeing her dear friend's silhouette in front of her.

Lucas walked straight for her and scooped her into his arms. "I'm taking Morgan back to camp if either of you morons care about anything other than your egos," he stated as he pulled her close to his chest and headed out of the clearing. They walked away leaving the two boys sitting dumbfounded in the dirt.

He held her tightly, with the big brother authority she had always loved about Lucas.

"How will we find our way back? It's pitch black out here," she asked quietly.

"I can see."

"In the dark?" she asked. When she looked into his eyes she saw that his pupils were dilated with a bright blue glowing ring, just like Ethan's. "I can't see in the dark," she said.

"I guess I'm just special," he teased as he gave her a little squeeze.

"How did you guys find us out here?" she asked curiously, knowing that even though they could see, she had traveled a long way into the bush following Ethan.

"Larrance felt it. He shot up at the campfire and said you were hurt and then he took off like a bolt of lightning into the woods. I just followed him."

They walked in silence for a few minutes avoiding the inevitable question. Finally Lucas mustered the courage to ask. "So, what's going on Morgan? Are you with Larrance or Ethan? You know you can't have both, right?"

She didn't know how to respond to his question because she didn't know the answer. She felt like her heart would burst. Tears spouted from the corners of her eyes. "I don't know Lucas, I wish I was home. I wish *we* were home and that this was just another one of my bad dreams. I miss mom and all our friends," she pouted.

"Hey, at least your best friend's here," he consoled her as held her tightly. "I know things have been weird between us, but they will get better. I wish I could take back that last morning in your bedroom. I know that permanently changed things between us in a bad way, and I want to put things back the way they were. I was so friggin' stupid. I really don't have those feelings for you either. I think I was just scared of losing you. We are just connected so deeply and the thought of you graduating this summer and leaving me behind scared me to death. So I thought a relationship was the only way to keep you in my life forever. I'm sorry I didn't tell you this sooner. I've just been so embarrassed."

He pushed a branch out of the way to keep it from scraping Morgan's dangling legs.

"You can tell me anything, Morgan. Trust me like you used to, please. I can't take this wall between us anymore. I love you. There's a reason we were hidden together and everyone else was separated. I know there is. I think it was so I could protect you."

She tightened her arms around his body pulling him in for a hug.

"Did Ethan hurt you?" he asked.

"Yes," she answered and Lucas came to a dead stop.

"No, it's not like that Lucas!" she quickly corrected. "He blasted me with a small amount of energy, but only because I was hurting him. I don't know what came over me, but I needed him to listen and he wouldn't. I got so angry I used my powers against him and pulled him unwillingly across the forest, towards me. It was bad of me Lucas. Real bad. I think I could have killed him. I'm just so frustrated; I don't know how to reach him."

"Do you really think he should be okay with this thing between you and Larrance?" he asked.

"No. Yes. I don't freakin' know! I thought he abandoned me. You saw how devastated I was. Larrance helped me through it and we bonded. Literally. Now I'm bonded to two men and I know I shouldn't, but I love them. Both of them." She sobbed against Lucas's bare chest. He gently stroked her hair. "I just need time to figure things out without them killing each other first. I'm so confused."

"I'm going to help," Lucas offered. As he continued to walk, the sounds of the group were getting closer.

"How can anyone help?"

"If time is what you need, I will keep them away from each other and away from you for as long as it takes," he said, setting her down before they walked into the clearing. "I'll get Tia to help, too," he offered, and they stepped into the opening where the group was gathered.

"Come on, come and sit with us," Lucas said, as he tugged her arm toward the pretty smiling girl warming by the fire.

She followed Lucas's stride and sat glumly beside the content couple.

"Here," Donovan said, handing her two small drumsticks cooked on a stick.

"Thank you. What is it?" she asked, regretting the question immediately.

"'Cuisses de grenouille," he answered.

She looked at him puzzled.

"It's his fancy way of saying Frogs legs," Lucas translated with a laugh.

"Tastes like chicken," Donovan answered defensively.

"That's what they always say after they feed you some nasty, crazy thing. The only thing I want that tastes like chicken--- is chicken!" Lucas commented.

Morgan chuckled as she ate the meaty little legs. *Hmm they really do taste like chicken*, she thought with amusement. Morgan looked up from the fire to see two sets of eyes fixed on her.

Larrance was on one side, gazing at her with love and desire through piercing green eyes that shone brightly against the flicker of the campfire. She could feel him willing her to come and sit beside him. She wanted nothing more than the comfort of his arms and the warmth of his touch.

Are you hurt? She felt his voice in her head.

I'm fine. I just fell over a log in the dark. Sorry if I scared you. She thought back to him as pleasantly as she could muster.

Yeah. Right. He looked away from her and gazed into the fire.

God, how she wanted his long strong arms around her. She started to get up, but Lucas's firm hand pushed her back in her spot. "No Larrance. No Ethan," he whispered the reminder in her ear sternly.

She felt like a chastised child as she sank back against her log. She turned to the other pair of eyes that stared at her from across the fire. These beautiful blue eyes were not as inviting. The look of hurt and betrayal bore a hole into her heart. She sent out a thought to him. She thought of their day at SeaWorld together and she felt his mind warming to hers. She thought of how she stayed by his side while he was in a coma for all those days and how happy she was when he woke. She then thought of the earth-shattering pain she felt when he swam away and abandoned her. She showed him the days she spent in bed in despair, not eating, not sleeping, just hurting all day and all night.

She felt all the information swirling around in his head as he began to truly see the ocean of true and deep feelings she had for him. She felt his resistance lower, and saw his thoughts of her and him kissing on the beach in Santa Monica, then in his car, and she could feel the love radiating between them until his thoughts shifted to her and Larrance in the cave. She suddenly felt a large impenetrable wall go up in his mind and felt it slam against her heart. She stared into his eyes and saw tears welling as he turned away.

"I'm going to try and sleep," she announced to the group as she stood.

"I made us each a bed with big leaves and stuff, they're over here," Donovan called to her.

She looked at the seven leafy mounds each about five inches thick and never thought leaves could be more heavenly. She headed toward them, looking forward to sleep.

"Wait!" Lucas shouted after her. "You can sleep with us so you don't get nightmares." He headed toward the makeshift beds with Tia in tow.

"You want her to sleep with us?" Tia asked, her voice sounding a little irate.

"She gets nightmares," Lucas pleaded with his little spitfire.

"I'm fine," Morgan interrupted the impending explosion. "I'll sleep over there," she said and pointed to the bed furthest from everyone. "I never had nightmares on the boat, and I'm sure I won't have them here either."

"That's because you always had a man in your room," Ethan's voice mumbled behind her.

She ignored them all and walked away overhearing Lucas growl some profanity toward Ethan as she passed by. She settled onto her bed, pulled one of the large leaves over her body and closed her tired eyes, waiting for sleep to take away her pain.

Chapter 18

The sounds and smells of the forest woke her early. Morgan realized that sleeping outdoors took some getting used to as she stretched out the kinks in her spine.

She smiled at the pile of leaves that were pulled close to her while she was asleep. On top of them lay Larrance. She looked down at his calm, large, manly features. His looks were often deceiving, but as he lay there peacefully sleeping, his serene features revealed his mere seventeen years.

She smiled to herself as she pulled a discarded leaf back over him. She headed for the woods to find a good place to pee.

"Good morning," she heard as she stumbled out of the bush.

Ethan stood in front of her with a pleasant, look on his face.

"Umm, hi, good morning!" she replied with excited disbelief, stumbling on every word.

"Sleep well?" he asked, carrying on the facade.

"Yes, surprisingly I did. It must be the fresh air. You?" she asked, desperate to keep the small but definite improvement in their relationship, going as long as possible.

"I slept fine. Thank you," he confirmed quickly. His gaze shifted from hers and the moment disappeared as quickly as it came.

She felt a hand on her shoulder and looked up to see Larrance. *That explains the sudden change,* she thought as she watched Ethan walk away and gather the rest of the group.

"Mornin' babe," Larrance proclaimed happily as he let out an exaggerated yawn then kissed her cheek like they were an old married couple.

Her arms flew up to push him away, but he was already out of hitting distance and headed to where everyone stood on the trail. She followed dutifully.

"So are we doing a little volcano jumping today?" Lucas inquired.

"No. Today we get to the top. Tomorrow we go in," Ethan replied.

"There's food and shelter up there so we can recharge. Oh, and they were putting Atlantean clothes up there for us as well."

"Awwww, you mean we have to wear clothes when we get there?" Lucas joked.

Everyone rolled their eyes at his lack of humor. Ethan ignored him and continued speaking as they began their walk toward the volcano.

"This is a long trek, so if we reach the top by nightfall we will be doing good."

The trail turned from sandy to rocky as they began to climb the steep narrow passage.

"We need to go single file from here," Ethan urged as Cleo and Tia formed a line behind him. Morgan looked at Lucas thankfully as he snuck in front of her and Donovan was behind her.

"Hey! Back of the line small fry," she heard Larrance's voice behind her.

"What? Why?" Donovan argued.

"I don't know why, buddy. Morgan just didn't want you walking behind her. I think you creep her out so she told me to make sure I was behind her," Larrance lied.

She turned to see the confused boy now pulling up the tail end of the line. "I never said anything of the sort, Donovan," she assured him and then ignored the boys as she began walking. She knew arguing the matter further was exactly what Larrance wanted. So she refused to say another word or even look behind her.

They walked for hours up the narrow winding path. Small rocks tumbled down the cliff side as they went.

"So how did you get to Atlantis and back so quickly if it is a three-day journey in and out?" Cleo asked Ethan as they climbed.

"This is not the only way into Atlantis. There are the water-runner tunnels. That's how most of us travel, but it would be far too dangerous for you guys," Ethan answered as he helped her over a rock that had fallen on the trail.

Morgan felt a roar of jealousy burning up inside her.

"It's so beautiful up here. The view is amazing," Tia chirped as they looked down at the jungle below and out to the ocean.

It is quite a view, Larrance sent from behind her and Morgan knew he was not talking about the landscape. She casually put her hand behind her back and flipped him the middle finger.

"Did you see that, Donovan? Man, she's really mad at you. She just flipped you the middle finger. What'd you do buddy?" Larrance teased.

"I don't...Did she?...I don't know what I did. I don't know," he answered in confusion.

"Not you, Donovan," Morgan groaned, not turning back to see what she was sure would be a crap-eating grin on Larrance's face.

The group came to a halt at the mouth of a well hidden cave after hours of vertical hiking on narrow, rocky trails. Morgan watched as each of the kids in front of her disappeared behind a bamboo-thatched curtain hanging in what looked like the doorway.

Larrance reached out from behind her and opened the bamboo curtain for them to pass through. Before them stood a large stone-carved room, in one corner, eight cots were made up with clean white linens. In the other corner sat a large trunk and a bamboo room divider. A large oval table with a basket of fresh fruit and vegetables greeted them close to the entrance. Beside the table sat an old green metal camp stove and boxes and cans of food!

"Wow! I think I've died and gone to heaven," Donovan said as he pushed his way past them. He snatched a banana from the basket then plopped his body onto one of the awaiting cots.

Morgan watched Lucas grab two apples. One for him and one for Tia, then he sauntered over and sat beside her on a cot where the two of them giggled and flirted quietly. She was truly happy for Lucas.

Hmmphh. Nobody's going to be getting me apples anymore. The self-pitying thought washed over her.

Larrance darted past her and grabbed the last two apples. He leaned against the table and held one out to her with a devious grin.

She slid around him, reaching into the basket as her body pressed against his and grabbed a star fruit from the basket instead. "Thanks, but I prefer something a little more exotic," she said as she bit into her fruit and walked away.

She turned back and leaned in again as she whispered threateningly into his ear. "Stay out of my head!"

She found a cot in the corner and plopped herself onto the soft mattress. She sunk into it and breathed in the scent of freshly-cleaned sheets. She marveled at the idea of something as simple as clean sheets being so heavenly, but after weeks of the same old grubby bedding and then the leaves they used last night, these were truly heaven sent.

"Did they do all of this just for us?" Cleo asked Ethan curiously.

"No, this cave has been here for a very long time, but they did add a few things especially for us," he answered as he looked around the cave. "The Atlanteans are very excited to meet you guys, especially the King. I know he's making sure that everything is perfect for your arrival."

Morgan noticed the warm glow across Ethan's face when he spoke of his father, the King.

"Our parents... or adoptive parents, I mean," Tia spoke up from her cot. "What do they think happened to us?"

"They think you drowned. You were all separate tragic drowning cases," Ethan answered, then looked over at Morgan sympathetically. "Even you, after our car accident they never recovered your body so you were considered deceased and washed out to sea."

She lowered her eyes as she lay back against her cot and tried to breathe deeply. She missed her mom so much. It had always been them against the world. Well, them and Lucas, she thought, looking over at him again. She was surprised to see him looking at her.

"You okay?" he asked with concern furrowed across his eyebrows.

She nodded and smiled the best she could, which seemed to be convincing enough for him to turn his attention back to Tia.

Donovan stood up from his cot. "I'm going to cook us a feast!" he announced, as he headed for the pile of boxed food and cans.

Morgan wondered how much of a feast you could get from the mismatched assortment of non-perishable food items she spied in the corner but she gave him an "A" for effort.

"Here." She heard Ethan behind her and turned to look up at him. He was standing with a pile of white clothes in his hands.

She looked at him questioningly.

"They left us clean clothes. This one was meant for you," he said, as he laid the gown on the cot beside her. "You can change behind that screen," he offered, then walked away.

Morgan gladly picked up the outfit. She wasn't much of a dress girl, but anything would be better than wearing the grimy clothes she had on for another day.

She slipped behind the screen and undressed. She slid the gown over her head and delighted in the soft buttery feel of the off-white silk. She looked in the small mirror that hung there and admired the beautiful gold stitching that spilled down the center of the dress and graced the seams. She couldn't believe how different she looked as she admired the floor-length Roman-style dress. It plunged delicately at her bust line and was gathered at the shoulders with gold ribbon attached to a delicate piece of chiffon that trailed down her back. The dress clung to all her curves in just the right way. She felt like a princess.

"Do you...Do you umm...Are you decent?" she heard Ethan muttering from behind the screen.

"Yes, you can come back here," she replied, then she heard the hesitant shuffle of his feet as he stepped behind the screen.

Ethan drew in his breath at the sight of her. "You look beautiful," he confessed in a low husky whisper.

"Could you, maybe..." she asked, turning around to show him the untied ribbon at the back.

"I will get one of the girls," he answered quickly backing against the screen.

"Don't be silly," she answered coyly. "It'll just take you a second." She backed up slightly, pinning him between her and the screen.

She knew she was not playing fair, but she was determined to end the fighting. She felt his fingers tremble as he fumbled with the ribbon on the mid-back of her dress.

"You look like a goddess."

She could feel the heat of his shallow breath on her bare shoulders. She felt his lips press against her shoulder and fireworks ignited throughout her body.

She couldn't help but let out a small moan as she leaned back further into the warmth of his body. He traced his fingers slowly up her arm, catching her neck and tilting it sideways as he laid another kiss behind her ear. She felt weak in the knees but she resisted the urge to face him. She wanted to pull him against her and kiss him passionately until he begged for more, but she knew things were too fragile between them for her to be abrupt. She could feel his aura reaching out and she welcomed it. She gave in to it, allowing him to be completely in control. She turned finally, wanting to kiss him with a passion deeper than the ocean itself.

She gazed into his fierce blue eyes, wanting him more than she had wanted anything in her life but the face that looked back at her was not filled with love or desire. She pulled away briefly to study the odd look on his face. His aura swirled around her in a turmoil of emotions and when she locked eyes with him all she could see was hurt, hate and revenge.

"Stop," she whispered, as she pushed him away. "Why are you doing this, Ethan?"

"It's what you want isn't it? Luring me back here? Isn't this what you want?" he demanded coldly.

She paused, choosing her words carefully. "Yes, Ethan, you're right, this is what I want," she said cautiously, as she moved the hand she still had pressed against his chest, up to his neck. She let energy flow from her fingers and dance down his back.

"I love you, Ethan. I don't want to love you *and* Larrance but I do. I'm in love with both of you and, no, I don't want to feel this way for two men but, yes, this..." she took a step against him. "You and me, is what I want. I want to be who we were. I need to know that it's not just in my head, that what we had is not gone, just a little broken. Please Ethan, this is it. I will not push you any further. If you still love me, then please be patient," she whispered as she desperately tried to find the boy she loved inside the scorned man in front of her.

Ethan pulled her into him and lightly kissed the tears from her cheeks. He pressed his lips to hers and kissed her softly and tentatively at first but as he lowered his defenses little by little, his kisses became deep with an uncontrollable passion and ferocious need. His large hands clung desperately to her body, moving to feel every curve of her beneath her satiny dress. She felt the wall that had been between them for days crumble at their feet as their energy fully combined around them swirling in a tornado of love and desire. She breathed in his scent of sandalwood and looked cautiously into his eyes.

"Your eyes are amazing, Ethan. They change colors from the lightest shades of the sky to the deepest shades of sapphire," she said looking at him in wonder.

"They do that when I'm truly happy," he whispered as he nuzzled her neck.

They wrapped their arms around each other. She leaned her head against his chest and they stood there silently enveloped in the warmth of each other's embrace. The emotions between them ran so raw and pure that neither of them wanted to pull away, so they stood there and allowed their energy to swirl freely around them.

Morgan finally broke away when a knock sounded on the outside of the screen.

"Hey, whatever you guys are doing in there," Lucas's voice called from behind the screen, "you need to cut it out! There are five uncomfortable people out here listening to the two of you making out. Seriously Morgan!" he reprimanded her.

Morgan felt the red hot heat of embarrassment rush from her toes to her cheeks. How could she have forgotten everyone on the other side of the thin screen?

"I'll go first," Ethan whispered as he cupped her reddened cheeks gently in his hands and nobly placed kisses on both of them. "I'm sorry for being such a jerk earlier. I'm trying to deal with this awkward situation we've all been thrown into, but it's incredibly hard. Please be patient with me Morgan, we'll work this out, I promise." he said and gave her one last peck on the cheek before he grabbed a pile of clothes from the chest beside them and slipped out into the open.

"I was helping her with her ribbons," he muttered. Morgan smiled at his schoolboy excuse as she stood behind the safety of the screen.

"Were you undoing them or doing them up because it sure sounded like you were..." Lucas started.

"I have clothes for everyone!" Ethan blurted, cutting off Lucas as he threw him a tunic.

Lucas held out the creamy white tunic with the elegant gold stitching and embroidered shoulders. "Okay, you're kidding me right? Tell me you accidentally handed me one of the girls'. These are dresses, dude!" Lucas complained.

"I think it's hot. You will have that whole Russell Crowe gladiator thing working for you," Tia piped up to everyone's surprise.

"Where's mine?" Donovan shouted eagerly.

Morgan finally slipped out from behind the screen. The room fell silent as all eyes turned to her.

"Wow!" was the statement in unison as they stared at her goddess-like floor-length dress that made her look every inch an Atlantean princess. She looked at Larrance, but he was not wowed by her new attire. He didn't even look her way.

I'm sorry Larrance. I had to talk to him. I didn't think you could hear my thoughts when I was with Ethan.

I couldn't hear you! he snapped, *but I feel your feelings, Morgan. I know you were doing a lot more than talking. Do you know how hard it was not to walk over there and slice his friggin' head off? How could you stand fifteen feet away from me and make out with another guy? Don't you know how I feel about you? Don't you care?* He questioned her with his thoughts then looked up briefly enough for her to see the anger he was fighting beneath his smiling facade.

I cannot apologize for something I cannot control. I don't want to hurt you, Larrance. There's something unbelievable between you and I, but there's also something unexplainably strong between Ethan and I. There's something that goes beyond even love when I'm near either of you; it's like we're a single person when we're together. Like our spirits join. The bond I have with both of you is special, and until we figure this out, I cannot break either bond, she spoke telepathically to him, hoping to spare him some embarrassment. She bravely slid into the chair beside him.

"You look like an angel," he whispered as he put his hand on her leg.

Normally she would have moved his hand away but tonight she knew he needed to touch her, so she just placed her hand on top of his and smiled at him lovingly.

Larrance let out a sigh of relief that she knew he had been holding in since she came out from behind the screen, and then he handed her a plate. One by one the group sat down dressed in their ancient Roman-style outfits. Morgan looked at Tia and Cleo in their pretty dresses—they were silky and flowing but not detailed like hers. Ethan had definitely made sure to give her the nicest dress.

Morgan loaded her plate with rice casserole, fruit salad and grabbed a bowl of chocolate pudding dessert. "Thank you Donovan, this meal looks amazing. I'm so glad you're here," she complimented the beaming freckle-faced boy across from her as she dug in.

Donovan nodded a thank you. He was the same age as them, but he exuded a childlike charm that the rest of them seemed to have lost through their teens. Morgan felt a bit sorry for him—the others were far more mature looking and seemed to have more life experience, and she could tell by the way he kept to the sidelines that he definitely felt like an outsider.

"Yeah, it's great Donovan, but where's the meat?" Lucas asked searching the table.

"We don't eat the flesh of our fellow warm-blooded mammals," Ethan answered dryly.

"Great, so now I'm a dress wearing, vegetarian, merman! Anything else you forgot to tell me?" Lucas raged as they all looked to one another.

Larrance broke the silence as a chuckle escaped him, and soon the whole table broke into hysterical laughter. Even Lucas couldn't help but laugh at the craziness of it all.

Chapter 19

Braced on the rocky ledge looking down into the vast darkness of the volcano's entrance, Morgan felt very small and human. They were dressed in their ancient Roman attire and covered by long velvety hooded capes Ethan handed out this morning, each one was a different deep jewel color.

"Shall we?" Ethan asked as he gestured to the hole.

"We just jump in?" Tia asked, turning pale at the thought.

"Yep," Ethan answered quickly. "Who wants to go first?"

"How about you?" Lucas asked as he held Tia protectively.

"I have to go last. I have to make sure everyone gets down all right. If there's a problem and I'm down there already, I cannot just crawl back out to help," he answered frankly.

"There's no way out? You just want us to jump into a dormant volcano with nothing more than blind faith? What proof do we have that you aren't just a nutjob or part of some 'Let's all drink the poisoned Kool-Aid' thing? This is your big plan? You've gotta be kidding me!" Larrance yelled.

"What's the matter? If you're scared maybe you should let the girls go first?" Ethan prodded.

Morgan saw the blur of Larrance's white tunic go by as he jumped blindly into the mouth of the volcano.

"Nooooo!" she yelled as she watched him disappear into the unknown. It felt like her heart had literally stopped beating until she heard his voice from down below.

"It's okay! I'm okay! It's not that far down. Jump next Morgan! I'll catch you!" Larrance yelled from inside the darkness.

She closed her eyes and took a big leap of faith as she jumped, feet together, into the hole. She fell for a few seconds (although it seemed much longer when she was in mid-air), then she landed softly onto a large net.

"You have to crawl down to the next net then slip through this hole," Larrance coached her.

"I can't see! It's too dark." she panicked.

She wondered if she was the only one of them who couldn't see at night.

"Just stay there," he reassured her. She felt for the edge of the net, but before she found it Larrance had her in his arms and carried her safely to the ground below.

"Okay!" they yelled above them, and waited as the rest of the group plunged bravely, one by one, into the netting below.

"Wow that was cool!" Donovan said as they all gathered.

"Yeah, except the whole wearing a dress while you jump through the air thing," Lucas grumbled as he smoothed down his tunic.

"I sure am glad it's dark or you all would have gotten an eyeful," he confided.

"Oh, believe me, I saw more than I care to mention," Cleo interjected.

Morgan was trying to get her eyes to adjust to the dark when she spotted a glowing passage behind them. "What's that?" she asked, walking cautiously toward the green glow.

"They're worms," Ethan answered as he slid past her and plucked one from the roof of the passageway. "Glow worms."

She looked at the large, pudgy, ribbed worm wriggling in his hands to get free. She watched as the tunnel's ceiling moved and rippled overhead. There were millions of fat glowing worms moving about. She swept her hand lightly across the glowing ceiling and the worms responded by brightening as she touched them.

"This is amazing," she said in awe. "Where did they come from? Did you guys put them here?"

"No, I think they just like the volcanic rock. I don't know where they came from. They have been here as long as I can remember," Ethan answered. "Come on," he urged, placing the worm back onto the rocky wall and taking her hand.

Cleo stopped short of the tunnel opening. "No way in hell am I going in there. What if they fall off the ceiling and drop into my hair?" she whined, stomping her foot childishly.

"It's okay Cleo, I'll protect you from those big bad worms," Larrance teased and she gave him a dirty look. He removed the burgundy cloak from around his neck and held it up over her head to shield her from any creatures that might drop from the ceiling.

"How's that?" He asked warmly.

"It'll do," she answered as she moved in closer to him. "I guess."

Morgan felt jealousy raging inside her although she knew she had no right to be jealous of anybody.

They all walked along the glowing underground tunnels. The trail twisted and turned in a maze of confusion, with side turnings and blind corners. Morgan knew there would be no way she would ever find the way back on her own. She breathed in the salty sulphur scent of the tunnel walls. After a long, stuffy, winding hike they finally reached a large room that consisted mainly of a large expanse of water. She looked around and didn't see any other tunnels for them to take.

"Perfect, dead end! We're lost aren't we, merman?" Larrance snarled at Ethan.

"No, fish-face! We're exactly where we need to be. Look." Ethan pointed to the water as it began to rumble and stir.

Suddenly, a massive dinosaur-like creature rose from beneath the surface. Its long neck and round head poked out toward them while its large body and finned feet remained in the water. It sniffed each one of them as its warm breath misted their faces.

When its gaze fell upon Ethan it stopped. "Hey there Calopia! How's my girl?" he asked, as he affectionately stroked her large cheek. "We need a ride. Are you up to transporting seven of us?" he asked warmly.

"Is this the Loch Ness monster?" Morgan asked innocently.

The creature raised its head snorting, in Morgan's face.

"This is Calopia; she's an Atlantean Water-runner. They do not like to be called monsters," he gently warned Morgan. "They've been sighted by humans a few times over the years and have developed many unwanted names because of it."

Lucas approached the water-runner alongside Ethan. He put his hand out to touch her and she swayed her body slowly against his touch.

"Wow, she likes you. They are usually so discerning when it comes to people," Ethan mused.

"Is she the one who brought all of us to the houseboat?" Lucas asked quietly.

"No, that was her son, Aeson. He is our Carrier-horse. Her other son is Argon. He is our Warrior-horse. You'll know him when you see him. No one rides him!" Ethan answered. He wrapped his arms around Calopia's neck and pulled himself smoothly onto her back.

He extended a hand to Morgan. She grabbed on and he pulled her up behind him. The rest of the group followed. Larrance went next, sandwiching Morgan between him and Ethan. Awkward!

"Now what?" Morgan asked apprehensively.

"Now, we hold on and take a deep breath!" Ethan shouted.

Calopia dove into the water and headed straight for the wall that stood solidly behind them, and then dove deeper into the clear cool water until they reached a large tunnel. She quickly swam through the circular opening and it opened up into a maze of tunnels. Instead of worm-covered ceilings, these tunnels were covered with flowing phosphorescent anemone-type creatures. The twisting corridors seemed scarily long, but the speed of the water-runner was deceiving, and they emerged into air pockets each time before they needed to draw another breath.

Morgan felt her air running short and was scared to try and take a breath. She knew she could breathe underwater, but she was scared to try it again. She held her breath for as long as she could and let out the last of her air as she felt the waterhorse begin to rise once more. They burst through the water and into daylight. The group gasped and choked, trying to fill their lungs with air as they looked around.

"Are we here?" Morgan asked.

"This is it, my love. This is Atlantis," Ethan glowed with excitement as he gave her a quick peck on the cheek.

She felt Larrance's arms tighten around her waist, reminding her that he was still there, holding on behind her.

"It's beautiful," Larrance gasped giving her another little squeeze.

Morgan felt numbed by the exquisiteness of her surroundings. She looked in awe at the large stone pillars, the manicured lawns and the rainbow of luscious flowers. Their surroundings were almost tropical, with large trees and vines covering ancient stone walls. She looked up as Calopia approached the shore. The ceiling was about a hundred feet overhead and sparkled with clear crystals that hung down like icicles, reflecting sunlight through each shard of stone.

"There's light. How? How's any of this possible?" she asked looking around in amazement.

Ethan jumped off Calopia's back as they reached the shore and helped Morgan down, leaving the others to fend for themselves. The excitement in his eyes bubbled over as he eagerly tugged at her hand, wanting so badly to share his entire world with her.

"The sunlight is absorbed from the water's surface and reflected by the crystal ceiling. I don't know exactly how it works, but it does. They say that when they threw the skulls into the volcano, they protected themselves by forming this giant crystal dome. I grew up here and I still think it's amazing. The crystal ceiling also works as a giant air filter, absorbing the oxygen from the water above and filtering it into the dome."

Morgan took in the people that began to crowd around her. They all had hair that shone like spun gold, sky blue eyes and pale ivory skin. They were dressed in tunics and gowns adorned with golden accessories.

"Oh Ethan, it's breathtaking," she gasped as she squeezed his hand warmly.

A group of young girls were the first to approach them. They hung braided wreaths of flowers around their necks, then stepped backwards and bowed to the seven of them. Soon, the rest of the gathering natives began to lower their bodies to the ground in a bow.

"What's going on?" Morgan asked.

"We are the Royal Council; they are showing their respect."

Ethan guided her past the bowing men, women, and children. The rest of the group followed silently, unable to put words to what their eyes were seeing.

They stepped onto an intricately laid cobblestone path that was crusted with gemstones and quartz. To their left, people were working a large, flourishing garden.

"Hey, *they're* wearing pants!" Lucas grumbled as he eyed the shirtless men in the garden with their white cotton pants.

"Royalty wears tunics; we do not wear pants." Ethan answered dismissively as he walked anxiously with his friends in tow.

"Well, royalty is going to start wearing pants! Even if I have to take them off the men in the garden myself!" Larrance argued.

"I bet you would like that. I kinda thought you swung that way," Ethan jabbed.

Morgan discreetly jumped in front of Larrance and put her hand on the fist that was about to strike Ethan in the back of the head.

There were loud splashes to the right of them. She looked at the large water-runner that snorted and thrashed in the otherwise peaceful blue lake. His body shone like polished silver and his eyes glowed hotly. She watched as the Atlanteans shouted and tried to get on top of the reluctant creature. They were trying to strap a saddle-like device to its back. Each one of them was unsuccessfully tossed and ended up soaking in the shallow of the lake without much progress.

"That must be Argon the warrior-horse," Morgan concluded in awe of the strength of will in the massive creature. She felt a twinge of pity for him. Nobody should try to break the spirit of such a strong and beautiful creature.

"That's him," Ethan beamed. "Don't worry; no one will ever break that horse. They have been trying for ages." He grabbed her hand quenching her anxiety.

Her eyes followed the trail to a round courtyard surrounded by a white marble and stone castle. Its ancient pillars and carved openings towered over them. It radiated breathtaking power and beauty. Strips of smaller houses flanked both sides of the castle and circled the courtyard. Morgan noticed that all of the houses seemed to span out in a circular formation with streams of crystal blue fish-filled waters flowing in waterways between the rows of houses.

"The layout of the city looks like a crop circle," Lucas spoke up.

"We aren't responsible for crop circles. I promise," Ethan laughed. "We built around the temple. The circle formation allows a consistent flow of energy throughout the entire city," As Ethan explained, Morgan could see Ethan's absolute love for Atlantis radiating across his face. She hoped she would soon feel the same way about her new home.

They stepped onto an intricately-carved wooden footbridge. Morgan could see a rainbow of exotic fish swimming leisurely beneath them. They passed three more passages of land each divided by a stream and connected by an elaborate footbridge. The group of Atlanteans that anxiously followed behind them continued to grow in size as they walked further into the city.

"Where is the temple exactly?" Morgan asked.

"Just a few more feet and…there." Ethan guided her across the perfectly manicured, lush, green lawn and pointed.

Morgan stepped forward and saw the courtyard descend into what looked like a natural amphitheater built into a large sinkhole. From a distance you couldn't even tell the temple existed. Rows of seating descended down and circled around the entire area. Everything led to the center where a large, ornate gazebo structure stood. A small moat of water surrounded it and large red roses had been trained to grow up the sides. The top of the gazebo was made of beautifully colored crystals of different sizes and shapes, all of which, pointed upwards toward the sky.

"It's stunning. I could imagine it was made by God himself," she whispered.

"We like to think it was. This was here after the cataclysm that dropped Atlantis to the ocean floor. There was nothing like it when Atlantis was on land but it appeared afterwards. The people gathered here in the very beginning of the cities rebirth and they built out from here." He led her down toward the temple's center.

"This may sound weird, but I can feel the energy. There is a great source of power here." Morgan crossed the moat on a tiny footbridge.

"I thought you would like this place. Your mother was Ashmana and she ruled this temple throughout her life."

Morgan looked around her. The others had wandered off to explore. Even Larrance had been pulled away reluctantly by Cleo. She sat at the steps of the temple.

"Ashmana? Isn't she the one who caused the fall of Atlantis, like 10,000 years ago? Is she still alive?" Morgan asked.

Ethan sat beside her. "She lived for thousands of years beneath the ocean. Trapped by the devastation she had created. She was cursed to live forever, trapped by the love she had for the two men who had destroyed her people. Her curse bound her to an eternity of loneliness and misery, but after ten thousand years of mourning, she managed to do the unthinkable. She fell in love with another, a commoner. They married right away and when they consummated the marriage on their wedding night, he died in her arms. Her curse taunted her still, but she discovered she was with child. When she gave birth, the curse lifted and Ashmana finally found peace. She died happily knowing she had passed on all of her goodness, strength and power into another. Into you," Ethan explained as he squeezed her hand gently.

Morgan wasn't sure how to feel after Ethan's revelation. Her mother had always been Lynn from Santa Monica, and she wasn't ready to share even an ounce of that love with a woman who almost destroyed Atlantis. She guiltily was thankful that Ashmana was no longer here. Lucas and she had both known they were adopted. This was one of the things she felt brought them together as friends when they were younger. They had spoken about their adoptions, but neither of them ever wanted to contact a birth parent. They looked at who they were as a direct connection to the great parents they had, and they did not want to mess with that by contacting some stranger who chose to give them away. Morgan knew that was no longer the case, but nevertheless, she considered herself to be Lynn's child not Ashmana's.

"What about our Atlantean parents?" Cleo asked.

"They're gone. The Triton attacked Atlantis only days ago. They kidnapped the entire Council. They have never been so brazen before. We have fought with them through the years but it was always out there, in the water," he pointed. "This time they entered our sanctuary. They managed to get into the main castle and kill many of our soldiers before they escaped with our Royal Council, your parents. Luckily, the King was away at the time." Ethan paused, "I'm sure they're still alive, though. I don't think the Triton were actually after them."

"I don't understand. Who would they be after if not the Council?" Morgan asked.

"Us," Ethan confessed. "Don't worry, once we're ready, we will make those dirty Triton pay for what they did and we'll get our parents back." Morgan could see a furrow in Ethan's brow and she could tell how much he hoped his words reassured the group.

"They aren't our parents," Lucas spoke up from the back of the group. "We all have real parents on land. These people may have given birth to us, but they chose to leave us on land. They chose to have us spend our entire childhood living a lie!"

"They didn't choose to send you to land. You were stolen," Ethan tried to reason with him.

"You're right, they didn't send us there, they just 'chose' to leave us there. It's kinda funny how they brought you back and let you grow up with your real parents, isn't it?" Lucas spat back.

Morgan knew how close Lucas was with his adoptive parents and she knew how much the idea of never seeing them again hurt him.

"You're here!" A jolly voice echoed across the temple, cutting through the rising tension.

They looked up and saw a stunning man with long flowing blonde hair. He beamed with power as he looked over them. Morgan guessed that he was in his forties.

"Hello, gorgeous!" Cleo purred at the god-like figure.

"Father!" Ethan shouted, as he sprang to his feet and headed back up to the courtyard where the grinning King awaited. The others followed taking two steps at a time. Cleo trailed behind in embarrassment.

Ethan shook the man's hand and then gave him a quick hug. "Any news on mother or the Council?"

His father shook his head sadly.

"Everyone, I would like you to meet King Nariedon. My father." Ethan beamed with the glow of a much-loved child.

Morgan bowed to the mighty man in front of her. She wasn't sure what the protocol was when you met the King of Atlantis, but a bow of the head and a curtsy (no matter how feeble) seemed like a good start. The others quickly followed her lead and bowed in an awkward unison. She felt Larrance protectively move to her side.

"Come, come my children!" the King beamed lovingly. "Let's get you to your rooms. You will stay with me in the castle until you are wed. Then you will be given houses of your own."

Tia came up beside Morgan and looked at her frantically. "Until we are wed?"

Morgan shrugged her shoulders, whispering back, "I'm sure he just means the castle will be our permanent home until we grow up and move out on our own."

They followed him obediently across the lawn. Morgan mused at how this man who was movie-star gorgeous talked to them as if he were a portly old grandfather.

Morgan looked at Ethan as he stood at his father's side. She hadn't even thought about the fact that his mother was probably on the Council and that she was one of the kidnapped Atlanteans. She wondered why Ethan hadn't told her before now. *This must be awful for him,* she thought to herself.

They stood at the chiseled steps of the enormous and elaborate castle as guards held the giant, intricately carved, wooden doors open for them to enter. Morgan took a deep breath knowing that this was it, there was no going back. Her life was about to change completely, and for better or worse, those changes were permanent. She took a step forward and slowly climbed the steps toward her new life.

Chapter 20

A slender, timid, young girl with a long silvery braid of hair hanging loosely down her back showed Morgan to her room. Her feet lightly skimmed the floors as she led Morgan down the marble floors toward the end of a long hall on the second floor. At the end of the hall was a large beautifully carved, dark, wooden door. The girl opened the door and revealed an enormous bedroom. In the corner, separated from the rest of the room by etched glass panels and a stone archway, was her bed. The bed was covered in gauze curtains and draped mounds of red silk. It had an oversized wooden headboard with ocean scenes delicately carved and spiraling up the pillars that formed a stunning canopy over the top.

Morgan delighted in the exquisiteness of it all. If she could have imagined Atlantis in a dream it would have looked like this. It was almost too good to be true. A large fireplace made from perfectly stacked, lightly colored, large field stones stood in the main part of the room. The stones were placed intricately up the wall and on the floor forming a large inviting hearth. In front of the already crackling blue-colored fire sat two of the coziest looking dark red velvet chairs she had ever seen. There was also a writing desk, a vanity, and three large carved wooden wardrobes with designs that matched her bed. She opened one of the wardrobe doors curiously and found it fully stocked with gowns. She grimaced. They were beautiful, but she was just not a gown-wearing type of girl. She knew it could be worse, though. She could be a boy forced to wear a tunic. She laughed at the memory of Lucas's horrified face when he held up his new attire.

She noticed there was a smaller room attached to hers.

"It's your bathroom," the girl told her.

Morgan approached with apprehension. She peeked inside and let out a sigh of relief when she saw a normal everyday porcelain toilet.

The girl smiled. "We can have things brought in from land. The Water-runners make weekly deliveries although we are pretty self-sustaining. There are some things humans have that we can't help but want down here. We grow all of our own food and make our own soaps, candles, clothing and more. We try to keep things natural and organic; humans use way too many chemicals and pollutants, silly people are going to kill off their entire species if they don't get their priorities straight. But their Internet sounds really interesting. My brother spent a week on land once and he told me that the Internet provided him with answers to every question he asked it. That sounds pretty cool. "

Morgan looked in awe at the tub in front of her. It was like nothing she had seen before. It was a giant clam shell!

"It's a little over the top, right? It reminds me of *The Little Mermaid,* but they say Poseidon himself found these clamshells and had them made into baths for his castle," the girl added.

Morgan thought of the boys having a bath in a giant clamshell and chuckled. "This was Poseidon's castle?"

The girl nodded.

"And you've seen *The Little Mermaid* movie?" Morgan asked in confusion.

The girl smiled. "We have a theatre downstairs that shows movies every week. Like I said, there are some things the humans have that we just can't resist." She winked at Morgan.

Morgan pictured a room full of Atlanteans eating popcorn and watching *The Little Mermaid* as they sat in their castle built by Poseidon beneath the ocean. It didn't get much stranger than that.

"You guys have power down here?"

"Yes, but not a lot. There are solar panels on the one side of the volcano overhead. King Nariedon had them installed and had the power cables strung through the tunnels, but it is seldom needed or used."

She headed for the door. "My name is Alea. I am your lady of court. My destiny is to serve you, so if there is anything you need, please allow me to assist you." She bowed her head and curtsied.

She pulled the door shut leaving Morgan alone in her immense room.

It is my destiny to serve you? Morgan shook her head. It was all just too much.

Exhausted from the day's events, she decided to head to her over-the-top-bathroom and bathe in her Clamshell. The handmade shampoo and soaps made her skin smell of sweet flowers and feel like creamy satin. After her long and much-needed soak, she dressed in another elaborate floor-length gown. The gown had a deep plunging neckline that revealed the necklaces of her two loves. The dress also had gold-crusted beading along the hemline and was covered in a flowing chiffon skirt. She swept her hair into a loose bun at the nape of her neck then sat at the makeup table. She was thankful to find a little welcome basket filled with goodies like mascara, lip gloss and even some pretty pearl drop earrings.

She stood up to check herself in the floor length mirror that hung on the wall beside her wardrobe. As she walked over to it, something caught her eye. There was a small blue velvet pouch on the desk. She picked it up and found a note attached to it. It read:

MY DEAR CHILD,

RULE WITH HEART AND COMPASSION AND BELIEVE IN YOUR POWER TO DO GOOD.

YOUR LOVING MOTHER - ASHMANA

Morgan's cheeks became wet with tears, she wasn't sure if she was crying over losing the mom she knew or the one she would never know. She had always felt like she was meant for more than the norm, but being the daughter of a powerful ruler like Ashmana exceeded anything she could ever imagine. She felt the weight of what was being passed down to her and didn't know how she could ever be the strong, effective leader she imagined her birth mother must have been at one time. She worried Atlantis would soon expect more from her than she could ever possibly deliver.

She opened the bag and poured out a long golden necklace with an upside down teardrop hanging delicately from the chain. It looked just like the ones she wore from Larrance and Ethan except her teardrop shape had a long straight line coming down from it. She slipped the chain over her head and let it fall against her chest. As it touched the other two necklaces, a light shot out, sending a shockwave through her body. She could feel heat against her chest at first, and then it spread across her body like wildfire. The light blasted her backwards, knocking her to the floor. She fought the pain desperately as burning jolts coursed through her body. The blasting power became too strong and she collapsed against the marble floor.

Morgan opened her eyes to Larrance's warm worried expression. "What happened?" he asked, catching his breath.

She realized he must have felt her pain and came running. She wrapped her arms around him carefully, still feeling the deep burning in her chest.

"I don't know, the last thing I remember is putting on a pendant my...Ashmana left me. It's like the ones you and Ethan had. Then there was this light and I felt like I was on fire. Next thing I knew I was here in your arms."

Suddenly, Ethan burst into the room with the King following close behind.

Larrance paid no attention to the intrusion. He pulled her away from his chest to look at her growing collection of pendants. He scooped them into his hand and gasped.

"What?" she asked, looking at his hand in confusion.

The King stepped forward and kneeled beside Larrance as he took the pendants from Larrance's hand. "It can't be," he mumbled. "It's not possible."

Morgan struggled to sit up. She reached out to the King, wanting her necklace back. "What is it?" she asked.

He opened his hand slightly to reveal a completely different, single pendant, and then let it dangle against his palm. "It is the Trident," he answered, his face masked with disbelief.

"There is a real trident in Atlantis? Where is it? Do you have it?" Morgan asked naively.

"There hasn't been a Trident in Atlantis for at least 10,000 years. I didn't even think those stories were true," the King answered as he lifted himself from the floor and made for the door.

"Morgan was wearing my royal pendant, Father," Ethan spoke up. "Then she was given another one that looked exactly like mine by this Triton." Ethan gestured to Larrance. "How is that possible? Was a pendant stolen by his father?"

The King stopped in the doorway, his face pale and sober as let out a large sigh. "No, Larrance has as much right to the royal pendant as you do Ethan. Larrance is my son, too," the King confessed. An expression of defeat spread across his face.

"But Thavan was his father! He was banished because of it! So how can this be? It doesn't make any sense. Did you have an affair with Thavan's wife?" Ethan fumed.

"No, I did not! I would never cheat on your mother, and before you ask she would never cheat on me either! We are soul mates." The King shook his head.

Morgan was in shock, and she could tell by Larrance's and Ethan's faces that they were just as stunned.

The King took a heavy breath and continued. "Larrance is the first Triton to be born of pure Atlantean blood. We have no Triton in our bloodline that we were aware of, but he was born Triton alongside you, his Atlantean twin brother. When this happened we could not tell anyone. Your mother was terrified that the Council would hurt him. We both were. When he was discovered they assumed he was Thavan's, so I am ashamed to say I did nothing. I let Thavan face the judgment and prosecution because I thought he would claim Larrance and raise him as his own. That did not happen. The Council took the boy and hid him on land to punish Thavan. Then they banished Thavan and his family. They were to never step foot in Atlantis again. Thavan and his wife were the last Triton in Atlantis, and they knew a lot was riding on them, so Thavan took the banishment very hard. I should have stepped in, but things had gotten so out of control I knew no one would have believed the truth, especially since no one, not even us, knew your mother was carrying twins.

"Once Thavan was on the outside he went to the Triton for help. They called him a traitor of his own kind and denied him entrance into their city. That night a group of Triton attacked them and killed his wife. Thavan went mad with anger and sought revenge on us for what we did to him." He paused. "For what I did to him. He kidnapped the six Council children as an act of revenge, but being the gentle person I knew him to be, he did not have the heart to hurt them, so instead, he hid them on land."

King Nariedon backed against the door opening it to leave. "Your mother and I have carried the burden of this terrible secret for seventeen years. I cannot change what has been done, but I will set things right. When your mother is rescued and back by my side we will announce the secret we have hidden all these years. We will tell the Atlanteans the truth and they will accept you as my son, Larrance." He took an awkward step toward Larrance.

Morgan felt Larrance go tense and she could see his eyes deaden with this stranger's confessions.

Nariedon stepped away, realizing it was still too soon to expect any kindness from his abandoned son, but Morgan could tell that the King felt the sting of Larrance's rejection just the same.

"In time," Nariedon nodded, and hurried out the door.

Morgan opened her mouth but Larrance just shook his head. She stayed quiet, knowing he needed time to process what just happened. She looked down at the pendant once again. The three upside down tears had opened up and changed, turning into what truly looked like a trident. The chains now hung from each end of the three golden spears. She held it up to examine it when Larrance winced.

"Your chest!" he exclaimed as he stroked the bare burning skin between her breasts. Morgan looked down bashfully. She could feel Ethan's unfaltering eyes glued to Larrance's hand on her chest.

"That's why it hurt so much. It felt like it was burning. I guess it really was," she said as she looked at the trident-shaped scar permanently blazed into her bosom.

"I...I felt it too," Larrance confessed as he unbuttoned his shirt.

Morgan noticed he had made good on his promise to find and start wearing pants. He stood before her bare-chested to the waist. Morgan looked nervously to Ethan then back at Larrance as he exposed his chest to her. Her heart almost stopped when Larrance took her hand and placed it against his chest. She tried to pull her hand out of Larrance's grip, then she stopped and stared as she saw what he was trying to show her. There, freshly burned into Larrance's chest, was a Trident-shaped scar.

Ethan turned without a word and stomped out of the room slamming the door behind him.

"Ethan!" she yelled as she pulled her hand away from Larrance.

"He's gone. Just let him cool off," he offered. "Here, come sit." He walked over to her fire place and turned her large velvet chair toward her. She looked at the longing in his face. She could see his need to connect with her.

"I can't, Larrance. I have to find Ethan," she answered, fighting the urge to wrap her arms around him and comfort him. But if she stayed, it wouldn't be fair to Ethan and if Larrance broke down and showed the emotions she knew he had brewing deep inside. She knew she would do anything to comfort him.

So she resisted, knowing that would lead to more, much more, and she would not have the strength to resist him tonight. She couldn't let that happen. She couldn't do that to Ethan. She turned away from his invite and threw on her long velvet cape. She walked out the door without another word and left the beautiful, vulnerable Larrance standing alone in her room as she chased after Ethan.

Chapter 21

Even the glamour of her new bedroom seemed jaded when Morgan returned from a fruitless search for Ethan. She knew she had to talk to Larrance about the matching symbols now burned on their chests, and about what that could possibly mean, but not tonight. She felt so emotionally exhausted, she decided to skip dinner and avoid any more drama. She slipped into her bed not even changing from her gown and let sleep quickly find her.

Dreams overtook her as she slept.

Morgan watched as bloodied, battered people ran chaotically around her, screaming with panic. She felt the earth rumble beneath her feet as she took in her surroundings. She was in Atlantis before the cataclysm. She took in the beauty of the structures as others screamed around her. "The Trident has broken!" they yelled through the streets. A deafening roar rumbled across the sky and shook Morgan to her knees. She looked up as the volcano to the north of the beautiful city erupted. Lava shot skyward turning the sky into a blood red fury—ashes began to fall around her like powdery snow, and lava raged down the mountainside burning everything in its wake. Morgan felt her legs quake as she tried to run alongside the hysterical crowd. The earth beneath her jarred and rumbled then it began to fall. The entire crowd was pulled to their knees by the sheer velocity of the rapidly sinking city. Screams deafened her as the crowd helplessly watched clear molten crystal shooting into arcs above them.

"Morgan, wake up! It's okay," Ethan gently nudged her back to reality as he stroked her forehead. His hand moved softly down to linger on her cheek before she opened her eyes to him.

"Shhh, it's okay," he repeated as he pulled her to him, wrapping his arms around her and rubbing her back gently.

"It was terrifying Ethan," she shuddered in his arms. "I was there. In Atlantis when it happened. The volcano erupted and Atlantis fell. I was witness to the sheer horror in their faces as they realized they were going to die. They were screaming about the Trident too. That it had broken. It was terrible!"

He laid her back down in the bed and curled in beside her, carefully staying on top of the blankets, "It's okay, I'm here now, go back to sleep." He stroked her tousled hair until she fell back into slumber.

Morgan woke in the morning feeling much better. She turned to face Ethan. She was glad to see he had not left her side. He was propped up on one elbow. She smiled as he continued to stroke her hair. His eyes were tired and wary and she was sure he hadn't slept the entire night.

"Thank you for staying with me," she whispered. "You haven't slept have you?" she asked, already knowing the answer. He looked away avoiding her question. "I tried to find you yesterday," she said.

"I know. I just had to clear my head. It all seems so unreal. I came to check on you when you didn't come down for dinner. You were already asleep so I sat by your fireplace for a while hoping you would wake up and we could talk. Then you started to scream, so I woke you."

"It was terrible, Ethan," she confessed.

The memories of last night's vivid dream came rushing back to her. She lowered her head against his chest, pushing him innocently onto his back against the bed. She listened to the steady drum of his heart as she spoke. "What do you think it meant?" she whispered.

"I have to show you something." He gently lifted her head up. She looked at him with a puzzled expression. He untied the neck of his tunic and tugged his shirt down revealing a trident scar on his chest. It was the same exact scar as hers and Larrance's.

Morgan gasped. "I think we need to find this Trident," she whispered, as she lightly touched his raised reddened scar.

Larrance shuffled his feet loudly to announce his arrival as he entered Morgan's bedroom. "I think we already have," he said as he approached the bed.

Morgan could see the anger in Larrance's eyes when he came around the bed curtains and saw Ethan sitting beside her with his tunic open. She looked at Larrance innocently, hoping the boys wouldn't erupt into yet another fist fight.

Larrance looked away as he spoke through clenched teeth. "I couldn't sleep so I did some reading last night in the archives downstairs. After a bit of searching, I found this…"

He held up the large antique book that had been tucked under his arm. "It says in here that Ashmana loved King Poseidon and the great warrior Ulysses, who it turns out, was Poseidon's twin brother. They ruled Atlantis together and they were called the 'Trident of Power' because they were unstoppable. The city grew and thrived. The advances in their civilization were astounding. Ashmana grew more and more gifted, until she possessed the powers of a goddess. She even grew powerful enough to turn Ulysses into the first Triton—the most powerful warrior the world had ever seen. She built him armies and he set out to conquer the world. While he was away, she married Poseidon. She felt the anger of Ulysses and tried to protect the Council and her new husband with the crystal skulls. As you know, it didn't work. Poseidon and Ulysses were killed in the cataclysm they caused and the Trident was broken. Ashmana was cursed by the gods for abusing her powers and forced to live an eternity never knowing love again and mourning her two true loves in the city the three of them had single-handedly created and destroyed."

Larrance sat at the end of the bed as he looked into their shocked expressions. "Do you get what I'm trying to say? *They* were the Trident. They built Atlantis, and when the Trident broke, Atlantis fell."

Morgan let what Larrance said sink in. She cleared her throat and asked, "So the Trident is back, but this time it's *us*?"

Larrance nodded. "Exactly."

Chapter 22

Morgan watched Larrance as he suddenly realized how close he was to the two of them lying on the bed. He stood abruptly and took a step back.

Morgan let her mind relax; trying to understand what Larrance was feeling. He was trying his hardest to accept the feelings between Ethan and Morgan, especially now that he knew they were all destined to live in this wretched love triangle. He tried to be understanding for Morgan's sake, but he couldn't help the urge that raged inside him to just slice Ethan's head clean off and be done with sharing the woman he loved.

Ethan, his brother. It still seemed so unreal.

Ethan reluctantly got up from the bed. "I have to ask the King about all of this. I will meet you guys downstairs after breakfast."

As Ethan drew in to kiss her, Morgan noticed Larrance out of the corner of her eye. His eyes swirled and dilated the way they always did when he was about to transform. He squeezed his eyes shut and she could tell he was fighting against the sudden urge to change into a Triton. He breathed in slowly, trying to calm the turmoil of emotions she knew he felt every time he saw Ethan touch her.

Ethan hurried out the door without giving Larrance the time of day.

Larrance turned his attention to Morgan. Her hair was messy from sleep and her full pouty lips were turned down at the corners the way they always did when she was in deep thought.

She patted the bed beside her and allowed her face to give way to an inviting smile. He sat close enough that she could feel his body heat radiating from through her thin gown. "Are you okay?" she asked, as she lightly stroked his arm.

He choked on the words he wanted to say. "I don't know. It's all so much. Do you think I'm him? Ulysses reincarnated?" He asked with vulnerability spread deeply across his wrinkled brow.

"No," she spoke gently. "I think you are Larrance. You are good, kind, smart and nothing like him. History would never repeat itself because you are not the monster he was. You are not a monster, period. Your father is an Atlantean, and you are an Atlantean above all else. You just possess a special gift. What you've become is beautiful, not bad, Larrance. I believe you being a Triton, has a real purpose. You were born this way without any Triton bloodline known in your family. That's a miracle, Larrance. I just know the gods have big plans for you." She wrapped her arms around him and pulled him against her. He held her, rubbing his hand softly against her back.

"Spoken like a true princess," Larrance smiled.

Morgan delved into Larrance's thoughts as he lay quietly beside her. He was surprised how much his feelings had changed toward her. He had felt wild, passionate electricity between them from the start and he had to restrain himself from ripping her clothes off every time she touched him. She made him feel like an animal, primal and territorial, but things were different now. For the first time he wanted nothing more than to simply hold her small vulnerable body gently in his arms. He wanted to feel her love for him and to give her love in return. He placed his cheek on the top of her head as she lay quietly in his arms. She pulled out of his mind not wanting to intrude any further.

"I love you so much Morgan, I probably would destroy the world if I ever lost you," he sighed. She pulled away, grabbing his head to face her. She looked him sternly in the eyes.

"Don't ever say things like that Larrance. Never! You would never harm innocent people for any reason, especially because of me. You don't want the idea of that hanging over my head do you?" she reprimanded him.

"No, I'm sorry. I just lose myself around you. It feels wonderful and scary at the same time. I should not have said that, I just wanted you to know how deeply I feel for you. It's like you possess my soul. I'm sorry, I feel like kicking myself for saying something so stupid. What the hell is wrong with me? I just lose all good sense when I'm around you."

He squeezed her in his arms gently breathing in her scent of vanilla and lavender. "I should go and let you get ready. See you at breakfast?" he smiled, reluctantly lifting himself off the bed. She nodded.

"Larrance!" she called out as he headed for the door. He turned to face her. "I love you too, more than I could ever put into words. Please don't ever doubt that."

She knew he wanted nothing more than to come back and curl up beside her, staying by her side all day and every day. She could feel his love and happiness coming at her in waves, until she felt surrounded by it. She wanted him. *Come to me,* she sent to his mind.

No! Not like this. Not as this! He looked at his forearms as the sting of the onyx fins burst from his skin. It was happening so naturally and rapidly now he barely seemed to feel it. Morgan knew the teeth would be through any second.

He turned his face from Morgan. He hated changing into a Triton in front of her. Correction, he hated changing into a Triton, period!

He quickly nodded goodbye, and rushed out of the room.

***

Morgan found Ethan in the hall on her way down for breakfast. He was sitting on a bench deep in thought. She nudged up beside him.

"Hey, what're you thinking about so intensely?" she asked.

"Everything, you, me, my…..brother." Ethan grumbled. Morgan almost fell off the bench when she heard the word "brother" come from Ethan's lips. "I spent my childhood dreaming of having a sibling to share my days with. I dreamt of a brotherly kinship that ran so deep we would rule Atlantis together and defeat the Triton once and for all. Imagine my surprise when my wish for a brother is granted, but the brother ends up being a Triton!"

"Ethan, you know he isn't an actual Triton, right? He is as much of an Atlantean as you are," Morgan argued.

Ethan dropped his head to his hands. "How did everything get so screwed up?"

Morgan followed Ethan into the King's study. They glanced across the poorly-lit room and spotted King Nariedon sitting behind his large marble desk. Ancient books and paintings were strewn around him and piled atop the desk. Morgan looked at the lines that formed beneath his eyes and the signs of worry that burdened his normally calm, but authoritative face. Ethan cleared his throat.

His dad's weary eyes lifted to meet theirs. "You know don't you?"

"We're the Trident," Ethan answered quietly in the affirmative. His dad nodded. "What does it mean, Father?" he asked as he pulled out a chair for Morgan and they sat across the desk from the King.

"I...I...don't know," Nariedon answered, shaking his head as if trying to physically gather his thoughts. "I know it is significant. The Trident has resurrected for a reason, I just wish I knew what it was. What I do know for sure is that history cannot repeat itself; Atlantis would not survive another devastating blow. Your mother studied the Trident's history for years. If only she were here."

"Why don't we send our warriors to the Triton city and end this, Father? If you sit around and wait for this new Council to be ready it could take months! You might as well sign Mom's death warrant," Ethan pleaded.

"I'm doing what has to be done! Do you think it's easy for me to make this decision? I can't send them before they are ready or they will all end up dead! The new and old Council! Our warriors are strong, but we need the power of a merged Council to defeat the Triton. You know this, my son. Do not let your love for your mother, cloud your judgment. I am doing what's best for her and our Atlantis," King Nariedon answered like a true King.

Morgan looked at Ethan carefully, she could tell he wanted to ask another question but was scared to hear the answer.

"Is a merge really necessary Father?" Ethan asked.

"You knew her destiny was planned. Although we did not know about the Trident, you still knew she was never meant for you." Nariedon rose from his desk passing them as he headed out the door.

Morgan's head was spinning. What were they talking about? Was the King talking about her? If she was never meant for Ethan, then who the hell was she meant for? Ethan chased after his father.

"We have shared our souls, Father, how can that not be our destiny?" Ethan shouted and his father froze. "She wears our family pendant, which can only be worn by the one I am meant to be with. Does that not show you that we are meant to be together? I love her Father, she is my soul mate. Please don't do this," Ethan pleaded.

"You need to stay away from her, son. You both do, or you will destroy us all! That much, I do know."

He turned around and added, "Don't forget that this young woman does not wear your pendant alone, my boy."

Morgan was speechless. She didn't know what was going on exactly, but she felt insulted and judged without jury. She reached for Ethan's hand, but he pulled away. She followed him to the breakfast area in an awkward silence.

Ethan stopped her in the doorway and spoke in a low tone. "I have been raised to think and behave like a future king, and I was taught to always put the good of Atlantis before all else. I have always done so without question, but just this once I want to say to hell with everything and go after what I want, which is and always will be, you Morgan. The minute I spotted the pretty blonde girl riding alone on the Ferris wheel, I knew it was you, the girl who has haunted my dreams since I was a child. The bond between us has grown stronger than I ever thought possible. How can denying this be what's best for Atlantis?" He saw the King approaching and lowered his eyes. Ethan said nothing more as he pushed past her and sat in a lone chair across the room. Morgan didn't know what was going on but she felt like something major was about to happen.

.

The rest of the group was sitting at the table when she walked in. She gestured for Ethan to sit beside her. He shook his head.

What's wrong? What's going on? she asked, as his father entered the dining room. He pretended not to hear.

She sat next to Larrance and he took her hand under the table giving it a friendly squeeze. He raised an eyebrow to her sensing something was wrong, but Morgan shook her head to signal that she didn't want to talk about it.

All eyes turned to Nariedon as he placed a large, gold bound, ancient book at the head of the table where he stood. "Good morning, my future Council. You all slept well, I hope," he began.

"Future Council?" Lucas asked.

"Yes, although we are without a Council at the moment, you cannot rule Atlantis until the proper steps are taken."

"What steps?" Donovan asked as he stuffed a chocolate scone into his mouth.

"We must merge the Council," Nariedon answered. "It has to be done as soon as possible so you will be at full strength when you are sent out to retrieve the old Council from the Triton."

They all looked at him puzzled.

"Each one of you has a pre-selected partner you are promised to. In Atlantis, we believe that each of us is born as half of a whole. Merging into a whole will allow each of you to achieve your most powerful state. Once you are merged you can draw from your partner's powers and strengths. It is how the Council has always ruled. I realize this will be a little different for all of you. In Atlantis the chosen partners are put together at a very young age and they grow up together and are usually very much in love by the time the merge takes place. Unfortunately, this is not the case for any of you. Well other than Lucas and Morgan, that is."

Morgan felt the color drain from her face and her cheeks burned like she had been physically slapped in the face. "This is insane! I'm not merging with anyone. Especially not Lucas!" she yelled. "I don't love Lucas! He's with Tia! Can't they merge? It's still within the Council's group of six?"

"It doesn't work like that. The connections are made when you are born. You don't have a say. You are all very young and this does not usually happen until you reach one hundred and the wisdom in our decisions is then obvious, but we need a Council now. I don't know how much longer they will keep the old Council alive. If they even are still alive. Besides, the idea of Lucas merging with Tia is absurd, she is his sister!" Nariedon grumbled.

Morgan watched Lucas's eyes widen as he shifted in his seat, leaning as far away from Tia as possible. She knew they hadn't done anything to feel guilty about, but she was sure they still felt a little foolish. Tia noticed Lucas's body shift and with that she jumped from her seat and shot out the door sobbing. Nariedon looked at Ethan expectantly. Ethan nodded as he rose from his chair carefully avoiding Morgan's confused stare and ran after Tia.

The King spoke as he looked at Morgan directly. "Ethan, as you may have just guessed, is and always has been, Tia's merge partner."

Morgan felt rage bubbling up from within as the pieces of the conversation all fell into place. She felt utterly betrayed. Ethan knew about the merges all along and never told her. Instead, he tried to lure her to Atlantis under false pretenses and allowed the relationship between them to grow, knowing that it could never be a reality! She closed her eyes and wished that it was all just a dream.

Morgan looked warily from person to person as Larrance still held her hand firmly under the table. "This is ridiculous! I refuse! I'm not even 'Council', am I? The Council is six and there are seven of us," Morgan continued to argue.

"You are our goddess. You must merge with the Council to prove to Atlanteans that you are not above them but one of them. You will have final rule when you take your seat as Queen, but you must always take the advice of both the Council and our King," Nariedon answered with a touch of agitation in his tone.

"Then I rule we get rid of this stupid law and merge when we want, with whom we choose!" she snorted.

"You cannot rule anything until you have merged. You are not our ruler until the ceremony has been completed," he said firmly.

"You have the power to change this!" she roared.

"I believe in the power and divinity of the merges. I know why you do not want to merge with Lucas, and believe me, Morgan, if I gave you what you wanted it would destroy us all, just like the first Trident almost did 10,000 years ago. I will not allow history to repeat itself while you are under my watch. Now, on with the pairings," he said as he turned the page of the large book in front of him.

"Let's see....oh, here it is. Larrance will merge with Cleo, Ethan with Tia, Morgan with Lucas, and Donovan will merge with an Atlantean from outside the Council, bringing new wisdom and blood into the group. So, choose wisely, son." The King nodded and smiled at Donovan, then shut the book and tucked it back under his arm.

"I will give you all some time to talk now. If anyone needs me I will be in my study." Nariedon stated his words dryly as he exited the room. He paused with a last thought. "Oh, the merging ceremonies will take place in twelve days," he added.

"We need to save the other elder Council now! We can't just sit around and wait twelve days for some crazy ritual. They will probably all be dead by then," Larrance spoke up.

"My wife is out there. Do you think I like the idea of her being held captive by some Neanderthal beasts? I can't just send some untrained children out into the ocean with their guns blazing, boy! You all need training, and you need to learn how to use your powers. Twelve days is still too short a time frame, but that is the best I can do." Defeat and worry pressed into his brow. He quickly left the room, avoiding any further arguments.

Morgan felt the world crashing in around her. Her only strength and power came from Larrance's hand that was still wrapped around hers beneath the table.

Cleo rose from her chair and crossed the room to stand behind Larrance. She smugly laid her hand on Larrance's shoulder and turned him toward her. "I knew we were meant to be," she said devilishly.

Larrance turned away from Cleo, completely ignoring her existence as he pulled Morgan's face toward his. "Can we get out of here?" he whispered desperately as he squeezed her hand.

She had no more words and no more strength to argue. She looked at Lucas who she knew she had hurt with her protests against merging with him. He would not even look in her direction. She felt tears filling her eyes and quickly nodded to Larrance. They rose without a word and headed for the door. Everyone else just sat there with the same blank expressions they had when King Nariedon announced his plans. Everyone except Cleo whose razor sharp glares and unrepeatable insults followed them out until they were through the castle doors.

Chapter 23

Larrance silently led Morgan through the courtyard, past the temple and the many stretches of lawn and bridges, until they reached the pond where they had entered Atlantis. He pulled her to a rocky area at the edge of the pond. He crawled up onto one of the large stones in front of them and reached down to help her. Morgan took his hand and crawled to the top of the eight-foot boulder. Larrance jumped off the other side of the boulder down into a shale rock bed with ease. He held his hands out to Morgan who hesitantly stood on the rock above him.

"Come on," he coaxed as he readied himself to catch her.

"Did I mention I'm scared of heights sometimes, too?" she confessed.

"It's only eight feet!" Larrance smiled at her neurotic cuteness.

"Yeah, I know, but look at all the sharp rocks at the bottom," she pouted.

Larrance quit smiling and his face turned serious. "Trust me, Morgan. I'll catch you."

She jumped into his arms, but he was not quite ready for her impulsive move so he fell over backwards with her on top of him. They laughed at the awkward position.

"You're right. These little rocks are sharp," he agreed.

"I think you planned that," she accused as she crawled off him and sat against the boulder.

"Maybe," he replied as he sat up and shrugged his shoulders.

Morgan looked around at the hideout she had jumped into. They were completely isolated with rock walls all around them. They were utterly and perfectly alone. She sat on the ground and rested her back against the large protective rock. "How did you know this was here?" she asked.

"I found it last night. It's where I sat and read all those books from the King's study." He sat down beside her with worry engraved deep into the creases of his face. "Are you all right, Morgan?" he asked, brushing his hand softly against her cheek. "I would never marry or merge or whatever the hell they call it with Cleo. I don't care if Atlantis is swallowed whole, I would never betray you. You know that don't you?"

She looked at the roar of green flames in his eyes. They burned so deeply there was no mistaking how he felt for her.

"Let me in, please, let me know what you are thinking. I've been trying to hear your thoughts all morning but I haven't been able to hear a thing since we arrived in Atlantis. I hate it! Talk to me, please," he begged.

She felt the walls around her heart fall away, just a little. "Do you think Ethan knew?"

Larrance's body grew tense at the mention of his brother's name. "Yes, why else would he have chased after Tia before Nariedon even announced that they were paired?"

Morgan felt her heart ache. "Why wouldn't he warn me? Why wouldn't he have told me ahead of time? I just don't understand. How could he let me fall in love with him if he knew we could never be together, if he knew he was partnered with Tia this whole time? How could he let Lucas fall for his own sister?" She tried to process the morning's events, thinking of how Ethan wouldn't sit beside her when she called him over. He wouldn't even look at her.

"He's an idiot, you don't need his lies anymore," Larrance fumed. He was done playing nice with Ethan. It was different when he thought Ethan had Morgan's best interests at heart, but now it was clear that Ethan had only been looking out for himself the whole time.

"What do we do? How do we get out of this?" Morgan asked him desperately as she skipped bits of shale rock in front of her.

Larrance stood and faced her. "We get out of here! We escape! We have twelve days before the merge, right?"

She nodded.

"Okay," he continued. "We just have to keep our ears and eyes open for a way out and when the opportunity presents itself, we take it."

"But even if we do get out, where do we go? Ethan said we can't be around humans while we transition. He said that we would drain the human's energy and kill them without even trying."

"We'll stay away from humans until we learn how to control it. You'll learn fast, I'm positive of that. We can make this work Morgan, I know we can. Do we have a plan?" he asked hopefully.

She looked at his large, perfectly toned body; he always stood with such a natural authority. His chiseled, lightly-tanned face radiated with power and knowledge. His gorgeous green mysterious eyes were framed with long dark eyelashes, but Morgan was surprised that when she looked at the hopeful face in front of her, she saw a boy instead of the man Larrance usually seemed to be. Right now he was definitely a vulnerable seventeen-year-old boy.

"Let's give it a shot," she answered. "But, we are bringing Lucas. I can't leave him here. He's my people."

"Lucas? Your future husband? Are you kidding?" Larrance growled.

"We get Lucas out or no deal," she said stubbornly as she crossed her arms firmly in front of her.

"All right, you, me and…Lucas," he conceded.

"Should we bring Cleo too?" he mocked.

Morgan kicked out her foot, striking Larrance in the shin.

"Owwww! I guess that's a NO!" he yelped, as he hopped around on one leg.

Morgan stood up and headed over to wrap her arms around the howling fool in front of her. She pulled him close and he responded, pulling her in tightly and wrapping his large arms around her, his howling and pain suddenly disappearing. He held her so tightly that she almost had to struggle for air, but she needed that. She needed to feel completely engulfed. Completely safe. She gently kissed his lips. She felt his body sigh in her arms. She had never given herself completely to a boy before, but she was ready. Larrance was who she had finally chosen, and she wanted him, here and now. She kissed him harder pushing herself into him as she fiercely pulled at his shirt. She struggled with his buttons as she slammed him desperately up against the boulder behind them.

She felt the Triton in him burst through as his forearms bore fins, his eyes began to storm in shades of green and blue, and then the fierce row of serrated teeth burst from the top of his mouth.

"Stop!" he panted, as he grabbed her fumbling hands from his shirt. He pushed her away, and threw his hands up to cover his face. "I just can't control it. I can't keep it from happening every time my heart races. Why can't I be like the rest of you? Why do I have to be the freak?" he brooded.

She ignored his ranting and pulled his hands away from his face, kissing him. She was gentle but urgent; she wanted to be with him, all of him. She did not care about him being Triton. If anything, it made him even more attractive. She wished he could see that.

"Not here, not like this Morgan, I love you too much for that."

She watched the swirling energy they had created around them begin to fade. She hadn't even noticed it was there this time. She let out a sigh and realized that what he was saying was true. Not here. Not like this. What was she thinking?

"*You* are not a freak, Larrance. We all have weird and crazy things happening to us. Your changes just show more on the outside," she took a step back. "I want to show you something." She had never intentionally tried to call on energy without Ethan around, but she felt confident that she could do it on her own.

She called the energy to her fingertips and watched as a small glowing ball appeared on her palm. She saw the look of wonder in Larrance's eyes and called more energy from her body and from her surroundings as the swirling sphere grew larger and more intense. She could feel the power of it in her hand. It reflected in

Larrance's eyes and she thought she could see a twinge of fear beneath his amazement. She began to pull the energy back in through her fingers like Ethan had showed her when she wanted to make the orb disappear. The ball of energy did not dissipate; instead it began to tremble against her fingertips.

"I don't know why it's not going away. It's supposed to absorb back through my fingers but it's..." Before she could finish her sentence the orb of electric energy shot from her hand and struck Larrance in the center of his chest dropping him to the ground.

"Larrance!" she yelled, as she ran to his still body.

"What the hell was that for?" he croaked painfully as he rubbed the charred circle left on his chest.

She fell to the ground beside him. "I don't know what happened, I'm so sorry. Does it hurt badly?" she asked as she wiped the char marks from his bare chest. Her hands passed slowly over his Trident scar and he placed his hand on hers.

"I'll live. Just don't try that again unless I'm safely behind a steel wall or something, please. You are a force to be reckoned with my dear. I'm just glad that I'm on your good side," he laughed.

They stayed in their little hideout for most of the day. When darkness fell they crawled out from behind the boulder and reluctantly headed hand-in-hand back toward the castle. The path was lit by the soft glow of candlelight.

"We need to act like we're going along with the merging ceremony," Larrance plotted. "We need to seem like we have accepted their plans for us so they don't suspect anything. I know you'll hate seeing me with Cleo as much as I'll hate seeing you with Lucas, but we need to play along until we find a way to escape, agreed?" Larrance asked, knowing how jealous they both got.

Morgan nodded and gave him a little smile as they parted ways at the bottom of the castle stairs. *This is going to be hard*, Morgan thought as she headed for her room. It physically hurt to even think of Larrance with someone else. How was she going to handle seeing him with Cleo for the next twelve days?

She shook the image from her mind as she opened her bedroom door. She would just hide out, that would make it easier. All she had to do was avoid everyone for a few days. That was her new plan.

That night, Morgan dreamt of Larrance. They were dancing and laughing in a large hall filled with Atlanteans when a group of Triton appeared in the corners. There were screams as the Triton attacked. Morgan looked up to Larrance for protection but his eyes had changed. The green had been completely replaced by black and his face was spread with an evil grin. She screamed as Larrance's mouth opened and his teeth sunk into her neck.

Morgan opened her eyes and rubbed her neck, trying to figure out her dream. She knew Larrance would never hurt her. How could she even dream such a thing?

Morgan jumped when she looked up from her bed to see a tall slender lady with a slim pointed face standing in her doorway.

"I am Lenora, and I will be your teacher. Please dress and meet me in the courtyard in fifteen minutes." The lady turned and disappeared from the room leaving Morgan speechless.

Morgan threw on the most comfortable and the least revealing dress she could find. She headed downstairs to find Cleo and Tia who also looked as if they had been given fifteen minutes notice since Cleo's hair was knotted and stringy and Tia still had sleep lines across her cheek.

Lenora was standing on the lawn waiting impatiently when the girls arrived. She looked like she was only in her mid-forties, but when she spoke she seemed more hardened and wise from experience. Her snow white hair was pulled back into a tight bun and she wore no makeup or jewelry of any kind. Her dress was simple and hung straight like a sack against her thin body.

"Well, let's get to it shall we? I only have a few days to teach you what most Atlanteans take years to learn. You must pay attention at all times as I do not repeat myself or explain myself. You are not children anymore, so do not expect to be treated like so. We will start with the basics today, and then I will focus on developing each one of your unique powers, and I will help you achieve greatness through them. Any questions?" she asked curtly.

"Where are the boys?" Cleo asked coyly.

"They are with a different instructor. Now, are there any questions that actually matter?" Lenora asked sharply.

The girls kept quiet.

"Okay, great, let's begin," she said as three bolts of energy shot from her fingertips knocking the three girls flat on their backs.

"That is an energy orb. Atlanteans have the ability to absorb and control energy. Some can send it as I just did, and some use it in other forms. I want each of you to focus on the energy that surrounds you and draw it into your bodies, then picture yourselves projecting it."

Morgan closed her eyes and concentrated. She focused on the energy of Atlantis; it was far more intense and powerful than anything she had ever felt before. She felt it flowing from the ground beneath her and the crystal ceiling above. She directed the energy to her fingers and slowly opened her eyes.

There, pulsing on her palm was a large energy orb. She looked over at Tia covered in a shield like the one she had conjured on the boat. Cleo was holding a white shaft of energy that formed the shape of a sword. Each girl had swirls of energy growing around their bodies radiating toward the teacher.

"Very good," Lenora praised while her face remained emotionless. "Now, absorb it, feel it and coax it slowly back into your body."

They all did as she asked successfully.

"Good, now do it again."

And they did, over and over for the entire day, stopping only quickly for lunch and dinner.

"You are a warrior, Cleo. You are a protector, Tia. And you," she continued, as she looked Morgan up and down dryly, "You are a lot of things, Morgan. I expect you all back here first thing tomorrow morning." She stated with the warmth of a drill sergeant and then she spun on her heel and disappeared across the courtyard.

Morgan was exhausted but happy for the full day's distraction. She found some contentment in knowing that she and Larrance had decided to escape. All they had to do now was come up with a plan. She hoped these next few days of training would reveal something they could use.

She shut her bedroom door and then gave a startled jump when she saw Lucas sitting in one of the velvet chairs in front of her fireplace.

"How was training?" he asked in a low, flat voice.

"It was good, and I think I surprised the teacher with my powers," she said honestly.

"Good for you," he snapped.

Morgan sat in the velvet chair and studied the look on Lucas's face. He was angry and in the mood to fight, and there would be nothing she could say right now that wouldn't set him off further. She sat there silently, waiting for the storm building around him to burst.

"Am I really that repulsive to you? Do I disgust you so badly that you would rather destroy an entire civilization than merge with me?" His face contorted with the pain of the rejection in his heart.

She remembered his eyes at breakfast yesterday and how her words were visibly hurting him. She knew she should have sought him out immediately afterwards and explained herself, but she just couldn't handle dealing with anything more than what she had on her plate already.

She regretted that decision because now he looked like a man on the edge of complete self-destruction and she was solely to blame.

"It's not you, Lucas. I'm seventeen years old. I'm not ready to merge with or marry anyone!" she argued.

"That's crap, and you know it Morgan. If Ethan or Larrance had been your chosen partner you wouldn't have had a problem, would you? Or maybe you would have had a problem because then you would only get one of them? I think maybe polygamy would have been your ideal arrangement, right? Then you could share a bed with both of them!" he yelled angrily.

Morgan knew she had hurt Lucas terribly and so she would forgive him for the mean and hateful things he was spewing, but she had heard enough. She flew from her chair and slapped him clear across the face.

"I'm sorry," he mumbled, realizing that he had gone too far as he rubbed the red handprint across his cheek.

"Do you want to talk about it? Really?" Morgan prodded him knowing there was so much more bothering him than he was saying.

"Do I want to talk about the girl I loved who crushed me by saying she thinks of me as a brother? Or how I moved on and found love again only to end up actually being that girl's brother? Is that what you think I should talk about? I think it's all pretty clear," Lucas confessed with anguish spiraling deep into his voice.

"Have you talked to Tia?" she asked.

"What for? What will it solve? She has tried to talk to me but I just can't bring myself to even look at her without feeling like a total pervert."

"You know she's going through this too, don't you?" she asked softly. She watched the walls fall around him and could see the hurt and vulnerable remains of her dear friend standing before her.

"She has the marvelous Ethan," he said dryly.

Morgan felt a pain in her chest, empathizing with Lucas's pain. "Maybe, but it's you she stares at and wants to talk to." She took a deep breath.

"How was your training today?" she asked, desperately wanting to change to a lighter subject.

"Oh, just great! I don't have a single power. I'm the only Atlantean without a special ability. Other than the ability to be completely inadequate, that is. Aren't I lucky?" he moped. He got up from his chair and headed toward her bed.

"What the heck are you doing? We aren't merged yet?" she asked, confused over his forwardness.

"I know I just...I was hoping I could sleep here, beside you tonight. I've been there for you, for the past five years, and tonight I need you to lie beside me. I just need you close to me. Is that too much to ask? Or have I become that repulsive to you?" he asked as he pulled the top of his smock off, leaving only a thin gauze layer on as his chest heaved furiously beneath it.

His words stung. They cut at her like knives but she knew she deserved every one of them.

"I would like it if you stayed tonight, Lucas. I could use the comfort of my dear old friend," she said, hoping he would hear the emphasis she put on the word 'friend' and not try anything foolish.

He did not answer; instead he slipped in her bed and patted the empty spot beside him. She climbed in the other side staying as close to the edge as she could without falling out. She felt his strong arm wrap around her waist as he pulled her across the bed and up against his chest. She froze in terror wondering if she was strong enough to fight him off if she had to.

"Do you really think I would try something or that I would hurt you?" She felt his breath hot on her cheek then he rolled over and pressed his back to hers.

"Goodnight," he grumbled.

"Night," she answered and went to sleep almost instantly.

***

Morning came quickly and Morgan was grateful now that Lucas had stayed. She hadn't slept that soundly since their last night together in her room. She nudged him awake and as he turned to her, he propped his head up with his hand. His face was soft now; the anger had given way to sleepy bliss.

"Morning," he whispered, slapping his dry mouth together.

She smiled at him, so happy that he was back to the old Lucas, her dear friend Lucas.

"I have something to tell you," she confessed, and then she explained her and Larrance's plans to escape from Atlantis.

"Will you come with us?" she asked hopefully.

"You, Larrance, and me, the third wheel? Wouldn't that be cute?"

She didn't respond, none of the words in her head seemed to be right.

They lay in silence for a few minutes then Lucas fell back against his pillow. "Can you see my aura?" He spoke slowly as he stared at the ceiling.

"No. I see light bits of energy around people, sometimes, but I've only ever seen Larrance and Ethan's actual auras. Their auras just seem to respond to my touch." She felt his disappointment as she spoke. "Let me try," she offered. "Here, take my hands."

She held his hands in hers as she pushed her energy toward him. She felt his energy grow around her and she opened her eyes.

"Wow! Lucas, I see it, and it's beautiful! It's gold," she said in awe of the warm swirling that surrounded his body.

"So, it's like a yellow color?" he asked looking at himself trying to see what she saw.

"No, I wouldn't even describe it as a color. It is like real liquid gold swirling around you. It's amazing."

She sent more of her energy out to him and tried to draw his toward her. Lucas was so unlike the others—his molten gold aura was warm and soothing. She could feel her body wanting to be wrapped in it. His energy did not seem to reach out to her; instead it seemed to pull her energy without offering anything back. Her energy pushed out a little further until it was wrapped fully around Lucas as he came closer to her. His energy still did not mix with hers. She could not pull from it the way she could with Ethan and Larrance. She felt her body giving way as more and more of her energy slipped toward him. It swirled around him, being steadily absorbed by the golden abyss of his aura. She was growing weaker and weaker until she thought she might pass out. She caught a glimpse of the pleasured look on Lucas's face and then heard a moan escape him. She felt the room rapidly closing in as the energy drained form her body. She called on what little strength she had left and shoved Lucas backwards, breaking the energy bond between them.

She fell weakly against her bed feeling vulnerable and confused. Lucas had drained her energy, easily. The thought scared her. Here she was, supposedly the most powerful person in Atlantis, and Lucas could drain the life from her body in minutes. She felt completely powerless with him, and she wondered if that was how she made Ethan feel when she had pulled so much energy from him in his car.

Lucas shook his head as if out of a daze. "Holy crap, Morgan! What was that?" he asked excitedly.

"What was what?" she responded coyly. But she was scared, no, terrified. She couldn't let Lucas know how much power he held over her. Not until she knew more about it herself.

"You didn't feel that thing between us? It was like a rush of energy and pleasure all rolled into one. You really didn't feel it?" he asked in confusion as he scratched his head.

"I have no idea what you're talking about," she lied as she hopped out of bed.

"We'd better get dressed and head downstairs," she asserted, then quickly rushed to the bathroom so he couldn't see the lies in her face. He knew her too well for her own good. She had never lied to him before. The minute he saw her face he would know she was lying. If he saw her right now he would see how much his aura had shaken her, how much she longed to merge with it even though it sucked the very life out of her? She still pictured the warm liquid gold that encompassed him and she longed to have it wrapped around her once more.

Could she have been wrong all along? Could Lucas really be the one she was meant to be with? She knew one thing was for sure, Lucas definitely had a power and it was a dangerous one.

Lucas stood up from the bed, looking himself up and down as he opened and closed his fingers. "Wow, I just feel so alive now, so energized! That was cool! You really didn't feel anything? You didn't even see the glowing light that came out of you and wrapped around me?" he asked.

"No, I felt nothing. I have no idea what you're talking about," she lied guiltily and quickly shut the bathroom door to avoid any further interrogation.

A few minutes passed before she heard a soft rap on the bathroom door. "I'll meet you downstairs for breakfast."

Morgan peeked out of her door as he walked away, and she noticed a pale glow still radiating across his arms. She could almost hear his trailing thoughts as he sauntered off and she knew he did not want to leave her right now. He had just felt a connection on the bed with her like nothing he had ever imagined. Morgan thought it felt as if they were connected from the insides of their bodies. She was unable to control the energy between them and that scared her to death.

Chapter 24

Morgan walked down the marble corridor toward the dining room for breakfast. She had stayed in her room all day yesterday after Lucas had drained so much of her energy, cutting class and pretending to have the flu. She was finally feeling a little better. There were a few knocks at her door, but thankfully Alea chased everyone away, allowing Morgan to rest and think. She would have loved to spend one more day in her room, but she knew the King would soon be sending doctors and she would have no real excuse for not having returned to class. She really was still quite weak, but some color had returned to her cheeks. She was not looking forward to the awaiting crowd behind the large dining room doors that stood before her.

She felt even more vulnerable being dressed in the ridiculous flowing gowns they had chosen for her. She decided she would ask Larrance where he kept his secret stash of pants. If he could break the rules and wear them, she was damn well going to wear them too; it was the twenty-first century for God's sake! Pants should be an option!

She pushed open the doors and quietly tried to slink past everyone unnoticed. She scanned the room quickly. She felt Ethan's eyes on her as he sat dutifully by Tia's side. She looked at him head on and expected him to turn away but he didn't. He stared back at her with such hurt and longing that she felt her cheeks redden. She gave him the meanest glare she could muster then sat in the furthest available chair and turned her back to him.

She felt successful in her attempt to avoid any drama. That was until she realized the chair she chose was right next to Cleo and Larrance without noticing!

Cleo rubbed Larrance's thigh as she whispered obscenities into his ear. Morgan thought she might get sick at the sight of the girl's nasty paws all over Larrance, until she caught a quick wink from Larrance to let her know he was sticking to the plan. She was seriously beginning to rethink their stupid plan if it meant some stupid cow got to maul her man while she sat two feet away. She sure wished Lucas would get there soon and sit with her. She was definitely the odd one out. Even Donovan was preoccupied in the corner. He had six girls standing behind his chair. Morgan chuckled to herself. Donovan had become the most eligible bachelor in the entire kingdom and his ear to ear smile showed he loved every second of it. She looked at the pretty girl on the left with her long flowing hair and realized it was Alea, her lady of court. Morgan gave her a smile and a wave and Alea quickly returned the gesture.

Morgan hadn't really noticed how beautiful Alea was. When she had first arrived, Alea was so sweet to her, and she would definitely be rooting for her to become Donovan's chosen partner.

King Nariedon walked in and sat at his usual spot at the head of the long banquet-like table. "Good morning, my future Council. We have big plans today," he beamed as he scooped fruit and porridge onto his plate.

"Ah, Morgan! You're feeling better I see," the King said as all eyes turned to her. Morgan nodded, keeping her eyes glued to the table and avoiding everyone's glances.

"Good to hear. I was going to send my doctors to come and see you today but now I see I should notify them that there is no need."

"I'm fine, your majesty. It must have been a twenty-four hour flu, but thank you for your concern," Morgan answered formally.

The King nodded and got down to business. "Yes, well, back to our exciting plans for today. There will be no school; Lenora has more important matters to attend to today. Instead, the girls are going down to see the city's seamstress and the men will come with me to the study so we can begin preparations for our work after the merge."

Morgan bit her tongue so hard it almost made her cry out in pain. She was going to be fitted for a wedding dress! She decided then and there that they had all been lying to her. This wasn't Atlantis, it was Hell!

Stop laughing at me! she sent to Larrance as she realized he had just heard her thoughts and his whole body now shook as he tried to hold in his laughter. He knew how much she hated wearing dresses and frou-frou things, and a day visiting a seamstress was like some kind of cruel and unusual torture.

Just remember, she continued. *The gown is for my merging with Lucas.*

Larrance's laughter stopped.

"Has anyone seen Lucas? I haven't seen him since yesterday morning. Why isn't he here?" she asked quietly.

"Last I saw him he was by the lake, but that was yesterday. He didn't show up for supper last night, either. We thought he was with you," Ethan answered, hoping she would look his way. She did not.

"Do you want me to help you look for him?" Ethan tried again.

She turned to face him. "You are the last person I need to help me find my merge partner," she spat cruelly.

Ethan's face turned white as his mouth opened to speak. He turned and looked at Larrance and then his father before he rose from the table. "Excuse me," he mumbled meekly and bolted from the room.

"Wow! That was a little harsh. Even I feel sorry for the guy," Cleo added with a snotty glare directed at Morgan.

"Come now, let's all just eat," the King encouraged.

After breakfast, as they all filed out of the room, Morgan stayed back and waited until King Nariedon was the only one remaining in the room.

He eyed her curiously then came over and patted her on the back gently. "I'm glad to see you're feeling better and to hear you now consider Lucas your partner. I know it is not easy for you, but it is necessary for all of your well-being."

"I need to know the truth about Lucas. He is different than the others. Why?" she asked, trying to be as direct and stern as she could muster.

The King eyed her and then nodded to himself as if he was giving himself permission to disclose the truth. "I should have known you would notice something different about him. He was chosen especially for you. He is an Utanican. They are very rare, and I do not think Atlantis has seen one in several thousand years."

"What's an Utanican?" she asked worriedly.

"He is the yin to your yang, my dear. He was conceived without special powers, yet with the most special of powers."

She looked at him confused. "I'm not good with riddles, King Nariedon," she growled, becoming very impatient with his devious answers.

"He absorbs. When there is too much power in a room he can naturally absorb and nullify it."

"Can he use the power he absorbs?" she asked.

"Some, I think, but not much. He will soon have the power to draw energy from half this city, but he would still have less power to wield than you do. His purpose is to rid us of too much power, not to create more. He's like an Atlantean surge protector. His job is to keep harmony and balance amongst those here that are the most powerful." The King turned, indicating that they should leave the room and head outside.

Morgan let everything he said sink in before she spoke again. "So, he's here to take my powers. To ensure I do not, and cannot, use them against Atlantis. That's it, isn't it?" she asked, feeling judged without jury.

"Yes, but not just you. I suspect he was born into this generation because this entire group of Council wields more power than I have ever seen," the King answered truthfully.

Morgan left King Nariedon on the castle steps as she headed for the lake. She felt betrayed by her own people. All they wanted was to harness and cage her! That's why they kept her and Lucas together on land and why they wanted to permanently connect them now. She was almost positive that if she merged with Lucas, she would permanently lose half, if not all of her powers. At one point that would have been the perfect solution, but not now. Her powers were hers for a reason and she wasn't ready to give them up just yet. She walked anxiously, searching for Lucas. She reached the lake's shoreline and did not see Lucas right away. It wasn't until she walked a little further that she seen a motionless body on the ground, partly hidden by large rocks that edged one side of the lake.

Panicked, Morgan ran to Lucas's body.

She knelt down over him, shaking with panic and almost blinded by the tears that streamed down her face. She shook his unresponsive body in fear. "Lucas! Lucas!"

He startled.

"Geez, Morgan! Are you trying to give me a freakin' heart attack?" he grumbled as he sat up and rubbed his eyes.

She looked at the silly boy in front of her with his blonde curls all tousled about. She grabbed him, giving him the biggest hug she could. "Oh my God, Lucas, I thought you were dead," she whimpered as she laid her head against his chest and tried to keep the waterworks from reappearing.

He stroked her back gently as he soothed her. "I'm fine; I was just having a nap. I was here all night. I'm glad to see you came looking for me, at least you still care. I should have waited to open my eyes, though," he said.

She looked at him curiously.

"Maybe I would have gotten mouth to mouth?" he grinned.

Morgan stood up and rolled her eyes. Their friendship had always been free from flirting and head games, and that was what was so great about it. She could tell those days were over.

She ignored his flirting and his ear-to-ear grin as she spoke. "Why did you stay here all night? I don't understand."

"Help me up and I'll show you," he said. He reached his hand out and she pulled him to his feet. He carefully led her hand-in-hand, past the growing piles of rock until they reached an opening in the stone wall.

Lucas picked up a pebble and threw it into the dark, well-hidden cave in front of them. The stone skipped three times then stopped with an unusual thud. "Watch this," he said and gave her hand a squeeze as he pulled her against him and away from the mouth of the cave. Morgan could feel Lucas's heart beating wildly as his chest pressed against her back. She turned her head to face him and his eyes shone with anticipation.

Morgan felt a low rumble as the ground shook beneath her. She tumbled backwards, further against Lucas as a gust of hot mist shot from the tunnel. Morgan jumped with surprise but Lucas wrapped his large, protective arms around her, holding her steadily against his chest. Seconds later, a primitive, angry looking Water-runner burst through the darkness of the cave.

Its long, jagged teeth were bared as it lunged towards them. Morgan didn't know whether to faint or scream but she did neither. Lucas held his hand out defensively in front of her. The Water-runner slowed but continued to move closer until its flesh was beneath Lucas's palm. He bravely stroked the Water-runner's neck. Morgan could see a shadow of light trailing Lucas's hand as it passed affectionately over the large beast's neck.

"This is Argon. My new friend," Lucas beamed, as he smoothly threw his leg over Argon's back and sat atop him triumphantly.

"Lucas, wait!" Morgan urged, but Lucas was already sitting easily atop the delinquent creatures back.

He reached out to Morgan. "Want a ride?" he asked.

"Isn't this the same bucking bronco that was throwing Atlanteans across the lake like wet towels, when we first got here? I think I'll just keep my feet right here on the nice, stable, ground," she replied.

"Come on, don't be such a chicken! Argon won't hurt you, I promise," he challenged.

"You'd better know what you're doing," she grumbled as she took his hand and he pulled her on behind him.

"Okay, now, hold on tight!" He barely got the words out before Argon's body bolted forward almost knocking her backwards to the ground. She wrapped her arms a little tighter around Lucas's waist as she let out a nervous laugh. Argon stealthily cut through the cool fresh water heading for the waterfall that covered the far wall of the lake. When they reached the flowing wall of water, Argon's head dove beneath it. Morgan braced herself as they lowered into the watery unknown. They were soon completely submerged and heading toward a glowing tunnel burrowed into the solid rock wall that surrounded Atlantis beneath the water's surface.

As they traveled through many rocky tunnels turning this way and that, Morgan was amazed that they did not struggle for air. They managed to breathe as normal as they glided smoothly through the long winding mazes of rock and water. Amazing vibrant multi-colored glowing plants lined the tunnel walls and provided a pale glowing light as they swayed in a dance of movements. With one final turn, Argon's massive body began to rise to the surface. Morgan was surprised to be back in the lake where they had started. She wiped the water from her eyes and tried to fix her sopping hair as best she could. Argon slid his bulky body to a halt atop the sandy shore. Lucas jumped off Argon then helped Morgan down gently.

"Thanks, that was amazing. I can't believe you can make him obey you like that," Morgan said.

Argon let out an angry huff in her direction.

"He wasn't obeying me. He's my friend. He doesn't like to be controlled, he likes to be understood," Lucas replied as he stroked Argon's side.

"Look at you Mr. Water-runner Whisperer," she laughed. "I'm so proud of you, Lucas," she beamed. "This is your power you know. The way you can connect with people, animals, amphibians or basically any living thing." She praised him as he shook his head in embarrassment and denial.

"I'm serious, Lucas! Look at the way you connected with Argon! He was a wild animal that no Atlantean could even approach, let alone ride, and you did it in one day. Anyway, thank you, I had fun." She headed for the grass feeling a little guilty about not sharing her knowledge of his actual powers, with him.

Lucas ran after her, stepping in front of her to intentionally block her way. "That was more than just fun, Morgan. Don't you see?" he asked as she looked at him in confusion.

"Argon is our ticket out of here. With his help, we can escape Atlantis through those tunnels!"

She pulled his head to hers and kissed him quickly on the cheek. "Oh, Lucas! You're a genius!" she raved.

"Yeah, I know," he gloated as he placed his hand in hers and led her back toward the castle.

"We should meet with Larrance later today and tell him the plan, but first I think I need a little shut eye." Lucas let out an overly-dramatic yawn.

Morgan rolled her eyes. "Yeah, I have to go to the seamstress and get fitted for my merging ceremony gown."

"Your wedding gown? Can I come?" he asked jokingly.

"I see that perked you up in a hurry." She laughed.

A giant smile spread across his eager face.

"The men are supposed to meet in the King's study. I think you should go and see what they have planned. If you are not too tired," she added.

"No, I'm not going to some stuffy meeting with the King. What does it matter? We won't be here after the merge. Who cares what his plans are?" he asserted. "I think coming with you and seeing you in a wedding gown would be much more amusing." Lucas childishly kicked at the path.

"Amusing for you, maybe," she said, growing short tempered with his teasing.

"Yeah, I always kinda' pictured you getting married in pants, possibly even sweats," he joked. "But I'm growing fond of this new Atlantean Goddess look you've got going on. You clean up pretty well," he eyed her, a little too slowly.

She felt awkward and miserable as she looked down at the slender ivory gown she was wearing. It was still damp and clinging to her body more than usual.

"When you're not sporting the drowned-rat look, that is," he teased as he lifted a chunk of her wet hair and then laughed as it made a slapping noise when it fell against her back.

She ignored his teasing. "We're sticking to the plan and doing everything they ask of us until we get our chance to escape. We cannot afford to stir up any suspicions."

"Okay fine, you win. See you this evening," he said as he leaned down and kissed her square on the lips.

She bolted backwards as if she had been slapped in the face as she put her hands to her lips and looked at him questioningly.

"What? You said we have to keep up appearances. We have to act like we're a happy couple right? To fool them?" he reasoned. He climbed the stairs to the castle with a nonchalant swagger.

"There's nobody around right now for us to fool," she said still holding her mouth.

"You never know. Better safe than sorry. Catch you later, sweetcakes!" he smiled and winked at her as he strode off into the castle.

She shook her head. "I think I've created a monster," she mumbled to herself and grudgingly headed to the seamstress shop.

Chapter 25

Morgan hadn't ventured very far behind the castle when she found what she guessed was Atlantis's Main Street. She admired the rows of quaint, colorful, neatly-kept storefronts. Each store was marked with a hanging, painted, wooden sign that displayed its name. There were no glass paned windows in Atlantis since bugs and weather were not an issue. There were just wooden shutters on each entrance and window, all open and awaiting business. Morgan was shocked by the hustle and bustle of the crowded streets. There were vendors for vegetables and fruit, pottery and paintings, even clothing stores that displayed many different versions of the same gown she was wearing, all in shades of white, of course.

She slipped into the clothing store for a quick look around. She spotted a young girl at the counter who jumped back seemingly startled by Morgan's presence. Morgan approached her slowly, trying not to spook the poor waif any further. She asked the girl if they had any pants for sale.

"You mean, for the gardeners?" she asked, confused by such an unusual request.

"Any pants would be fine," she suggested.

The girl quickly skittered across the store. She opened a drawer of an old wooden wardrobe that was sitting in the corner and pulled out a pile of neatly-folded white linen drawstring pants.

"Those are perfect! But, oh, I don't have any money," Morgan said now feeling quite foolish.

"We don't use money here; we work on a credit system. As we work toward the betterment of our city, we earn credits toward food and clothing and specialty items. You, however, are our future Queen, so credits are not an issue. Anything you desire in my store belongs to you," she said kindly.

"I am no Queen, but thank you for your kindness. Can you spare four pairs of large and two pairs of small?"

The girl nodded happily, then quickly bundled up the six pairs of pants and handed them to Morgan. Before Morgan left the store the girl directed her to the seamstress shop, which was only four doors down.

Morgan passed a quaint little diner and bakery where Atlanteans sat at small wrought iron tables, gossiping as they sipped steaming hot cups of coffee and tea. The atmosphere reminded her of her weekly trips to Starbucks with her friends back home and it made her miss them dearly. The smell of fresh baked bread reached her nostrils as it wafted out the open windows of the corner bakery. It was made her stomach rumble. She decided to pop in and admire the pastries. The baker recognized her instantly and doted on her like a true princess. He stuffed her with sample after sample of all his delicious baking and insisted she take a loaf of fresh sourdough bread wrapped in paper, before she headed out the door.

Try as she might, she couldn't put it off any longer. Morgan shuffled her hesitant feet in the direction of the seamstress shop.

Bolts of white and cream material were piled in each corner of the elegant Seamstress shop. There were colorful tapestries hanging on the walls and beautiful large gilded mirrors surrounding a pedestal in the center of the room. Soft emerald-colored couches lined the far side of the shop. Morgan spotted Tia sitting next to Alea and another small blonde girl. Alea smiled from ear-to-ear when she saw Morgan in the doorway and waved her over.

Morgan set her packages on the floor and sunk into the pillow-soft couch that was positioned across from the three girls. "Alea! Does this mean Donovan has chosen you? I knew he would choose you," Morgan said happily.

Alea looked uncomfortably at the girl beside her. "Not exactly, he has narrowed it down to the two of us," she gestured toward the frail girl sitting beside her. "This is Mintin."

"Oh, I'm sorry. I didn't realize there were still two of you. But that's good, right? That you have a little more time to get to know

Donovan before you have to commit to spending the rest of your life with him?" Morgan asked, feeling completely embarrassed by her earlier assumption.

"Don't be sorry. We are both honored that he would even consider us. Whoever is chosen will serve him to her best ability. To even be considered worthy of a Council member's affection is beyond words," Alea explained.

Morgan shook her head in disbelief at the old fashioned way of thinking, but she decided she would be better off keeping her opinion to herself. She was, however, happy that Alea was there with them despite the circumstances.

Morgan noticed that Tia's large doe eyes were glued to the floor and her small body was curled up against the arm of the sofa. "How are you doing, Tia?" she asked apprehensively.

The sweet girl raised her eyes and Morgan could feel the sadness radiating from them. "I'm fine," Tia said, "Thanks for asking. How are you? Did you find Lucas?"

"Yes, he... " Morgan was interrupted when Cleo burst into the room.

"Oh great, the 'Queen' has blessed us with her presence," Cleo chided, as she rolled her eyes in Morgan's direction.

She stood over the four of them wearing a glamorously sleek pink velvet floor-length gown with a diamond encrusted deep plunging neckline. The pink streaks in her hair matched her dress perfectly, and her silver hair shone elegantly against her glowing pale skin. Morgan would never admit it to anybody, of course, but at that moment Cleo was the most beautiful girl she had ever seen. On the outside.

"I know right? I look totally amazing!" Cleo gloated. "Larrance is one lucky man," she bragged as she brushed her hair away from her shoulders and admired her reflection in the large gilded mirror. She stepped on the podium in front of the mirror as the seamstress chased after her.

"You'd better stay still, Cleo, I wouldn't want the seamstress to stab you with a pin or something," Morgan chided as she stood up from the couch. "I'm going next door for a coffee." She refused to sit and watch another woman being fitted for a wedding dress intended for the man she loved. She knew they were escaping long before the merge, so the stupid dress didn't matter, but she couldn't take any more of Cleo's insinuations and crap.

The seamstress nodded for Morgan to go. The seamstress then turned her attention back to Cleo and was frantically trying to place pins in Cleo's dress as the self-loving diva turned back and forth admiring her own reflection.

"Wait up!" Tia shouted, as she joined Morgan outside the shop. "I needed to get out of there for a bit before I choked Cleo with my bare hands. She keeps going on and on about her and Larrance. Can't she see that he's not even interested in her? I don't even think he likes her as a person, let alone someone he would ever date. I don't know why she can't see it. It's obvious to everyone else that he's madly in love with you. They both are," Tia admitted as she walked past Morgan and into the coffee shop.

They grabbed their coffees. So many words ran through Morgan's head, as she tried to find the ones she'd wanted to say to Tia for so long now. "Tia, I...I'm sorry about Lucas and Ethan, and everything for that matter! I'm sure Ethan has moved on though, since he hasn't even talked to me since the merge was announced."

They sat at one of the little tables on the patio.

"He loves you more than I've ever seen a man love a woman, Morgan. He is hurting, badly," she confided.

Morgan said nothing. She wanted him to hurt because he had betrayed her and he deserved to hurt the way she was hurting.

"How is Lucas? He won't talk to me," Tia asked on a sadder note.

Morgan stretched her hand out and placed it on Tia's. When they touched she could see her aura and it glowed as blue as her sapphire eyes. "He's confused and needs a little space to figure things out. He's a good person, Tia, he just doesn't know how to deal with this impossibly difficult situation. These wounds will heal in time, they have to," Morgan consoled her.

"I just wish he would talk to me," Tia said sadly.

"He will. Just give him time," Morgan said optimistically.

"Well, I guess we should get back. Hopefully Cleo the Cow is done with her fitting," Tia said as she pushed her empty cup in front of her.

Morgan looked at her with surprise; she had never heard Tia talk badly about anyone before. She explained to Tia that "cow" was still much too nice of a euphemism to be used on Cleo.

"Come on, you are the last one to be fitted. I can't wait to see your gown, I bet it's amazing," Tia said with a genuine sweetness in her voice as she tugged at Morgan's arm.

Morgan rolled her eyes. "I hate dresses," she grumbled as they entered the seamstress shop.

Cleo was thankfully finished and was now in the changing room. The seamstress promptly pulled Morgan away from the entrance and shoved her into a vacant change room.

"Here, put this on and come out as Lady Morgan," she said as she bowed her head and handed Morgan a giant heap of purple velvet, silk, and chiffon.

Morgan took the dress and resisted the urge to complain. She knew the seamstress must have spent hours upon hours creating the ornate gown she held in her hands. Morgan figured that if she even let out a groan of displeasure over the dress she would be the one getting stabbed with a pin.

She pulled the gown gently over her head. It ran down her body with soft silky smoothness and hugged her breasts and hips, perfectly. It flowed away below the hips and rippled gracefully around her feet. The deep purple color of the fabric made her hair shine in contrast like spun gold, and her cheeks glowed in just the right shades of pink. The bodice of the dress was low cut enough that the trident burn showed. She lifted the necklace out from beneath the material and let it dangle over her chest.

She opened the door of the changing room and headed for the fitting pedestal. She heard the girls gasp as she entered the room. She looked to see if she had missed a button or something.

"What?" she asked worriedly.

"You look like royalty! You look stunning, flawless!" Tia exclaimed as the other two girls just sat with their mouths open in awe. Cleo, of course, had already left.

"Yeah, right," Morgan argued. "Flawless is the last word a person would use to describe me."

As much as Morgan protested, she did feel pretty when she looked at herself in the long mirror. She imagined herself walking up the aisle in the heavenly, custom-made dress with the chiffon train trailing delicately behind her. She pictured Larrance at the end of the aisle waiting for her, his eyes shining happily as she approached. Then she pictured Ethan and Lucas standing confused and dejected in the corner. She shook her head to clear the image from her mind.

"I thought everyone wore white here," she asked the portly seamstress woman, who worked with quick precision on the train of her dress.

"The Council is always married in their royal color. You're family color is purple. Purple has always been the highest sign of royalty," she answered as she turned and tugged Morgan's body to comply with her wishes.

"I don't like dresses," she confided, regretting saying the words as soon as they left her mouth. The seamstress pulled to a stop. "But this is definitely the most beautiful dress I have ever seen. Thank you," she said honestly, trying to smooth things over.

The seamstress nodded, satisfied, and finished presenting the train.

The four girls headed back to the castle that evening after grabbing supper in the courtyard. The mood was light as they giggled and joked like the teenagers they were supposed to be. Alea did her best "Cleo in the mirror" impression as Tia pretended to be the seamstress pinning the swirling diva.

Morgan laughed loudly and was extremely thankful for the lighthearted banter. She couldn't remember the last time she had laughed. She missed her girlfriends back home so much.

The girls spent the evening telling stories in the Great Room of the castle. The fireplace welcomed them as it burned brightly with a soothing white light. They curled up on the large couches in front of the fire and picked at plates of fresh fruit while they talked.

When the boys were finally freed from the King's planning session, they looked tired and worn. They joined the girls, sitting comfortably on the floor in front of them. The boys were so completely drained of energy that none of them said a word; they just sat there quietly.

Morgan decided to break the silence and lighten the mood by telling the group about her and Lucas's first rollerblading experience down the Santa Monica Boulevard. She told them how Lucas decided to pick up speed once he'd got the hang of the blades. He immediately lost his balance and crashed into her, sending her careening into a hotdog vendor and his cart. She knocked the whole thing over, and the middle-aged hotdog vendor was furious! He chased after the two wobbly skating teens for three blocks, chucking ruined hot dog buns at them until they finally managed to duck down an alley and get away.

Lucas laughed at her recollections until tears streaked down his face. Morgan noticed Larrance and Ethan both had warm smiles on their faces and it warmed her heart. Tia carried on the momentum by sharing one of her own embarrassing childhood stories. Morgan could tell that the boys were thankful for the light and happy evening.

They all sat up until the small hours of the morning, none of them wanting to leave the comfort and warmth of the simple friendly conversation. Even Cleo snuck in and sat quietly beside Donovan.

When the morning light began to appear through the castle windows, Morgan stood up. She was exhausted and ready for bed. The others followed her lead. She looked around at all of her new friends sadly. She would truly miss them when she left this place.

She crawled into her large welcoming bed and let sleep overtake her.

****

She ran through the city hand-in-hand with Larrance, clad in her purple gown. He pulled her faster as the walls around them crumbled. She frantically jumped right and left, dodging the pieces of crystal that rattled free from the ceiling and shattered at their feet. She heard screams echoing across the dome as Atlanteans ran desperately for shelter. Larrance pulled her to the altar of the temple. Everyone was gathering there as the world crumbled around them. They lowered their bodies in a bow to her as she stood in the center of the gathering crowd. "Help us please!" they begged. The crystal dome echoed with a powerful crack, and water began to run from the ceiling.

Morgan shot up in bed, screaming. Sweat covered her trembling body. She tried to slow her rampant heartbeat as she took long, deep breaths. She heard a soft knock at her door.

"Come in," she said, thinking Alea must have heard her screams.

It was Ethan. He came rushing to her. "Are you okay?" he asked with worry as he gently swept the hair from her face and tucked it behind her ears. "You're soaked," he said, looking at her gown.

She was damp with sweat, and so chilled, her teeth began to chatter. He pulled her blanket back up around her body and then rubbed her arms and shoulders briskly.

"You're ice cold. I'll light your fireplace," he said tenderly and headed across her room.

The stones in her fireplace were soon glowing with a warm blue light and she felt her body calm as she began to warm up.

"What are you doing here?" she asked as she came across the room and joined him in front of the fire, still bundled with blankets.

"I thought we should talk," he said and moved to sit across from her.

"I have nothing to say to you, Ethan. Not anymore," she said, trying as hard as she could to seem indifferent.

Ethan nodded. "I don't blame you for being angry with me. After all, I knew I was supposed to partner with Tia, but what you don't understand is this—I knew I was *supposed to* merge with her, but I didn't think I would *have to* merge with her. I thought that once we got back here I would approach the Council and tell them that I love you. That I want to be with you. That I am meant to be with you, and I knew that if the Council had a chance to hear my pleas they would allow us to be together. I thought that even if I couldn't get them to agree right away I would have a hundred years or so before the merge to persuade them. Please understand that I was positive that by the time we were ready to take our seats on the Council we would be merged to one another. You have always been the only girl for me, Morgan. It has been you since I first heard stories of you as a child. I couldn't have foreseen how wrong things would go. You can't blame me for the kidnapping of the Council, or the quick and necessary merges, or for the Trident! I know you want to blame somebody for all your sufferings, but please don't let it be me."

She looked at the exhaustion in his eyes, his unkempt hair and wrinkled clothes, and saw for the first time the toll this was taking on him.

"How could you let Lucas fall in love with Tia if you knew they were brother and sister? Do you know how wrong that is?" she shot at him, trying to stay mad at the broken boy in front of her.

"I didn't know they were brother and sister any more than I knew that I had a brother! Do you think I'm that twisted?" he asked.

"You gave me your pendant and made sure we were bonded for life without ever mentioning the merges. You let me fall in love with you when you knew there was a chance that we would be merged to other people. I don't know how I feel about you anymore Ethan. I don't even know who you are; I never did though, did I?"

"You've seen inside my very soul. How can you say you don't know me? You're the only one in the world who has ever really known me," he argued sadly.

"I think you should leave. I don't think Tia would approve of her merge partner spending time in my bedroom," she asserted as she stood.

He grabbed her by the shoulders, his lips mere inches from hers. "Please don't push me away Morgan. I can't fathom a life without you in it," he murmured softly against her earlobe. He slowly dropped his hands from her shoulders letting them glide lightly down her arms.

Morgan bit back tears. She needed to be strong.

"I can live a lifetime on the mere memories of kissing you. On the perfect memory of the sweet taste of your lips," he confided as he rubbed his cheek longingly against hers. "But I could never live if I thought you really truly hated me or blamed me. Do you Morgan? Please tell me the truth. Do you really, truly, hate me? Tell me you do and I will never bother you again. Tell me you blame me for everything. Tell me you despise me. Tell Me!" he growled, grabbing her wrists and holding her roughly against him.

She said nothing. Instead, she gathered her energy and sent it out around him. She needed to feel the gentleness of his soul one last time before she left him and Atlantis behind forever. She wanted to hate him for putting duty first, for choosing to merge with Tia because his father commanded it instead of fighting for their relationship. For telling her that they were meant to be together when he knew the Council would never allow it, and for always choosing the betterment of Atlantis over her. But she didn't hate him. She wasn't even sure if she was capable of hating him since, like it or not, the Trident connected them, forever.

She felt his tensed, rejected body soften beneath her energy as it grew around him. Soon his own energy rushed from his body to meet hers and the joined auras spun around them in coils of color. She pulled at the soft white light inside of him and felt his soul before her. She met it with her own as the two ribbons swirled between them. Sparks shot through her entire body as she bathed in the light of their deep connection. She looked at him and saw tears streaking down his perfect face. She leaned forward and kissed the salty droplets from his cheeks. He wrapped his muscular arms around her and pulled her desperately against his chest. The swirl of energy suddenly fell away and they were left standing there alone and raw with emotion.

Morgan's instincts told her that she should pull away but her body refused. She snuggled herself deeply against his chest.

"I want to hate you; I want to forget I ever met you. Every time I see you with Tia it's like having my heart ripped from my chest over and over again. I don't know how much longer I can do this, Ethan. My wounds can't heal when they keep getting re-opened. Like it or not, you are with Tia now and I need space and time to get over you."

"This is not what I want. I want you, not her. You hold my heart along with my soul. Nothing can or will, ever change that. I may be forced to merge with her, but I will never touch her, I can promise you that. It will always only be you and me. Even if it is only in my heart and mind," he confessed as he laid his cheek tenderly against the top of her head.

Morgan pulled away feeling sorry for her new friend Tia, the sweet young girl about to enter into a loveless relationship. "You cannot be cruel to Tia, she's a good person and this is not her fault either," she said.

"I know, but I'll never fully merge with Tia. You must know that. How can I when you and I have already joined souls? I'll always be a part of you, and in my mind, I will always belong to you, Morgan, even when I'm forced to stand beside another woman. I'm yours. I need you to know that. We may not be allowed to be together right now but, my heart, my soul; they're yours—now and forever."

He stared longingly into her eyes. "When we met with the King today, he said that after the merge ceremony, when we are at full strength, we'll attack the Triton and retrieve the old Council. When we return with the Council, I plan to overturn the laws of marriage. Even though we will be merged, I'm going to demand that we still be given the choice to marry whomever we wish. I'm going to tell them how I feel about you and that we have shared our souls. I'm going to show them that we're destined to be together despite the merge. Do you understand what I'm saying?" he asked.

She did not gesture either way but waited for the words to fall from his lips.

"There's still hope. I'm not giving up on us. Not ever," he declared.

"Even if they grant marriage outside our merge partners, your father said the Trident is forbidden to be together. That it would destroy Atlantis," she said in a whisper.

"We will find a way my love," he whispered as he tenderly stroked her hair. "We have to."

***

That night Morgan dreamt of Lucas and the merge. He was standing at the altar and she was at the back of the aisle dressed in her purple gown. When the priest called Lucas's partner forward, Morgan began to take a step when another girl stepped out in front of her toward Lucas. Morgan looked carefully at the blonde hair of the girl but wasn't able to tell who it was. The girl wore a dark green gown that flowed perfectly against her petite frame. Morgan waited patiently for Lucas to lift the girl's chiffon veil. He reached out to lift the veil and Morgan could see pure and true happiness beam across his smiling face.

Morgan woke completely frustrated by the inconvenient end to her dream. She wanted to know who the girl in green was. She lay there a while longer trying to retrieve the dream and continue on with it, but it was no use. She hauled herself out of bed and began to get ready for another grueling day with drill sergeant Lenora.

Morgan spent the day learning about the indigenous plants and fish of Atlantis. They examined dinner-plate sized butterflies with brilliant colored wings of blue and yellow. They also studied pudgy caterpillars, much like the ones in the volcano, but they glowed in a rainbow of different colors. The plants they learned about were all large, lush and almost luminescent in color. Morgan imagined they would look at home in a sci-fi rainforest. The many fish they studied were all stunningly beautiful as they swam leisurely along the numerous streams that encircled the city. Morgan's favorites were the Corplat fish. They were a deep crimson red with purple stripes and long blue fins, and when she dipped her fingers into the water they would swim up and nudge her with their little fish noses.

"Atlanteans are the only warm-blooded creatures down here I'm afraid," Lenora explained.

"Well, besides the Water-runners, and Ivan the blacksmith's, Labrador retriever. Don't even bother asking me how he managed to get that mangy thing down here," she said. She led the girls back to the community kitchen. Morgan noticed Lenora's face tighten more than usual when she mentioned the Blacksmith's name, she wondered if the poor man had crossed the wrong path with this obviously scorned woman.

"Here we will learn the power of herbs. We will learn about herbs from the land, which you are probably familiar with, and then we will learn about the herbs you will only find here in Atlantis." Lenora opened the door to the large greenhouse building, revealing a jungle of lush herbs. In the middle of the room full of mysterious plants sat a table with beakers and mortar and pestle sets.

"You mean, we're going to learn how to make potions?" Cleo asked.

"I suppose you could say that. Today we will learn how to make a sleeping potion and a truth serum."

"I didn't think those things were actually possible," Tia added.

"When you live as long as we do, my dear, anything is possible," Lenora replied as she stood eagerly in front of the mixing table like a mad scientist.

"Finally, something interesting!" Cleo babbled.

"Here, put these on," Lenora said as she handed each girl a goofy-looking pair of safety glasses.

They worked all day perfecting their potions, and when they got them right, Lenora made them dump their awesome concoctions down the sink! She even checked their pockets before they left the building to make sure they didn't take anything out of the greenhouse. When they left, she locked the greenhouse door behind her.

"Just when I thought we were going to do something worthwhile," Cleo complained. "What good is knowing how to make potions if we aren't allowed to have them? We don't even have access to the herbs we need to make them. This sucks. It's just a bunch of useless information." She stomped off.

Tia stood beside Morgan and inconspicuously nudged her as she lifted her hand slightly out of her pocket revealing the tops of two full potion bottles she had smuggled out of the greenhouse. She winked before she walked away innocently.

Morgan laughed to herself. No one would ever suspect that quiet little Tia would completely disobey or steal anything. She was the perfect outlaw. Morgan felt a new respect for the blonde little wolf in sheep's clothing and she decided to keep a closer eye on her new friend from now on.

***

The next day, Lenora ordered the group to meet by the lake for class. The boys huddled together and skipped stones across the lake's still surface while the girls lazily stretched out on the sandy shore.

"Okay everyone, pay attention," Lenora commanded as she approached them, disturbing their leisurely morning. She stopped at the water's edge and extended her right hand. She moved her fingers slowly and the group watched in awe as small streams of water danced along the top of the lake.

"Some Atlanteans have the ability to control water. We call it 'water dancing.' It's a very hard skill to learn and takes years of practice. Ethan has been my prized pupil at this over the years. He has more natural ability at water dancing than I have ever seen. Ethan will you show the class how it is done please?" she asked. She closed her hand, lowered her arm and the water streams she'd created dropped instantly. The lake was placid once again.

Ethan stepped forward and stretched his hand out with the same ease and confidence as Lenora had just demonstrated. Morgan watched as water began to swirl and dance atop the lake's surface. Ethan steadily danced the spiraling streams inwards until they were on the shore dancing around all of them. The group ran their fingers against the wet spiraling tendrils in amazement until Ethan let the water drop to the ground.

"Thank you, Ethan," Lenora said. "Okay, you will each attempt it now. Don't be too disappointed if you don't get it right away. As I said earlier, water dancing takes years to master. You must see the water's inner energy. Focus on every tiny droplet of that makes up this body of water. Each minuscule droplet is a tiny source of energy that is yours to communicate with and control."

Morgan went next. She reached out her hand and closed her eyes, trying to picture the energy within the water as she attempted to pull it toward her hand. She opened her eyes and found what looked like a glowing energy orb in her palm. This orb was made up completely of water. It swirled slowly in front of her as it rose an inch or so above her hand.

"That is very good, Morgan. Now I want you to send that ball of water to the back wall. Aim at that purple flower on the rock ledge," Lenora instructed.

Morgan focused on the flower and pictured the ball of water hitting it. The orb flew from her hand and hit her target perfectly. She stepped back, satisfied with her success.

Larrance stepped forward now eager to try.

"Triton people do not possess these powers," Lenora snarled disapprovingly.

"Larrance is Atlantean!" Morgan shouted angrily at the prejudiced teacher.

Larrance ignored the commotion and stretched his arms out toward the water. His fins shot from his arms and the group gasped. Morgan noticed his feet moving awkwardly then watched as his toes spread to reveal a thin skin webbing between each toe.

"Larrance, your feet!" Morgan blurted in shock.

Larrance looked down, leaving his arms still fully stretched out. "Holy crap!" he exclaimed, staring at his mutated feet.

"Young man!" Lenora scolded.

Larrance paid her no attention. "Great! Perfect! Now I look like a friggin' frog!" he complained to Morgan. He wiggled and lifted his webbed toes as he studied them in despair.

"Young man," Lenora yelled again.

"It's not that bad, hardly even noticeable." Morgan lied.

"Yeah, right," he sulked.

"YOUNG MAN!" Lenora fumed.

"WHATTT!" Larrance yelled, finally acknowledging the annoying voice behind him.

"Put...down...the lake...RIGHT NOW!" she growled.

Morgan and Larrance both turned to where the lake had been. The entire body of water was arched upwards revealing a dry lake bottom in front of them. The fish were oblivious to all the commotion and were calmly swimming back and forth overhead in the flowing glass-like arch that stood before them.

Lucas stepped forward, onto the lake's dry, sandy floor and raised his hands to the giant roof of water that rippled over his head. "This is amazing," he said and swirled his hand along the water ceiling.

"Holy crap!" Larrance and Morgan said in unison.

"Now! Triton! Put it down NOW!" Lenora shouted.

Larrance released his control and the water slammed down with a giant sloshing.

Lucas was standing in front of them, now knee deep in water and sopping wet from head to toe. He grumbled as everyone laughed at his soggy body. "Really? You couldn't say, 'hey Lucas get back to shore'? You couldn't have given me a little heads up before you dumped a lake on me?" he whined as he wrung the water from his tunic.

"Where's the fun in that?" Larrance taunted him.

"Come with me young man," Lenora ordered as she yanked Larrance by the shoulder. "King Nariedon's office. NOW!" she commanded. Her angry face was an unnatural shade of red.

Larrance shrugged his shoulders and followed behind her like a problem child heading for a routine trip to the principal's office, still completely unaffected by the teacher's furious demeanor.

Morgan and the rest of the group followed too. Morgan watched Larrance's fins retract into his arms and his feet change back to normal as he walked dutifully toward the castle.

Larrance and the group sat on the floor against the walls of the King's study quietly as they listened to Lenora's furious ranting.

"I refuse to waste my time teaching some insolent Triton! I refuse to show him our powers and abilities so that he can turn around and use them against us! The Tritons are evil, unholy beasts!" Lenora fumed.

"That is enough, Lenora! You will not talk about my son that way," the King roared.

Morgan was sure she could hear the shock of the King's words physically hitting Lenora from out in the hall.

"Your son? But he's a Triton. How?…Who?" Lenora stammered.

"He is Ethan's twin brother. He is not a Triton; he is something new and something special," the King explained.

"How is this possible? He looks exactly like one of them?" she asked as the group all moved in closer to the door to listen.

"I don't know, Lenora, he was born Triton without a drop of Triton blood in his lineage. It is, as it is meant to be. He is my son and he is part of the Trident, and you will treat him with the respect and love a future King of Atlantis deserves," the King yelled angrily.

"The Trident? It has returned?"

"Yes. Ashmana's daughter, Morgan, Ethan and Larrance, they all bear the marks," he said in a calmer voice.

"This is serious, your majesty, this could mark the end for all Atlanteans. We have to tell the others," she stated.

"No. We will wait until the Council is rescued from the Tritons and they will decide what is to be done about the Trident," Nariedon argued.

"*If* the Council is rescued," Lenora snorted.

"You are forbidden to speak a word of any of this to anybody," the King threatened.

Lenora stomped from the room not even glancing at the pile of teenagers pressed against the wall eavesdropping.

"Let's get out of here before the King comes out," Donovan whispered, yanking at Larrance.

They all got up and ran from the castle like naughty school children. Nobody spoke about the conversation they had just heard.

They returned to the lake. Donovan and Lucas ran into the clear water deliberately splashing the rest of the group. Cleo and Tia accepted the obvious challenge and ran after the boys spraying them with water, too. Ethan turned to Morgan as she sat on the shore with Larrance. Ethan nodded at her in understanding, and joined the rest of the group as he splashed them repeatedly with large conjured-up waves of water. Tia created a protective dome around herself and Cleo as the water spilled away leaving them dry underneath.

"No fair!" the boys all teased.

Morgan watched Larrance. His face was blank, completely vacant of emotion. He had not spoken a word since Lenora dragged him to the castle. She reached down and took his hand in hers. He did not respond in any way. He just kept looking straight ahead; he looked so distant that a chill shot up Morgan's spine.

"Talk to me, Larrance," she whispered.

He said nothing.

"Please don't shut me out. I don't care if you are a Triton or Atlantean or human, I love you," she said pleadingly. Still no response.

"Lucas has a plan, Larrance. He's going to get us out of here. We can go home and none of this crap will even matter anymore," she reasoned.

"I can't go home," he said quietly, breaking his silence but still staring straight ahead.

"What do you mean? I thought that's what you wanted?" she asked.

"I said, I wanted to get out of 'here.' I didn't say anything about wanting to go home. I have no home. I never have. While you all were enjoying your new adoptive parents and new homes I was in an orphanage waiting to be doled out to the first interested prospect. I spent my childhood being tossed from foster home to foster home. Nobody's wanted me my entire life. I have no place to go." Larrance's normally unaffected demeanor was betrayed by the signs of emotional torture that now invaded his face. He refused to look at Morgan as he continued.

"When that thing snatched me from the water, I was on the run from child services. I had finally found a way out. I had a place of my own and real job at a mechanic's shop. I was going to be eighteen soon and I was finally on my way to having a normal life. But now all of my work was for nothing. My job will be gone already and soon my apartment. I am back at square one. The things I have spent so long to accomplish were destroyed when that thing kidnapped me and brought me here. I would be returning to nothing and no one. You and Lucas should go without me. I don't want to drag you down into all of my drama. You truly are a goddess, Morgan, and you deserve better. I'm just an orphan, a delinquent and a fish-toed freak." He jerked to his feet and abruptly walked away.

The rest of the group was still carrying on in the lake. When they noticed Larrance storm off, they fell silent. All eyes turned to Morgan. Ethan moved toward her wanting to come to her aid. She shook her head at him and then chased after Larrance. She tried to catching Larrance but he was too fast. She couldn't see him anywhere. She went to his rocky hiding spot but it was empty.

She felt so bad for him. She had just assumed that Larrance had grown up the same as the rest of them. Boy was she wrong and now he was hurting so badly, she could feel it in her own soul. She searched the city streets until her feet ached. She was exhausted and starving, but she did not stop. Her heart hurt just thinking of the emotional pain Larrance was in.

She peered around the wall of the café and her heart jumped as she caught a glimpse of him darting behind a building.

"Larrance, stop!" She was chasing him down an alley when she heard a loud siren echoing through the city. She felt Larrance rush up behind her. He placed his hand on the back of her arm and steered her forward.

"Come on," he said.

"What is that? A siren?" she asked.

"I don't know, I'm taking you to the safety of the castle until I find out," he spoke without even glimpsing in her direction. Morgan obeyed, marching forward.

"Larrance, I'm so sorry about your rotten childhood. I had no idea, but you're not alone anymore. You have me and the rest of the group."

"Hurry up!" he scolded, yanking at her arm, pretending as if she hadn't spoken.

They reached the steps of the castle where a large crowd had gathered. They pushed through the circle of onlookers until they came upon a small woman, broken and bloodied, cradled in the arms of the King. He sobbed as he rubbed his cheek against her perfect, lifeless face.

The doors to the castle burst open and Ethan jolted through, breathless and crazy-eyed. He ran to his father's side. "Tell me it's not her Father! Tell me it's not her! You promised this wouldn't happen!" he yelled.

He fell to his knees beside his father and began gently assessing the poor woman's many wounds.

"Mother, it's Ethan, I need you to hold on! Please hold on. You can fight this!" Ethan sobbed and the crowd of Atlanteans sobbed with him.

The woman moved her head slightly, showing she was still alive. Her lips moved and her throat gurgled with blood as she tried to speak. She opened her eyes and turned her head from Ethan and the King to look weakly through the crowd. "Is he here?" she beseeched them painfully.

The King looked directly at Larrance. "Yes, Love, he's here and he's a magnificent and powerful young man, you will be proud." the King answered softly.

Morgan pushed Larrance closer to his father's side even though she could feel his immense apprehension. The King reached out to Larrance and pulled him downwards until he was kneeling alongside the suffering woman.

"This is Larrance, Love. Your son," The King attempted to smile through his worried tears.

The woman's bloodied arm rose to touch Larrance's face. Morgan watched Larrance freeze in fear as his eyes widened like a cornered animal.

"You are as magnificent as I knew you would be. You are so special, my dear son, you will change the world," she whispered through her pain. "But I see such sadness in you, Larrance. I'm so sorry for that. Don't ever think that I didn't love you. Not a minute in a day went by that I did not think of you." Tears streaked down her dirt and blood covered face.

"I'm so happy you're home and that I had this chance to see you one last time. I...love...you, my son." The words fell weakly from her lips as she released her final breath.

The short, gray-haired man, wearing a white coat that had been hovering over them, grabbed the Queen's delicate wrist. Morgan guessed that he was a doctor.

"I'm sorry your majesty. She's gone," he announced.

The King roared with a heartache that echoed across the entire city. Ethan's face streamed with tears as his body crumpled inwards.

Ethan looked in Morgan's direction and his face was twisted and crazed with sorrow.

"You can save her Morgan! You have the power! You have to save her!" he demanded.

Morgan looked at the glimpse of hope in his face and it crushed her. She stepped forward clumsily. "I'm so sorry Ethan, but she's already gone. I don't think there's anything I can do for her. It's too late."

"You have the power to save her, Morgan. I know you do!" Ethan begged, staring up at her from his mother's side. Morgan couldn't refuse Ethan's desperate pleas. She kneeled beside Ethan and placed her hands on his Mother's blank, pale face.

"I'm not very experienced with my powers yet, but I'll try my best Ethan. For you" Morgan hoped for the best but to her regret, she felt nothing. Not a drop or even a glimmer of life remained inside the woman's body. Morgan pushed her energy further into the woman but still felt no response. She was about to pull her hands away when she sensed a small flicker in the woman's mind. Morgan grasped onto it instinctively and tried to pull it toward her.

The Trident will save the world. They will triumph...join...and rise above...the glory will be... Morgan heard the weak voice come reciting inside the woman's head but the small flicker of life quickly slipped away.

Morgan lifted her hands away and looked into Ethan's grief-stricken eyes. "I'm sorry, Ethan. I really tried but she's gone."

"NOOO!" Ethan yelled, yanking savagely at Morgan's hands and shoving them back onto the woman's cold body. "Try harder, Morgan! You have the power! Try harder!" he demanded.

Ethan was deliberately rough. His large merciless hands gripped her wrists so tightly her fingers were beginning to numb. Jolts of pain streamed up Morgan's arm as Ethan squeezed even harder. She let out a whimper.

Larrance jumped forward shoving Ethan away with one arm and pulling Morgan to him with the other. "That's enough. She already tried to help your mother, like you asked her to. Now leave her the hell alone!" He took a threatening stance between Ethan and her.

Ethan's eyes went to the purple, finger-shaped bruise marks beginning to form on Morgan's wrists. "I...I'm sorry," he stuttered blankly. His face was so clouded with torment and despair that it had become barely recognizable. He knelt down and lifted his mother's lifeless body from the ground, turning without a sound; he carried her toward the castle.

"The Trident will save the world. They will triumph, join and rise above, the glory will be..!" Morgan blurted out behind him.

Ethan froze but did not turn to face her.

"Those were the last words in her mind. The last thoughts I found in her!" Morgan shouted, taking a cautious step toward him. She desperately wanted to reach out to him.

He continued walking, not once turning back to look at her. His father joined his side and they quickly and sadly disappeared behind the castle doors.

Morgan turned to Larrance, but he had already disappeared into the crowd. She rubbed her sore wrists and looked at the castle's closed doors. She had wanted to save the mother of the two men she loved, more than she had ever wanted anything in her life, but it had just been too late.

She felt Lucas's friendly hand casually squeezing her shoulder. "Hey, you tried. You tried hard. Everyone could see that, there was nothing more you could've done to help her. Don't beat yourself up over this, none of it's your fault Morgan." he said and wiped at the tears she didn't even know were running down her cheeks.

"Don't cry sweetie. You know how much I hate seeing you cry. Ethan doesn't blame you, he's just a little crazy with grief right now. And Larrance, well I'm not sure why Larrance is being such a tool but he'll get over it too, I guarantee it." he comforted her.

Morgan looked into Lucas's warm friendly face and her heart melted. She stepped forward without speaking and wrapped her arms tightly around him. Lucas hugged her back in the same kind, gentle, supportive embrace he had held her in so many times throughout the years. She felt so safe in his arms that she finally let her shields down. The flood gates opened and she sobbed against his chest.

She felt like such a failure. She had the ability to save lives, yet she couldn't save someone as important as the mother of the two men she loved. How could either of them ever forgive her?

"It's not your fault. You didn't hurt her; you tried to save her. I'm sure they are grateful to you for at least trying, Morgan." Lucas soothed as he stroked her head.

Morgan wiped at her tears with the back of her sore, throbbing hands and pulled together enough strength to stand on her own once again.

"Come on, let's get you out of this crowd," Lucas suggested. He placed his arm protectively over her shoulder and led her into the castle. The rest of the group followed closely behind. They pushed through a swarm of armored soldiers that were quickly gathering at the castle's entrance.

Morgan wondered where this army of men had come from. She hadn't seen a single one of them in Atlantis before this moment. She decided that if Hercules had ever existed, these massive, muscle-bound men could easily be his children.

"Where did they find her?" Donovan asked the group curiously as they entered the den.

One of the soldiers stepped out of the stiff formation of marching men and slipped into the den's entranceway. He looked to be in his mid-thirties, but Morgan knew that looks were deceiving in Atlantis. He had shaggy golden blonde curls and a short sandy blonde beard, which was the first facial hair Morgan had noticed on a man in Atlantis since she'd arrived. He stepped closer to them and she could see an old scar that spread from his forehead down to his cheekbone. It was subtle, not scary, but it made him look the part of a hardened warrior.

"I'm sorry to interrupt. My names Ulysian. I'm with the Atlantean guard. I've been posted here for your protection," he announced.

The group snorted at the idea of a babysitter and turned away from him.

"We found her at the bottom of the Volcano," Ulysian blurted out to the group, trying to regain their attention. "The King's wife. We found her at the bottom of the Volcano," he said, drawing them all in as he sat on the couch in the middle of where the group was gathered. He spoke with a familiarity that Morgan couldn't quite put her finger on.

"When the Triton attacked last time, they came in through the Water-runner tunnels, so we have been guarding them night and day. We didn't even think the Triton knew about the volcano entrance, but apparently they do and they want to make sure that we know that they know about it. They're trying to get our attention. They want something from us pretty badly. Enough to break the peace between Triton and Atlantis, forever." Ulysian stated confidently.

"What do you think they want so badly?" Donovan asked.

"I think they want the Triton boy that is here in Atlantis," Ulysian confessed.

"Larrance?" Morgan felt her knees weaken.

"Yes, Larrance, the King's Triton son. We think that's what this has been about since the very beginning. We even think he's the reason you were all stolen seventeen years ago. It all boils down to him. I don't know why the King doesn't just hand him over. He doesn't belong here anyway," Ulysian said barbarically.

"He's one of us! The Council isn't complete without him!" Cleo yelled at the soldier.

"He's also part of the Trident. He bears the mark and possesses power. He's part of the most valued and legendary prophecy in Atlantis. Do you not think that makes him worthy of a place here? If you're planning on handing Larrance over to these beasts you better be prepared to send me too, because he and I are connected. You can tell *that* to whomever the 'we' you're referring to is." Morgan fumed. The soldier's mouth dropped open and his face paled, he knew he had overstepped his boundaries.

"I...I..." Ulysian bowed his head in Morgan's direction attempting an apology.

"You..you...are exactly *right*, my lost for words friend" Larrance interjected as he strut into the room with a cocky swagger, biting into the apple he held in his hand. He didn't look in Morgan's direction even once. "I don't belong here. I can feel that. I was not made to save the Atlanteans. I was made to save the Triton," he stated in a firm, unchallengeable tone.

His eyes flared with an emotion Morgan couldn't even identify.

"I need you to take me to them. Ulysian, is it?" Larrance asked. "Well, Ulysian, if I'm all they want, then I will go to them. I will agree to give myself over to them freely on the condition that they will let the rest of the Council go unharmed. You look like a smart man. I think you know it's the only way the rest of the Council will return to Atlantis alive," Larrance suggested and then arrogantly patted the man's armored chest and took another bite of his apple.

"No, Larrance! You can't do this! Don't do this! Please," Morgan felt her knees weaken at the thought of Larrance being handed over to the Triton monsters. She reached out to grab Larrance's hand but he pulled away from her hastily. Still not willing to look into her eyes, he kept his head down as he started toward the door.

"I don't think the King will go for it. You're his son and I just found out you're also part of the Trident. There's no way the King will release you," Ulysian argued as he stood. He turned to face Larrance ignoring Morgan completely.

"I'm going to the Triton with or without the help of the Atlantean guard. You know as well as I do that they are ready to attack at any moment. You come up with a better idea within the next 24 hours and I'll be happy to listen. If not, it was nice knowing ya' and thanks for nothing!" Larrance growled and disappeared through the doorway.

They were all left standing there looking at one another dumbfounded.

"That hothead is going to get himself killed! There's no way I'm sending my men out on his kamikaze mission," Ulysian grumbled. "We need the combined power of the entire Council to defeat the Triton. Without all of you, none of us stand a chance."

"He would never agree to any of us coming along," Lucas spoke.

"What if he didn't know?" Ulysian plotted. Morgan noticed how the warrior's face changed from looks of uncertainty to that of a man with a devious plan.

"We can't just let Larrance serve himself up to those monsters and sign his own death warrant. He's not a Triton. He's Atlantean. The Triton will see that as plainly as we do and they'll kill him!" Morgan pleaded, hoping to convince the others to follow along with Ulysian's sudden plan.

"We need to go with him. As a group we're already very strong. We can protect him and bring him back," Tia suggested.

"I agree," Lucas said, sending his sister a smile.

"You agree with Tia? I didn't think you knew she existed anymore," Cleo jabbed.

"Are you in or out?" Lucas snarled.

"Me? Pass up an opportunity to kick some butt? I was in way before you or your girlfriend, oh sorry, its 'sister' now right?" Cleo chided.

Lucas bolted across the room at Cleo, but Morgan stepped in front of him. "Just ignore her Lucas. She's just a mean-spirited bully. She's jealous that you and Tia are on the path to becoming friends again, and she doesn't have a single friend here!" Morgan said. Despite Morgan's efforts to intercede, Tia's cheeks were flushed red with embarrassment.

"Get out, Cleo! No one needs your kind of help!" Morgan screamed at the evil pink-streaked vixen in front of her.

Cleo stumbled backwards a little surprised by Morgan's brutal retaliation.

"GET...OUT...NOW!" Morgan screamed again.

Cleo took the hint and stomped out the door.

"Wow, you're even scarier than she is," Donovan chuckled as he patted Morgan on the back. "I'm in, too. In case anyone was wondering," he said. "I'll go check on Larrance and let you guys know when he's planning on leaving. I'll talk to Cleo, too. I know she can be a total bitch sometimes, well most of the time, but we need her," Donovan added and headed for the door.

"I'll make arrangements for some of my men to go with Larrance to the Triton City. Once they're out of sight, I'll lead the rest of you there. The King refuses to speak to anyone; he's so overcome with grief. So this decision falls on me. I knew your mother Ashmana quite well, Lady Morgan, and if you have even a fraction of the power she possessed I know we can come away from this situation victorious. I'll begin preparations immediately," Ulysian said, then gave a bow before exiting the room.

Chapter 26

The day dawned as bright blue sparkled across the crystal ceiling, but Morgan was grim-faced and tired. She'd tossed and turned all night. She had thought about asking Lucas to stay in her room like he used to, but she was worried about being that close to his golden aura. She was not sure how to deal with it yet, and she didn't want to be in any kind of weakened state for what was to come.

As she headed across the courtyard, she thought about the dream she had last night. She had dreamt about battling the Triton. There was no victorious ending for either side—only death and chaos in the blood-clouded waters.

She looked in fear at her new group of friends; they were gathered and peering at her anxiously from the shore of the lake. Each person was vital and needed to come but she was so afraid for them, she felt sick. She couldn't stand the idea of any of her new friends possibly getting hurt or even killed today. She didn't want them to go and she had a bad feeling about the war-like atmosphere she could feel slowly building around them.

Morgan noticed Larrance standing across the beach from the group. He stood with two dozen Atlantean Guard soldiers. The soldiers were rushing about, packing up weapons and armor as they prepared for battle. Morgan walked deliberately and directly in front of Larrance. He purposely busied himself with the side straps of his hard bronze Atlantean armor, trying not look at her.

"Look at me Larrance," she demanded.

He turned his head up toward her but kept his eyes to the ground.

She took a step forward and placed her hand under his chin. "Look at me," she whispered, and after another moment of hesitation, he did.

His eyes raged in a beautiful but dangerous looking storm of green and blue. Beneath the ocean that swirled on the surface of his eyes, Morgan was sure she could see sadness and worry breaking through.

"Please don't go, Larrance. Stay here, with me. This is where you belong. You're not a Triton, and you don't need to be ashamed of what you are," she pleaded.

"But, I am a Triton, Morgan. And you're right; I don't have to be ashamed of who I am any longer. I don't think I ever really felt bad about who I was. I think it was you who's made me ashamed of what I really am! But no more. I'm going where I belong and you need to go back to your little castle and leave me alone Princess." he snapped.

She felt his words hit her like a physical slap across the face. "Larrance, what's going on? This isn't you. How can you say that I'm ashamed of you? I love you! Why are you being like this?" she pleaded.

"This is who I've always been. Don't presume to know me, Morgan, because you don't," he answered defiantly.

She fought the tears that were beginning to build beneath her lids, not wanting to give him the pleasure of seeing her cry. "We are the Trident, and we're connected on the deepest spiritual levels, so how could I not know you? You can lie to yourself all you want, but I've seen your very soul and I do know you. Yes, maybe I didn't know about your terrible childhood and the torments you have endured in your life, but I know you even deeper than that. You belong here with me, and beside me, forever. You're not one of those evil, murderous creatures, and you're not an unwanted child somewhere in San Diego. You're a powerful Atlantean now, like me and with me....forever." She cupped his chin, demanding that he face her.

She could see the pain and doubt in his eyes and she felt a small bit of the wall he had put up begin to crumble. She sent her energy out and felt it swirl around him. She wanted to reach inside his mind to show him how much she loved him. She wanted to show him how much she needed him to stay with her, but his silvery white aura held firm around his body like an impenetrable shell.

"Stop it," he whispered futilely as she completely enveloped them in a glowing cocoon of energy.

"No one can hear us now, so tell me the truth. Why are you doing this?" she implored.

"I have to do this, Morgan; it's important. I know that you and the group are planning on following, but you need to promise me that you'll keep them here. I don't want anything bad to happen to them...or you. It's your duty as future Queen to protect them and keep them here where they are safe," he answered sternly.

"If you care about us so much, then why are you leaving us and joining a society that would like nothing more than to make our extinction real?" she demanded.

"It's the only way we can save the rest of the Council. They won't quit hurting people until I'm in their possession. I spoke to Lucas earlier, and he understands what is necessary to keep you safe. Stay by his side today. Promise me you'll do that?" He pulled her into his arms. Catching her pleasantly off-guard.

She felt their energies combine for a brief second and then he pulled away. He placed his hands firmly on her shoulders. The energy cocoon she had formed around them fell away and the group of soldiers all stopped what they were doing and stared at the vulnerable couple.

"There is nothing between us anymore Morgan, you need to move on. I can't be bothered by you anymore," Larrance snapped then walked past her coldly.

Morgan hoped he was putting on a show for the soldiers, but she wasn't sure anymore. She felt her body weaken and she involuntarily fell to her knees. What the hell was happening? Did he actually just break up with her? Was that possible? How could he just walk away when they were connected for life?

Once again, Lucas came to her aid, pulling her to her feet and leading her back to the group.

The soldiers began to dive one-by-one into the lake, and they all soon disappeared beneath the water's surface leaving Larrance to stand alone on the other side of the beach. He gave a quick nod to the group as fins burst from his forearms. He dove willfully into the calm water leaving his new group of friends behind forever.

"We have to follow him!" Donovan shouted as he dashed toward the water.

"Not yet!" Lucas shouted sternly as he gently lowered Morgan to the ground.

Lucas dug behind a pile of rocks at the corner of the shoreline.

"Here," He said tossing a pile of burlap bags onto the shore. A clanging pile of swords spewed out. "With any luck we won't need them, but I thought we should be prepared, just in case."

"What the hell are you planning on doing with those?" a voice echoed across the grassy bank above them.

"Oh God, Ethan!" Morgan gasped. Her heart sunk at the sound of his voice. She hadn't seen him since he carried his mother away yesterday. She knew he was mad at her for not saving his mother and now he would be furious at her for sneaking off to save Larrance. But Larrance's life was at stake so if that meant tying up and gagging Ethan to escape, and save Larrance she would do it. She would hate it, but she would do it.

"Going somewhere?" he asked dryly. "Despite everything, you and I are connected, Morgan. Did you think I wouldn't know something was going on here?"

Morgan handed her bag of gardener pants to Tia. It was her pathetic contribution to their escape. Lucas brings swords, she comes armed with pants.

"Here, you guys can put these on if you want. I thought it would be easier to ride the Water-runners in pants. I'll be right back," she said. She headed up the grassy hill to where Ethan stood over them.

"You're not going after Larrance." Ethan ordered.

"You knew about it? You knew your own brother was planning to trade his freedom and possibly his life for the Council and you did nothing to stop him? He came to you and told you his plans and you told him he should do it, didn't you? Didn't you?" she shouted.

"He wanted to, Morgan! It was his idea. He is one of them. He'll be fine. If he doesn't make this sacrifice, the rest of the Council will die, just like my mother," he added.

"He's not one of them! *He* is one of us! I don't just mean an Atlantean or the group either. I mean that he is one of the three of us, the Trident. And if anything happens to him Ethan, or if you try and stop me, I'll never forgive you," she threatened.

He reached for her hand but she pulled away from him quickly. He looked down and saw the purple finger-shaped bruises on her wrists.

"Oh god, I'm so sorry. I can't believe I did that to you. Please forgive me, I don't know what to say or think or do anymore. I've become the monster you once thought Larrance to be." He timidly tried reaching for her hand again and this time she let him take it. He held her palm against his chest with both of his hands.

"I know I should have argued with Larrance and stopped him, but I wanted him gone, I wanted him away from you. I know you two are still seeing each other despite the fact that our father forbids it, and I admire him for breaking the rules and I hate him for it, too. I can't break the rules the way he does; it's just not in me to disobey my King like that. And I can't help but feel like, well, if I can't be with you, then he shouldn't be either," he confided.

She stared into his face, watching his crystal blue eyes grow shiny from tears.

"I know I've turned into a horrible jealous monster, but I don't know how to stop. Just like I don't know how to stop loving you or how to stop thinking about you every second of every day. I don't hate my brother, Morgan. I'm not sure what I feel for him, but I know it isn't hate."

A large splashing sound echoed behind them. Morgan turned to see Ulysian and three Water-runners in the lake. She panicked as she turned back to Ethan. She could see the realization of their escape across his face.

"I won't stop you," he assured her and lightly ran his hand up her arm to rest on her shoulder. "I want to come with you. I need to come with you and help you save the Council and Larrance. Please say you'll allow me to come, Morgan. I know I've asked too much of you already, but please grant this favor."

Morgan could see the desperation in his face and she felt the honesty in his words, he wanted to make amends, how could she deny him that? She gave him a nod of acceptance.

She knew how hard it was for Ethan to go against his father's wishes, and King Nariedon would definitely be against their last-minute rescue attempt. But Ethan showed up, and for once she felt he was willing to put her before his duties to Atlantis. She wished she could enter his thoughts instead of only hearing them when he directed them to her, but she was desperate to save Larrance so she had no other choice than to trust that Ethan's intentions were good. She hoped the unruffled flow of his aura proved he was being sincere. She hadn't totally forgiven him for his past discretions, but if he was really there to help, this would definitely be the olive branch their relationship desperately needed.

They walked side-by-side toward the shore. The group looked stunned to see Ethan heading their way. Their expressions were like kids caught with their hands in the cookie jar.

"It's all right, he's not here to stop us. He's coming with us," she stated.

Ethan hopped on the back of Calopia, the Water-runner that brought them to Atlantis and he reached a hand out for Morgan.

Lucas stepped between them displaying a perfect, football-player block. "She rides with me," he said with a fierceness that surprised Morgan.

Ethan nodded, too vulnerable to argue. He turned his hand to Tia instead. She took it without hesitation and slid on behind him. Cleo and Donovan boarded another Water-runner. Donovan took the back and with a polite gesture left Cleo the driver's seat.

"Smart man," Lucas chuckled as he helped Morgan onto Argon's back.

"What about Ulysian?" she asked realizing they were short a Water-runner.

"Don't worry about me, Princess, I brought my own ride," Ulysian said. He whistled and seconds later a large dolphin popped its head up from the water. It eagerly nudged Ulysian's leg.

"Hmm, big masculine warriors riding dolphins. That's...umm..well, who knew?" Donovan mumbled fighting the urge to further harass the giant warrior's choice of ride.

Ulysian ignored Donovan's obvious mocking tone. "Everyone stay close behind us and we should all get there in one piece." He threw himself into the water, hoisted his massive body onto the dolphin's back, and took off with a splash.

"Hold on," Lucas yelled to Morgan as Argon bolted into pursuit of the dolphin.

They dove deep into the lake and were soon racing one after another through the maze of water-filled tunnels. They raced up and down through the rocky passages with the fast jarring movements of a gut-wrenching, underground amusement ride. Morgan's stomach was spinning as she clung to Lucas's waist urgently trying to keep her breakfast down. Just when she didn't think she could take anymore rollercoaster torture, they burst through the tunnels into open ocean waters. Argon's massive body burst above the water's surface. Morgan let out a sigh of relief.

She scanned the area as she drank in the warming sun on her wet skin. She looked gratefully at the blue, barely-clouded sky above her. She took a deep breath of fresh salted air and welcomed the light breeze that spread goose-bumps across her skin. She was surprised how much she had missed these small things and taken them for granted before Atlantis. The castle was beautiful, like a dream paradise, but nothing could replace the sky, the sun or fresh air.

"Are you okay?" Lucas asked, trying to turn himself to face her for a full assessment.

"I'm fine. That was quite a ride," she mumbled as the other Water-runners and riders surfaced behind them.

"I know, hey? That was wicked!" he chimed, patting Argon on the neck.

"Not quite how I would describe it, but it was definitely something." She groaned, still feeling her stomach churn. "Larrance said he talked to you about something? Did you know he was going to do this?" she asked quietly.

Lucas was silent as he led Argon out of listening distance of the rest of the group. "When we dive again and the group heads toward the Triton city, we can make our getaway. That's what Larrance came to talk to me about. He knew you would follow him and he asked me to talk you into using this opportunity to escape. That's what he wants us to do," Lucas answered quietly.

"Are you kidding me? We can't just ride off and abandon everyone!" she yelled smacking his back.

"Shhhh! Larrance did all of this for you. We have to go now or he did it all for nothing," Lucas argued.

"No, we are going stay and fight with our friends. We can't just turn and run, it would be like feeding them to the wolves! When we save Larrance and the Council, we'll have another chance to escape, and then, me, you, and Larrance will leave together! Just like we planned all along," she ordered.

"This is why he made me promise not to tell you," he groaned.

She smacked his back again.

"Oww, quit hitting!" he whined. "I agree with you, okay? I don't want to leave them like this either! Fine. We save everyone first, then we escape. Deal?" he bargained.

"Deal," she answered triumphantly.

"Stop smirking," Lucas grumbled, knowing her well enough that he didn't need to turn around to know the expression on her face.

"We'll be at the outskirts of Portugan, the Triton city in about an hour," Ulysian announced to the group. "The Water-runners should be able to get us to the Triton's main house undetected. From there we'll be on foot. Stay close and stay quiet," Ulysian plotted.

The Water-runners dove again, this time deep into the depths of the ocean. They traveled fast and mostly straight, which Morgan's tummy was thankful for.

Morgan spotted dim lights in the distance, and as they drew closer she gasped at the breathtaking beauty of Portugan. There were faintly lit domes in a rainbow of colors all around the ocean's base. She could see angelic-looking Triton children chasing each other through the water and playing in the distance. A coral reef wrapped around the outskirts of the city, and delicate-glowing sea plants grew alongside the sandy pathways that led from one dome to the other. The children, Morgan noticed, were not all dark haired like Larrance—some were blonde, some were redheads, and some were brunettes. They all had small iridescent fins poking out of their forearms and they swam with the grace and speed she had seen in Larrance.

Seeing the children play like human school children was unsettling for Morgan. She had expected to swim into a horrible sinister place full of death and Neanderthals, whereas Portugan was the exact opposite. It radiated a tranquil beauty.

They managed to reach the large iridescent dome in the city center, undetected. It was about the size of a football stadium. Ulysian jumped off his dolphin and onto the roof of the dome. When Argon stopped, Morgan and Lucas jumped off of his back and onto the dome. Once the rest of the group arrived, they headed for what looked like a submarine hatch. Ulysian cranked the stiff wheel with a lot of effort, he yanked and pulled for several minutes, making Morgan a little nervous, but the door finally released and opened to a small metal-walled room. They swam inside the little room and Ulysian shut the hatch behind them. It was pitch black and Morgan shuddered with panic until she felt Lucas's hand on hers. Ethan hit a switch and lights went on lining the floor of the underwater room. Ethan pulled a lever that was positioned next to the large steel door in front of him. When the lever went down, water began to drain out through the floor grates.

When the water was gone, Morgan spoke. "Thank goodness the castle is dry. I hate being in water all the time, it freaks me out."

Ulysian turned to look at her in disbelief. "But you're the future Queen of the Ocean!"

"Yeah, go figure," she said, shrugging her shoulders.

The group laughed but Ulysian shook his head in disbelief.

"Okay, quiet," Ethan ordered. He opened the steel door that led into the Triton castle.

Morgan kept hold of Lucas's hand, as they cautiously walked down the white marble hallway. Large wrought iron candelabras hung from the ceilings overhead and lit the halls with in flickering candlelight. Ulysian was busy sneaking in and out of several rooms along the lengthy hallway, rummaging his way around each of them until he returned triumphantly with an arm full of velvet cloaks. They each draped themselves in a cloak and pulled the large hoods up to cover their faces.

"I've studied the layout of this place from floor plans that we …" his wrinkled eyebrow revealed a bit of his wickedness as he searched for an appropriate word, "…attained. I think the main hall is just up ahead. Keep covered, keep quiet, and for God's sakes don't do anything without my say so. Got it?"

They nodded obediently and then followed Ulysian up a flight of stairs and onto a small veranda that looked out over a large Triton-filled ballroom. Morgan spotted a man who she couldn't help but assume was the Triton King, since he was sitting on a throne at the far end of the room. He looked large and fierce. He had long straight black hair and his deadened eyes glowed toxic green. His emotionless face was pulled and hard, like stone. There was chaotic crowd of commotion on the floor in front of him.

"Bring him closer," the vicious looking King bellowed. His deadly fins shone like jagged black onyx atop his forearms.

The room's audience of Tritons fell silent and most of them meekly backed away, cowering along the walls. Guards entered the far doors with Larrance. They forcibly pushed him ahead, throwing him to the carpet at the foot of the stairs leading to the King's throne.

Larrance lifted himself up, standing willfully straight, and turned to face the King without fear. Morgan was so scared for him she couldn't breathe. She had seen how slowly he had gotten up and she knew he must be hurt already. She fought the urge to speak to Larrance telepathically but she didn't want to distract him. She didn't want him worrying about her safety when it was his life she needed him to concentrate on saving. She struggled to keep the wall up in her mind knowing that Larrance would sense her presence as soon as she dropped the mental barrier.

"How nice of you to join us, boy. Larrance, is it?" the Triton King spoke in a smooth deep tone like a fox before pouncing his prey.

"We've been waiting for you, for a long time, son," the King continued, his voice commanding the room. He stepped toward Larrance.

"*I* am not your son," Larrance said coolly.

"Now, now. What I meant is, you're the son of the Triton people. You've come to us with a great destiny, Larrance. A Triton prophecy has been passed down through the ages. It tells of a Triton child being born in Atlantis. That child grows up to be a great warrior that brings Atlantis to its knees. Do you understand what I'm saying, boy? You're the Triton's chosen one, and with you in our midst, the Triton will finally regain our rightful place. The time has come for the Tritons to destroy every last one of those arrogant Atlantean assholes. Atlantis will no longer rule the seas and the time of the Triton will begin," the King preached.

"I'll never help you. You're a primitive monster!" Larrance spat. He struggled against the two soldiers who now had him in their grips.

"Silly boy. You've helped us already," the King smirked. He waved his hand at the guards on his right.

Morgan heard a rustling behind the long velvet curtains that hung beside her. In a matter of seconds, the hall they were standing in was swarming with sword-wielding Tritons. The crowd below was now looking up at Morgan and the group and gasping with shock.

"Aaah, right on cue. My fellow Triton, may I present to you---the future Council of Atlantis." The King pointed to the Atlantean teens. "So glad you could join our…festivities. Come on down here so we can talk. Face to face," the King crooned.

The guards shoved at the group, poking swords at their backs as they forced them down the stairs to stand alongside the wearied elder Council on the main floor.

"You see Larrance, we now have the entire Atlantean Council, young and old. Thanks to you we can wipe out their entire chain of royalty without even having to leave the comfort of our own home." The King laughed an evil chuckle that echoed ominously across the hall.

"You will not touch them!" Larrance lunged forward, but the King moved with lightning speed. He pulled a dagger from his cloak and held it hostilely to Larrance's chest.

"Or what, Larrance? Are you willing to give your life for those pretentious leviathans?" The King snarled, his rage so apparent it practically seeped from his skin.

Larrance stood firm, not flinching away from the jagged dagger that was cutting into his chest.

"Larrance! No!" Morgan shouted.

The King looked at her and his face paled. "Ashmana?" he whispered. To Morgan's relief, the Triton King finally pulled the knife away from Larrance's chest He studied Larrance in confusion, trying to piece the connection between him and Morgan. Larrance's torn shirt fell open and the Triton King spotted the symbol on Larrance's chest.

The King reached out in amazement and touched the trident-shaped scar. "The Trident? It can't be!" he shook his head as he took a step back from Larrance. He looked back and forth from Morgan to Larrance, his mind reeling from the shock of the resurrected Trident.

"The Trident was our creator and then our executioner. I will not let it hurt our people for a second time. You are not the prophecy I thought you were, boy." The King raised his dagger once again, and lunged towards Larrance.

"Nooo!!" Morgan screamed.

She felt her body shake and barely felt the ball of energy blast from her outreached hands. The blast flew through the air and startled everyone as it struck the King square in the chest, knocking him backwards.

She was too late. Morgan winced when she saw the King's dagger already buried deep into Larrance's shoulder, just inches away from his heart.

"Larrance!" she yelled.

The King lunged at Larrance again. Larrance swiftly yanked the dagger from his own body and drove it straight into the Triton King's heart.

"Kill them, kill them all!" the King commanded with his last breaths and then he fell hard against the throne stairs. The Triton soldiers formed a circle around the Atlanteans and pulled their swords readying themselves to attack. The Council, young and old, huddled tightly against each other in fear. All at once, a dome of webbed light came down over top of them. Tia had created a shield to protect them.

Morgan looked at her thankfully until she realized that Larrance was on the outside of the shield. "Tia! What about Larrance?" she asked frantically.

"I can't reach him!" she yelled over the roar of Tritons now attacking the shield.

"Let me out, Tia!" Morgan yelled.

"I can't let you out without letting them in!" Tia answered.

"Enough!" Larrance's voice boomed. It was so loud and commanding Morgan could of swore she felt it rumble the floor beneath them.

The Tritons stopped slashing at the protective dome and all attention turned to Larrance who was standing brazenly at the head of the throne.

"My fellow Tritons. I am Larrance, the first Triton son born in an underwater Atlantis. I possess the power of the Trident." He pulled his tattered shirt from his body completely, exposing the blood-stained Trident marks to the entire room. The Triton were motionless as they listened to the boy (who now looked entirely like a man), he commanded their attention at the throne.

"Your King has died by my hands. I am in charge now, unless there is someone here who wishes to challenge me?" he growled with a fierceness that made their bones tremble.

"As your new King you will obey my wishes. I want the Atlanteans released."

The Triton stood in silence; it seemed they were still trying to process all the events that had just passed.

"Now!" Larrance roared with king-like authority.

The Tritons stepped away from Tia's shield. She let it drop and fade away. Morgan stepped forward, about to run to Larrance, who was still bleeding from his shoulder where the King had stabbed him.

Ethan grabbed her arm, stopping her. "You have to stay here. They can't see you with him,. He can't appear vulnerable." he whispered.

She stopped and saw Larrance nod to her, confirming Ethan was right. She noticed the slight quiver of his hands and tremble in his legs. She felt the flurry of emotions in his head although he would not let her in. He had just killed a man and although he was hiding his anguish from the others quite well, Morgan knew better.

"You," Larrance bellowed, pointing at a young Triton soldier. "Remove the Atlanteans from my castle immediately! Then free the Atlantean guards that brought me here, they're being held in the dungeon."

"Yes, sir," the boy answered, and he proceeded to guide the group down the hall.

"Wait!" Larrance boomed behind them. "I will come along and make sure everything goes smoothly," he grumbled with a fake annoyance.

Morgan tried to walk slowly so that she would end up alongside Larrance but the cluster of people around her kept shoving her forward.

They soon reached the airlock where they had entered and Morgan looked desperately at Larrance. Their eyes locked and she wanted to cry out to him. She wanted to pull him into the room with them. She wanted to yell "Stop he's coming with us!" to the boy shutting the door to the room. She at least wanted a chance to say goodbye to the man she loved, but she knew any sort of commotion could compromise Larrance's new position with the Triton. She watched agonizingly as the door began to close and Larrance's face disappeared behind it.

"Wait!" she heard Larrance bellow from behind the door. "I need to speak to the Atlantean girl with the necklace. Bring her to me."

The door opened and the boy gestured for Morgan to come with him. She followed obediently. Larrance was standing by himself in the first room down the hall, waiting for her. It was a small room with a couple of chairs and a large window that had fish of every color swimming past, like a giant aquarium, though Morgan knew they were swimming outside on the coral reef.

"Shut the door behind you. I need to speak to her alone," Larrance commanded the Triton boy. She watched the boy open his mouth to object, but he changed his mind and obediently closed the door, leaving Morgan alone in the room with Larrance.

She ran to Larrance and immediately wiped the blood from his wound to examine it. She placed her hand atop the puncture point and the blood pooled against her fingers. "OH, Larrance! This wound is really bad," she gasped.

"I know," he whispered and placed his hands on top of hers. She sent her energy into him seeking out his wound to heal. She felt him wrap his arms around her waist and pull her into him.

"That's enough, Morgan, it'll heal now. I'll be fine. Thanks to you." He pulled her hand away and looked at the bright red scar where the hole had been.

"You need to conserve your energy for your trip back to California. Lucas will take you tonight," he instructed her.

She pulled back from him slightly and they locked eyes. "I won't leave you behind, Larrance. I can't. You have to come with us. Please," she begged.

"I have to stay here. It's the only way I can make sure everybody is safe."

"What about you? How do I know you're going to be safe?" she fought back.

"I'll be fine, and when things calm down I'll come find you. I promise Morgan. This is only temporary. Go home with Lucas. He'll keep you safe, and when the time is right I'll come for you." He stopped speaking and ran his hand across her cheek, tucking a small piece of hair behind her ear. "I love you, Princess Morgan. I've loved you since I first laid eyes on you, since the day I walked in your room and you screamed at me!" he flashed a smile. "And

I'll continue to love you until I take my last breath on this earth," he promised. He pulled her back into his embrace and laid a soft desperate kiss on her awaiting lips.

The door creaked open and they pulled apart quickly.

The soldier cleared his throat awkwardly as he stood in the doorway. "Sir, I mean um...your majesty, the Atlanteans need to leave now before the Triton soldiers have a change of heart. The Atlantean guard has been released from the dungeons and they're all waiting for the girl. They won't leave Portugan until she's with them."

"Yeah, take her, I'm finished interrogating her," he lied to the suspicious soldier.

He grabbed Morgan's hand and snuck one last touch between them, giving it a quick loving squeeze as she passed by.

She fought every urge in her body not to turn around and cling to him. She wanted nothing more than to hold him and never let go, no matter what. But she knew she couldn't risk the lives of the rest of the group or the elder Council. She couldn't be selfish even though she wanted it more than anything.

She followed the soldier and walked solemnly into the room with the hatch. She turned and stared sadly into Larrance's eyes until they sealed the door between them. Tears began to stream uncontrollably down her face as the cool water gathered around her ankles. The water rose up her body as the room de-pressurized.

She felt arms wrap around her sides and she turned to find Ethan locked around her.

"He did the most unselfish thing I've ever seen. He sacrificed everything for us. Don't worry love, once we get everyone back safely, we'll figure out a way to bring him home, too. You're right; he belongs with us," Ethan whispered.

She felt the floodgates release in her heart and all the tears she had been holding back came bursting forth. Her body was racked with emotion.

Ethan pulled her securely against him. "It will be okay, Morgan. Larrance isn't in any immediate danger. Everything will be okay." He soothed her as the water reached their necks.

She wrapped her arms around him and she took her last breath of air as the water covered their heads and reached the hatch. Ulysian opened the top hatch and they swam out one by one. The Atlantean Guards were outside the dome waiting dutifully alongside the Water-runners and Ulysian's dolphin. Morgan panicked when she saw the army of Atlanteans waiting for her. If the Atlantean Guard was traveling back with them, there would be no way she and Lucas could sneak off unnoticed.

I will take care of it, you and Lucas head west, while I distract them.

Morgan spun toward the voice she heard in her head and found herself facing Ethan in disbelief. *You know about our plan to return to land? You're not going to try and stop us?* she sent back to him.

I only want you to be happy Morgan, that's all I've ever wanted, and yes, I've known about your escape plans for quite some time. I just hoped that you would change your mind, but I see that your desire to leave is too strong to dissuade you. I now realize that this is something you have to do. You have to leave Atlantis to truly realize how much it is a part of you. . I can't make you stay in Atlantis even though it is where you belong. I can only hope that you'll realize how much you're needed in Atlantis and how much you need Atlantis, on your own. When you do, I'll be there waiting for you. Go now Morgan, nobody will stop you, I'll make sure of that.

She stared at Ethan for a moment, their eyes lingering. She felt the love and pain in his heart. She carefully studied every curve of his face, promising herself to never forget a single detail. He looked like an angel as his blonde hair floated around his head like a halo.

Ethan signaled her to go then turned away and began directing the soldiers to leave, creating Morgan's distraction.

Lucas rode up to Morgan on Argon's back. He pulled her up in front of him, wrapping his arms on either side of her. Morgan stared at Ethan, wanting to see his face one last time but he never turned around in time. With a sudden jolt, her and Lucas were speeding away from the other Atlanteans. They were soon miles away from Portugan without any trace of being followed.

Morgan and Lucas traveled for hours but it felt more like days. They were traveling extremely fast beneath the water, making it hard for them to move or breathe. They were joined by dolphins first, then whales, and finally seals. When the seals joined their group of escorts, Morgan knew they must be close to shore.

Under the cover of night, they finally arrived on shore. Argon pulled himself onto the city's sandy beach. Morgan and Lucas slid from his back, and when their feet hit the sand after hours of high speed water travel, their legs wobbled unsteadily. It took their bodies a few minutes to acclimatize to the solid ground. Argon gave Lucas a little nudge of affection.

"Thank you, buddy, we couldn't have done this without you," he said. He rubbed the prehistoric mammal's cheek affectionately.

"You have to leave now Argon. I don't want anybody to see you." Lucas said.

Argon gave a disobedient huff.

"Don't worry, we're safe now Argon. But if you're spotted here, you'll be the one in danger. I'll miss you buddy but you have to go." Argon rubbed his large, wet cheek against Lucas and then turned and abruptly disappeared back into the ocean.

Morgan and Lucas were alone on the vacant shore. Morgan searched the area unable to spot any familiar surroundings. "This isn't Santa Monica, is it?"

"San Diego, actually. Larrance gave me the key to his apartment. He thought we should lay low for a while until we figure out our power-draining abilities. We don't want to hurt anyone."

"But how will we live on our own? We don't have any money," she argued as she combed through her wet, tangled hair.

"With this." Lucas pulled a plastic pouch full of money out of the backpack he had been carrying since they left Portugan.

"Ethan gave it to me. Wait, there's something else in here... What the?...Oh Gross!" He pulled out a furry, brown dripping mess that resembled a wet carcass. He twisted and wrung the water from the sopping lump of fur.

Morgan stepped forward to get a closer look and then her face dropped. "Stop!" she blurted as she pulled the victim from Lucas's hands.

She peered into the large glass brown eyes of the wet, plush seal looking up at her. Morgan hugged it tightly against her chest. It was the seal she had dropped in the tunnel at the aquarium! Around its neck was a little bow that held a flat silver heart. Morgan turned it over and read the engraved inscription:

Morgan,

My Love, My destiny, My Soul mate.

Till we are together again.

Ethan.

She hugged the soggy stuffed animal even tighter, trying so desperately to not cry.

Lucas took her hand. "Let's see if we can find our new home shall we?" he said.

He led her off the beach, then added with a grin, "How do you like that, you and I are gettin' shacked up!"

She offered a small smile as she gently rubbed the Trident scar on her chest and blindly followed her dear friend into their unknown future.

She knew that with Lucas around to absorb her powers they would find a way to control her energy and they would be able to be a part of the real world again soon. She was happy to be above ground, although her feet felt heavier with each step she took away from the ocean.

Morgan searched the shoreline one last time with foolish hopes of seeing Larrance or Ethan, but she saw nothing but calm waves lapping at the distant shore.